PUSHKIN PRESS

22·6·'21

THE
PAS

n Stock

"This is history as told by someone right in the middle of it. The breathless escape from hotel to hotel, from city to city, and, above all, from train to train... is conveyed almost physically to the reader"
—*Frankfurter Rundschau*

"Thrillingly topical... *The Passenger* will soon be read and discussed in schools"
—*Die Zeit*

"An incredibly gripping rediscovery"   —*SRF Der Literaturclub*

"There is no literary novel on the year of 1938 or the pogroms (Night of Broken Glass). *The Passenger* fills this gap, transferring the documented horror and mass suffering into the free space of fiction. It's a story about emigration and deportation, about new beginnings and failed hopes: one of the many tragedies of exile"
—*Frankfurter Allgemeine Zeitung*

"One of the most important books of the year... the insight into the atmosphere of the times is so deep, so immediate, it will make you feel as though you'd accompanied the hero yourself" —*Stern*

"A tragicomic fable of the human condition and a comedy of morals and characters of exceptional psychological acuity"   —*Le Figaro*

"A masterpiece"   —*L'Avvenire*

"Although written more than 80 years ago, this book qualifies as a 'breathtaking thriller'. It is as if Kafka and Tom Clancy were sent together as reporters into the abyss of Germany in 1938"
—*Corriere della Sera*

ULRICH ALEXANDER BOSCHWITZ was born in Berlin in 1915. He left Germany in 1935 for Oslo, Norway, studied at the Sorbonne in Paris, and wrote two novels, including *The Passenger*. Boschwitz eventually settled in England in 1939, although he was interned as a German "enemy alien" after war broke out—despite his Jewish background—and subsequently shipped to Australia. In 1942, Boschwitz was allowed to return to England, but his ship was torpedoed by a German submarine and he was killed along with all 362 passengers. He was twenty-seven years old.

THE PASSENGER

ULRICH ALEXANDER BOSCHWITZ

TRANSLATED FROM THE GERMAN BY PHILIP BOEHM
WITH A PREFACE BY ANDRÉ ACIMAN AND AN AFTERWORD BY PETER GRAF

PUSHKIN PRESS

Pushkin Press
71–75 Shelton Street
London WC2H 9JQ

Copyright © 2018 by J. G. Cotta'sche Buchhandlung
Nachfolger GmbH, gegr. 1659, Stuttgart

This edition published by arrangement with Literarische Agentur
Michael Gaeb and Regal Hoffmann & Associates LLC

English translation © 2021 Philip Boehm

Preface © 2021 André Aciman

The Passenger was first published in German as *Der Reisende* in Stuttgart, 2018

First published by Pushkin Press in 2021

The translation of this work was supported by a grant from the Goethe-Institut.

The translator thanks TOLEDO, a program of the Robert Bosch Foundation
and the Deutscher Übersetzerfonds, for their support of this project.

1 3 5 7 9 8 6 4 2

Hardback ISBN 13: 978-1-78227-538-1
Trade Paperback ISBN 13: 978-1-78227-684-5

Offset by Tetragon, London
Printed and bound by CPI Group (UK) Ltd, Croydon, CRO 4YY

www.pushkinpress.com

CONTENTS

Preface by André Aciman   ix

The Passenger   1

Afterword by Peter Graf   257

PREFACE

———

André Aciman

Berlin, just after Kristallnacht: Nazis everywhere, Jews being hounded, picked up, beaten, and arrested, their stores ransacked and vandalized, every Jew in Greater Germany now terrorized. Not a shred of humanity or shame left in this wide country, except in scant, totally insignificant gestures— the occasional tap on the shoulder, *No worries, you don't look Jewish*, or the unctuous but ultimately malevolent *Would love to help, but under the circumstance, surely you understand*. Everyone—even people you once thought were your friends and partners—will fleece you or rat on you, or both, and if you call them out as the barefaced rogues they are, they'll only reply with the one infallible curse: *Jew!* You've become a swear word on two legs, and your only hope is that no one nearby heard it spoken, because informants and plainclothes policemen are stalking everywhere, in trains, hotels, street corners, cafés. Anyone who looks at you is dangerous, and if he looks twice, you know you'd better scram; a third gaze can mean the unimaginable. You try to blend in but, as Otto Silbermann, the protagonist of this remarkable novel, realizes soon enough, you look most suspicious precisely when you're trying not to.

This is 1938, and World War Two hasn't erupted yet, but everyone knows it's coming, and though no one has the merest foreboding that what's about to happen will turn Europe into a slaughterhouse, Germany has already started its single-minded war against its Jews. The death camps haven't been built but concentration camps are already fully operational. Yellow stars have yet to make their appearance, but it would help, says a waiter to Silbermann, if Jews were asked to wear a yellow band on their sleeve to make it easier to spot them. Meanwhile, the German bureaucratic machine leaves nothing to chance: your passport bears a loutish red *J*, your phone may be tapped, and even if you have "Aryan" looks, your name instantly identifies you as a Jew. With the dragnet closing in, you realize you're trapped and have nowhere to go, and as for fleeing the country, well, you should have thought of that months earlier, now it's too late. Germany won't let you out, and other countries don't want to let you in. In the words of novelist Ulrich Boschwitz, "For a Jew the entire Reich [has become] one big concentration camp."

So you're on the run, in a state of panic-stricken paralysis, holing up in a series of improvised but bungled hiding places. When you stop to catch your breath in some spot that seems safe enough for a fleeting few hours, the question inevitably comes back: why *didn't* you flee when you could easily have done so? The answer couldn't be more galling: because you thought things weren't as bad as all that, because you continue to believe that this foul phase can't possibly last much longer, because you cling to the conviction that Germany is still a democracy, not a madhouse. In Silbermann's words, we're "in the middle of Europe, in the twentieth century!"—not some backwater where laws are the whims of the lawless. Surely this can't be happening.

But of course it is, and Boschwitz mines the irony for nuggets of the darkest Kafkan humor, even as his not-exactly-lovable hero insists on living according to middle-class conventions that have long ceased to have any meaning.

When the storm troopers come knocking at his door, Otto Silbermann manages to slip out the back of his comfortable bourgeois home, leaving behind all of his belongings, while his Christian wife helps hasten his escape. He has a decent amount of cash, he knows his way around, he could even pull a few strings, and a number of people owe him favors. Besides, all this is bound to blow over soon: after all, he served on the front in the Great War, he dutifully pays his taxes, runs a respected business; in short, Otto Silbermann is a thoroughly upstanding citizen.

Of course, the fact that he doesn't look Jewish helps. When he boards a train, he is the sort of traveler who gives every indication of knowing where he is headed. And his fellow passengers feel free to engage him in conversation. A man with a Nazi lapel pin suggests they play chess, a stenotypist whose leftist boyfriend served time in a concentration camp confides her problems, and the estranged wife of a lawyer is happy to flirt with him. He listens to disgruntled miners and regales lighthearted soldiers. And so we, too, meet a cross section of the populace—"regular" Germans pursuing their everyday affairs, minding their own business, going about their lives with nary a care in the world.

While his looks succeed in deceiving others, over time he begins to see he may simply be deceiving himself. A traveling Aryan speeds ahead, but as Silbermann finds out, a Jew on the run hurtles and jostles his way about, follows one alleged escape route after the other, but is basically buffeted about by an evil wind, and—if he survives the storm, which so many will not—he will likely wind up years later in another kind of camp, for "displaced persons." Meanwhile here in 1938, Otto Silbermann is already displaced. And so he travels from Berlin to Hamburg, from Hamburg back to Berlin, then from Berlin to Dortmund, Dortmund to Aachen, back to Dortmund, on to Küstrin, Dresden and eventually back to Berlin. With each frenetic trip—in first class, or second class, or third class—he ends up shedding one more of the delusions that had protected and prevented him from recognizing the inevitable. He can no longer pass for who he always thought he was: "The truth is I don't have the right to be an ordinary human being."

Ulrich Alexander Boschwitz (1915–1942) was born to an affluent and secularized family. Boschwitz's Jewish father, who had converted to Christianity and married a Protestant woman, died just weeks before the birth of his son. In 1935, following the promulgation of the Nuremberg Laws, Ulrich and his mother escaped to Sweden, where the young man wrote and published his first novel, *Menschen neben dem Leben* (*People Parallel to Life*), under the pseudonym of John Grane. His sister had already emigrated to Palestine in 1933 and settled in a kibbutz. From Sweden, Boschwitz moved to Paris, where he studied awhile at the Sorbonne, before moving on to Luxembourg and then Belgium. In 1939, shortly before the outbreak of the war, he joined his mother in England.

Deeply affected by the events of Kristallnacht, he worked feverishly on what would become *The Passenger*, finishing a first draft in barely four weeks. In England he was able to publish an early version of the novel, which was also brought out in France, though barely noticed in either country. As an official "enemy alien," Boschwitz was interned following the outbreak of hostilities in a camp on the Isle of Man, along with thousands of other refugees from Germany and Austria, as well as a small number of actual Nazi sympathizers. As the war progressed, male refugees, along with newly captured prisoners of war, were shipped off to various British dominions. Boschwitz had the ill fortune to be deported to Australia aboard the HMT *Dunera*. The passage was brutal, as the passengers were robbed and subjected to gross indignities regardless of whether they were Jewish refugees or Nazi sympathizers. In Australia the detainees were interned in a prison camp in New South Wales. Following the attack on Pearl Harbor, the authorities reclassified actual refugees as "friendly aliens" and so Ulrich Boschwitz was freed. With some trepidation he boarded the troopship MV *Abosso* bound for England, but that was torpedoed by a German submarine, and Boschwitz perished, along with 361 of his fellow travelers. He was twenty-seven years old.

In a last letter to his mother, Ulrich Boschwitz signaled his desire to overhaul the manuscript of *The Passenger*, noting that she should expect to receive the first 109 pages of his reworked version from a fellow prisoner who was on his way to England. In the same letter he advised her that in the event of his death, she should undertake to have an experienced person of letters implement these changes. Alas, his revisions have never come to light.

But what did turn up, some seventy-plus years after his death, was Ulrich Boschwitz's original German typescript, in an archive in Frankfurt, thanks to a tip from the author's niece. With the support of Boschwitz's family, and interpolating what he knew of the author's wishes based on what he had communicated to his mother and others, the German publisher and editor Peter Graf revised the rediscovered typescript. And so the novel finally appeared in its original language in 2018, under the title *Der Reisende*, and was translated and acclaimed throughout the world. This translation by Philip Boehm is of that revised original.

Boschwitz has given us the first fictional depiction of Jewish life in Germany in the final months before the war, a keenly observed sociological snapshot as well as an insightful psychological portrait of the protagonist. *The Passenger* is a disabused, prophetic, and flawlessly penetrating glimpse of what, in retrospect, was to be the unavoidable outcome of the persecution of Jews under Hitler's regime. Boschwitz's tale of an individual scurrying from train station to train station across a homeland that is no longer home could not have been more prescient of the terror the Nazis would unleash on every Jew. The author's own peregrinations from Germany to Sweden and on to France, Luxembourg, Belgium, England, and finally to Australia could not have failed to give him a firsthand feel for Silbermann's own desperate itinerary. What Boschwitz saw clearly enough was the utter despoliation of one's identity, of one's trust in the world, and ultimately of one's very humanity: "They'll slowly undress us first and then kill us, so our clothes won't get bloody and our banknotes won't get damaged. These days murder is performed economically." How could he have known all this so early in the tragedy? Or, to turn the question around, how is it that so many can still claim never to have known what was done to the Jews in Hitler's Europe?

THE
PASSENGER

ONE

Becker stood up, stubbed his cigar in the ashtray, buttoned his jacket, and placed his right hand reassuringly on Silbermann's shoulder. "So then take care, Otto. I think I'll be back in Berlin by tomorrow. If something comes up, you can simply call me in Hamburg."

Silbermann nodded. "Just do me one favor," he said, "and don't go gambling again. You're too lucky in love to have luck in cards. Besides, you'll end up losing . . . our money."

Becker laughed, annoyed. "Why don't you just say your money," he asked. "Have I ever once . . . ?"

"No no." Silbermann quickly cut him off. "I'm only joking, you know that, but even so: you really are on the reckless side. If you start gambling again you won't be so quick to stop, especially if you have all the cash from this check . . ."

Silbermann stopped in midsentence and went on calmly. "I have complete confidence in you. After all, you're a reasonable fellow. Still, it's a pity to lose a single mark at the game table. And even though it's your money at stake, now that we're business partners I'd feel just as bad if you lose as if it were my own."

Becker's kind, broad face, which for a moment had turned sour and furrowed, brightened.

"We don't need to pretend, Otto," he said, now at ease. "If I lose then of course it's your money I'll be losing, since I don't have any." He chuckled.

"We are partners," Silbermann insisted.

"Of course," said Becker, once again serious. "And so why are you talking to me as though I were still your employee?"

"Have I offended you?" asked Silbermann. His tone was part gentle irony and part mild fright.

"Nonsense," Becker replied. "Old friends like us! Three years on the western front, twenty years working together, sticking together—you can't offend me old fellow, at most just annoy me a little."

He again placed his hand on Silbermann's shoulder.

"Otto," he declared in a forceful voice. "In these uncertain times, in this unclear world, there's only one thing that can be relied on, and that is friendship, true, man-to-man friendship! And let me tell you, old boy, for me you are a man—a German man, not a Jew."

"But I am a Jew," said Silbermann, who knew Becker's fondness for proclamations that had more pith than tact. He was afraid his new partner might go on expounding in his coarse-but-heartfelt way and so miss his train, but Becker was having one of his moments of feeling, and he wasn't about to give up a single second of it.

"I'll tell you something else," Becker declared, ignoring

the nervousness of his friend, to whom he had opened his heart more often than Silbermann would have wished. "I am a National Socialist. God knows I've never misled you about that. If you were a Jew like other Jews, a real Jew, in other words, then you might have kept me on as general manager, but you would never have made me your partner! And I'm not just the goy of record, either. I've never ever been that. I'm convinced there's been some mistake and that you're actually an Aryan. Marne, Yser, Somme, the two of us, man! So just let anyone try to tell me that you . . ."

Silbermann looked around for the waiter. "Gustav, you're going to miss your train!" he interrupted.

"I couldn't care less about the train." Becker sat back down. "I'd like to have another beer with you," he declared with some emotion.

Silbermann rapped his fist on the table. "Go ahead and have another then, for all I care, just drink it in the dining car," he snapped. "I have a meeting to go to."

Becker first let out an offended huff but then said, more compliantly, "As you like, Otto. If I were an anti-Semite I wouldn't put up with that tone. Like you're some lieutenant barking orders. The truth is I never put up with it! Not from anyone! Except you."

He stood up again, took the briefcase off the table, and said, laughing, "And a man like that claims to be a Jew!" He shook his head with feigned amazement, nodded once more to Silbermann, and left the first-class waiting room.

Watching his friend leave, Silbermann was dismayed to notice he was weaving slightly and bumping into tables, with the same stiffly erect posture he always assumed when seriously drunk.

He's not well suited to being a partner, thought Silbermann. He should have remained a manager. In that capacity he was reliable, quiet, and respectable, a very good colleague. But his newfound fortune doesn't become him. If only he doesn't wind up ruining the business. If only he doesn't go gambling!

Silbermann wrinkled his forehead. "His good fortune has made him unfit," he mumbled, annoyed.

The waiter Silbermann had been looking for earlier— without success—finally appeared.

"Are guests meant to wait for service here or for the trains?" asked Silbermann, his sharp tone expressing his disdain for anything that approached slovenliness or exuded an unfriendly air.

"I beg your pardon," answered the waiter. "A gentleman in second class was complaining because he thought he was sitting across from a Jew. But it wasn't a Jew at all, the man was from South America, and since I know a little Spanish I was called in to help."

"I see."

Silbermann got up. His mouth contracted into a line, and his gray eyes fixed the waiter with a severe look.

The waiter tried to smooth things over. "It really wasn't a Jew," he assured Silbermann. Evidently the waiter considered his guest to be a particularly staunch member of the party.

"I'm not interested in that. Has the train for Hamburg already left?"

The waiter glanced at the clock above the exit to the platforms.

"Seven twenty," he thought out loud. "The train for Magdeburg is just leaving. Hamburg leaves at seven twenty-four. If you hurry you can still make it. I wish that someday I could go running to catch a train, but people like me . . ."

He brushed a few bread crumbs off the table with a napkin.

"The best would be," he went on, picking up the previous subject, "if the Jews had to wear yellow bands on their arms. Then at least there wouldn't be any confusion."

Silbermann looked at him. "Are they really so terrible?" he asked quietly, regretting his words even as he spoke them.

The waiter looked at Silbermann as though he hadn't understood him right. He was clearly surprised, but also unsuspecting, since Silbermann had none of the features that marked him as a Jew, according to the tenets of the racial scientists.

"The whole thing has nothing to do with me," the man said at last, carefully. "Still, it would be good for the others. My brother-in-law for example looks a little Jewish, but of course he's an Aryan, it's only that he has to constantly explain and prove everything, over and over. That's too much to ask of anyone."

"Yes it is," Silbermann agreed. Then he paid his tab and left.

Unbelievable, he thought, absolutely unbelievable.

After leaving the train station, he climbed into a taxi and headed home. The streets were full of people, many in uniform. Newsboys were hawking their papers, and Silbermann had the impression they were doing a brisk business. For a moment he considered buying one for himself but then decided against it, since he figured the news was bound to be bad, and almost certainly hostile, at least as far as he was concerned. He would undoubtedly be experiencing it all firsthand soon enough.

After a short ride the taxi pulled up in front of his building. Frau Friedrichs, the wife of the concierge, was lingering in the stairwell. She greeted him politely and Silbermann was somehow glad to see that her behavior remained unchanged. As he stepped onto the red plush runner and climbed the stairs, he once again had the sensation that his life was only half real. Recently such ruminations had become a habit.

I'm living as though I weren't a Jew, he thought, somewhat incredulously. For the time being I'm simply a well-to-do citizen—under threat, it's true, but as of yet unscathed. How is this possible? I live in a modern six-room apartment. People talk to me and treat me as though I were one of them. They act as if I'm the same person I used to be, the liars—it's enough to give a man a guilty conscience. Whereas I'd like to show them a clearer picture of reality, namely that as of yesterday I'm something different because I am a Jew. And who did I used to be? No—who am I? What am I, really? A swear word on two legs, one that people mistake for something else!

I no longer have any rights, and it's only out of propriety or habit that so many act as though I did. My entire existence is based solely on the faulty memory of people who essentially wish to destroy it. They just happen to have forgotten about me. I've been officially degraded, but the public debasement has yet to take place.

Frau Zänkel, the councilor's widow, was just stepping

out of her apartment. Silbermann doffed his hat and greeted her with a "Guten Tag, gnädige Frau."

"How are you doing?" she asked kindly.

"I'm fine, by and large. And yourself?"

"Tolerably well. For an old lady."

She held out her hand in parting.

"These must be difficult times for you," she added, regretfully, "terrible times . . ."

Silbermann contented himself with an attentive little smile that was both cautious and thoughtful, neither agreeing nor disagreeing. "In essence we've been assigned a peculiar role," he said at last.

"But they're great times, too," she consoled him. "There's no doubt that you're being treated unjustly, but that's exactly why you need to be fair-minded and compassionate in your thinking."

"Isn't that a lot to ask, gnädige Frau? Besides, I don't think at all anymore. I've given that up. It's the best way to deal with everything."

"They'll never do anything to you," she assured him, and banged the umbrella she was clenching in her right hand resolutely on a stair, as if to signal that she wouldn't allow anyone to get too close to him. Then she gave him an encouraging nod and stepped on by.

As soon as he was back in his apartment, he asked the maid if Herr Findler was already there. She said he was, so Silbermann hastily took off his hat and coat and stepped into the study, where his visitor was waiting.

Theo Findler was examining a painting with clear disapproval. When he heard the door open, he quickly turned around and smiled at the man entering.

"Well?" he asked, knitting his brow as he always did when he spoke, thinking that the wrinkles added weight to his words. "How are you, my friend? I was afraid something might have happened to you. You never know . . . Have you given my last offer some more thought? How is your wife? I haven't seen her at all today. So, Becker's off to Hamburg."

Findler took a deep breath, because he was only at the beginning of his monologue.

"Well you two sure are clever! A person could learn from you. Becker has a Jewish head on his shoulders. Ha ha, he'll manage all right, he'll manage. I'd have been happy to join in the business, but too late is too late, right? By the way, where did you dig up these awful pictures? I don't understand how anyone could hang rubbish like that on their walls. No order to the things, you old culture-Bolshevik you. Now don't go thinking that I'll be raising my last offer even by just another thousand marks. Not on your life, I can't do it.

"You think I'm a rich man, Silbermann. Everybody does. If only I knew where they came up with that idea. And here I'm having a hard time paying what I owe in taxes. Speaking of taxes, can't you find me a clever bookkeeper or point me to someone? I mean I know my way around a little bit, but I don't have time to take care of all that properly. These taxes, these goddamned taxes. Tell me, am I supposed to support the whole German Reich all by myself? Well?

"You're not saying anything? What is it? Did you think things over? Are you going to take my offer? Your wife must have something against me. I see she's kept herself completely out of sight. I don't understand it. Is she upset with me because we didn't say hello to you the other evening? But good grief, how could we have? The place was teeming with Nazis! Later my wife pestered me that we should have said hello. But I told her that Silbermann's far too reasonable. He realizes I can't compromise myself on his account. Well?

"So, Silbermann, out with it. Do you want to sell or don't you?"

Findler seemed to have finished talking—in any case he was now looking expectantly at Silbermann. They sat down at the smokers' table, but Findler must have moved too abruptly, since he winced and, with a concentrated expression, started rubbing his left hip.

"Ninety thousand," Silbermann said, ignoring all the various questions and remarks he realized were mostly meant to throw him off guard. "Thirty thousand in cash, the rest secured by mortgage."

Findler started up as if he'd been given an electric shock.

"You've got to be joking," he shouted, sounding offended. "Listen, it's high time we stopped all this dithering. Fifteen thousand on the table, you hear? What on earth—thirty thousand marks! You know, if I had thirty thousand marks lying around, I could think of better things to do than buy your place. Thirty thousand marks!"

"But consider the net income from rent. And since the sale price is already ridiculous, the least I have to have is a decent down payment. The building's worth two hundred thousand marks, you're buying it . . ."

"Worth, worth, worth," Findler interrupted. "What do you think I'm worth? Except nobody would pay a thing for me. Nobody can pay what I'm worth, and nobody would even think of putting down just a thousand marks. I'm unsaleable. And so is your building. Ha ha ha, Silbermann, and I say it as a friend. I'm taking the shack off your hands, and if I don't then the state will. And they won't give you a lousy pfennig."

The telephone rang in the next room. For a moment Silbermann wondered if he should answer it. Then he jumped up, excused himself, and left the study.

I'll probably take what he's offering, he thought as he picked up the receiver. After all, Findler's still a relatively decent fellow.

"Hello, who is this?"

The long-distance operator answered. "Please hold the line, you have a call from Paris," said a cool female voice.

Silbermann felt a flash of excitement and lit a cigarette. "Elfriede," he called out in a low voice.

His wife, who had stayed in the salon just as he'd suspected, came in, quietly opening and closing the door behind her.

"Hello, Elfriede," he said, covering the receiver with his hand. "I just arrived five minutes ago. Herr Findler is here. Won't you go in and talk with him?"

She stepped close and they exchanged a fleeting kiss.

"It's Eduard," he whispered. "The call is coming at an awkward moment. Please go talk with Findler, otherwise he'll listen in. It's already practically a crime to telephone with Paris."

"Tell Eduard hello from me," she said. "I'd really like to say a few words to him myself."

"That's out of the question." He warded her off. "The lines are all being tapped. And you're too careless. You'd say something you shouldn't."

"I should at least be able to say hello to my own son."

"I'm afraid you can't. Please understand."

She looked at him beseechingly. "Just a few words," she said. "I'll be careful."

"The answer is no," he said firmly. "Hello? Hello . . . Eduard? Hello Eduard . . ." He pointed imploringly at the door of the study.

She went.

"Listen," Silbermann said, going back to the phone call. "Have you managed to arrange our permit?" He spoke very slowly, weighing each word before he uttered it.

"No," Eduard answered on the other end. "It's extremely difficult. You can't count on getting it. I'm trying everything I can, but . . ."

Silbermann cleared his throat. He decided he had to be more forceful.

"That's unacceptable. Either you're making an effort or you aren't! And I'm sure you realize the matter is of some importance. I don't even know where to start with these lazy excuses."

"You're overestimating what I can do, Father," answered Eduard, upset. "Six months ago it would have been a lot easier. But you didn't want to. And that's not exactly my fault."

"It's not a question of who's at fault," Silbermann snapped back, fuming. "Your job is to see to the permits. And be so kind as to spare me your wisdom."

"Listen, Father," Eduard said, indignantly. "You want me to get you the moon and the stars and you're bawling me out because I haven't delivered them!" Then he added, "But how are you both doing? How is Mother? Please give her my best. I would have been happy to speak with her."

"Fix the permit and do it quickly," Silbermann repeated sternly. "That's all I'm asking! Your mother sends her best. Unfortunately she can't talk with you right now."

"I'll get it done," answered Eduard. "At least I'll try everything I can."

Silbermann placed the receiver back on the hook.

That's the first time in my life I've wanted something from my son, he thought, disgruntled and disappointed. And I know for a fact he's bound to fail! If I had a business friend in Paris, he'd be able to come up with the entry permits in a few days, but Eduard . . . I shouldn't expect too much. He's simply not accustomed to doing things for us. When someone's used to you always being there for them it's very hard for that person to switch roles. Eduard's used to my helping him and now I'm asking him to help me. And he's not well suited to his new part.

Then Silbermann shook his head, ashamed of his own ruminations. I'm being unfair, he thought, and what's worse, I'm being sentimental.

He went back to the study.

"I was just explaining to your wife," Findler said, by way of greeting, "that it's very careless of you to keep going to the same old places. If you run into some acquaintance who isn't kindly disposed toward you, you could wind up in a lot of trouble. Your wife is an Aryan, she can go anywhere she wants, but you . . . God knows I'm not approving of the circumstances that make such advice necessary, but I'm speaking with your own interest at heart. The best would be for you to stay home or with friends. Of course no one can tell by looking at you that you're Jewish, but why tempt the devil? Incidentally what's Sohnemann up to? He hotfooted it, and in the nick of time, too. Ha ha ha, funny times we're living in, right?"

"Listen, Findler," Silbermann began, "I'll let you have the place for a down payment of twenty thousand marks, just so we can finally come to a deal."

"Don't talk nonsense. Why would you want to hoodwink your old Findler? Besides they'll take whatever money you have at the border. For you I'd even chip in a few marks more than what the joint's worth to me, but to pay extra just so it winds up in the state treasury—I have no interest in that."

"For the moment I don't have any intention of leaving Germany."

"Well, children, do as you like. I really wish something better for you than the current circumstances. It's Jewish blood that's bringing the German people together. And I fail to see why my friend Silbermann of all people should wind up as glue. Running for your life, on the other hand—that I understand completely."

"Don't you think what's happening to the Jews is a horrible crime?" asked Frau Silbermann, who was horror-stricken by Findler's proclamation that "it's Jewish blood that's bringing the German people together," and who still hadn't given up searching for some moral in the events of the times.

"Of course," Findler said dryly. "A lot of bad things happen in the world. And some good things as well. Today it's this person, tomorrow that one. One person's consumptive, another's a Jew, and if they're really unlucky they're both at once. That's the way it is. How much bad luck do you think I've had in my life? There's nothing you can do about it."

"I knew that you aren't exactly the most tactful person, Herr Findler," said Frau Silbermann, indignant, "but that you're so cold inside and so . . ."—here she swallowed the word "brutal"—"indifferent, that is something new to me."

Findler smiled, unmoved. "I love my wife and my little daughter. As far as the rest of humanity goes, everything is strictly business. There you have my entire relationship to my surroundings. I don't love the Jews, I don't hate the Jews. I am indifferent to them, though as capable business-men I admire them. If an injustice is being done to them, I'm sorry, but it doesn't surprise me, either. That's the way of the world. When the time comes, some fail and go bankrupt while others prosper."

"And if you were a Jew yourself?"

"But I'm not! I've given up racking my brain about what might be. I have enough to deal with what actually is."

"So do you always think only about yourself? Are you incapable of sympathizing with the tragic plights of other people?"

"Who the devil worries about me when I have bad luck? Theo Findler doesn't have anyone but Theo Findler. And those two have to stick together thick as thieves. Ha ha."

"Yet you claim to love your wife and daughter." Frau Silbermann was becoming more and more agitated. "I can't believe that someone who's so . . . bestially indifferent is capable of . . ."

"Hey, listen, that's going too far. I have pretty thick skin and can stand a lot of joking, but I don't like being insulted!"

Frau Silbermann stood up. "You will excuse me," she said frostily to Findler. Then she left the room.

"Good God, you are a sensitive bunch." Findler laughed. "My heavens! Well, honest people like myself have to put up with a lot. Back to business! So what's the score? Well?"

The phone rang once again.

"Twenty thousand," Silbermann insisted, "the rest secured by mortgage."

The door opened, and Frau Silbermann asked her husband to step into the next room. She was apparently still agitated, and he did not appreciate the new disturbance. "Think about it," he said to Findler as he left the room.

"What is it, Elfriede," he asked his wife.

She pointed to the telephone. "Your sister's on the line. Speak to her. She'll explain everything . . ."

He reached for the receiver.

"Hilde?"

"Yes, yes?" his sister stammered, clearly upset. "Günther has been arrested!"

Silbermann was so surprised he didn't know what to say. "How so?" he finally asked. "What happened?"

"Don't you know—all Jews are being arrested."

He pulled up a chair and sat down.

"Calm down please, Hilde," he said. "There must be some mistake. Now tell me everything once more, nice and quietly . . ."

"There's no time for that. I only called to warn you. Four men in our building were arrested. If I only knew what was happening to Günther."

"But it can't be! People don't just go hauling off respectable citizens from their homes! They can't do that!"

He was silent. Yes they can, he then thought, they can.

"Shall I come over?" he asked after a while. "Or do you want to come to our place?"

"No, I'm not leaving the apartment, I'm staying here. And you shouldn't come, either. That won't help anything. Good-bye, Otto." She hung up.

Distraught, he looked at his wife.

"Elfriede," he whispered, "they're arresting all the Jews! Maybe it's just a temporary scare tactic. In any case Günther has been arrested, but you already know that."

Silbermann paused for a moment.

"What should we do? What do you think is best, Elfriede? Should I stay here? Maybe they'll forget about me. I've never been seriously harassed before. If only Becker were here. He has a whole slew of party connections. He could intervene in an emergency. Of course if the arrests are coming from above, then he can't do anything, either. And by the time he gets back from Hamburg I could have been beaten to death by mistake. Ach—nonsense! Nothing's going to happen to me. In the worst case you'll just ring up Becker and ask him to come back immediately."

"Six months ago we still could have gotten out of Germany," his wife said slowly. "We stayed on my account, because I couldn't bear to leave my family behind. If something happens to you it will be my fault. You wanted to go, but I . . ."

"Ach." He brushed aside her self-reproach. "It's no one's fault. Is someone who forgot to put on a bulletproof vest at the right moment to blame if he gets shot? That's all nonsense. Besides, you were more for leaving than I was. If you'd had your way we would already be out of the country. You would have left your family more easily than I would have left my business. But it didn't happen. And at this point the whys and wherefores don't matter."

He gave her a kiss, then went back to Herr Findler. He attempted to appear as calm and composed as before, but something in his face, some excessive tension, a smile that seemed forced, made the other man suspicious.

"What's going on?" Findler asked. "Bad news?"

"Family matters," said Silbermann, and sat back down at the table.

"I see," said Findler, drawing the words out, his forehead more furrowed than usual. "Well, I'm sure it's bad news, right? Family news is always bad. Believe me, I know."

Silbermann opened the cigarette case that was lying on the table. "Shall we get back to business?" he asked as calmly as he could.

"Well," Findler replied, "I'm really not so tempted. I'm not even sure if it's still possible to buy property from Jews. No idea. If you had your way you'd flimflam me before I could count to three. Well?"

This constant "well," which sounded so fat and smug, was gradually bringing Silbermann to the point of despair.

"Do you actually want to buy the building or just talk about buying it? What do you want to do?"

"Well," said Findler as he stretched in his armchair. "I really wrenched my hip earlier. What do you say to that? Wouldn't it be better if we waited to see what new regulations are coming? It's too risky for me. I pay for a place and end up not getting it. The government has in mind all sorts of things for you Jews."

"All right then fifteen thousand!"

"I don't know, Silbermann, I really have no idea if I should or not. What say we wait a few weeks, and if nothing happens in the meantime I'll still be able to buy the place. First I also have to speak with my lawyer, absolutely."

"But ten minutes ago . . ."

"Since then I've started to have some doubts. I also don't want you to have any trouble because you're selling your home. But most of all I don't want any trouble myself."

"Just so we can finish this: I let you have the building for a down payment of fourteen thousand marks. But you have to agree now."

"Is that so? Well . . . let's talk about it again tomorrow. Fourteen thousand marks is a heap of money, that's for sure! I'm not an ogre. I don't want something for nothing. But I have to ask myself whether this place is really worth a fourteen thousand down payment. And of course you realize that the payment could only be made after the deed gets notarized and registered. And in case of any force majeure the whole transaction would be void. Fourteen thousand marks . . . Do you honestly believe I'm getting a bargain if we shake on it this evening and call it a deal?"

"You wanted to pay fifteen thousand marks and now you're hesitating at fourteen?"

"I'm just thinking there are other deals I could make with the money, maybe better ones. You just always have to see for yourself where you are in life. Well?" He sighed contentedly.

Silbermann jumped up.

"Of course I can't influence your decision," he said impatiently. "But since I don't have any more time I'd appreciate it if you could make up your mind right here and now. Otherwise please consider my offer as no longer valid. I don't even know if you're seriously interested in the purchase or not."

"There's no need to sound like that," Findler replied testily. "I've always known that you Jews aren't cut out for doing business, at least not with people who know what they're doing, well . . ."

Silbermann saw how much Findler was enjoying this extortion—the man was even proud of it. Silbermann had a sharp response on his tongue, something to the effect that he, Silbermann, couldn't compete with blackmailers and had no desire to, and that he was used to conducting business in a decent manner. Except there are times when the most simple-minded swindler has the edge over the most intelligent and decent person.

But he didn't manage to spit out the uncivil thoughts that were bubbling up inside him or even to answer Findler more mildly—which would have been far more reasonable— because suddenly there was a wild ringing at the door. Without paying attention to his visitor's bewildered face or excusing himself even with a single word, Silbermann hurried out of the room into the hall, where he met his wife.

"You have to leave," she whispered, upset.

"No, no, I can't leave you here alone!"

Not knowing what he should do, he headed toward the door. She stopped him.

"Nothing can happen to me if you're not here," she assured him, blocking his way. "Spend tonight in a hotel. Now be quick and go."

He thought for a moment. The bell rang again and fists began pounding at the door.

"Open up, Jew, open up . . ." several overlapping voices bellowed. Silbermann's jaw dropped. He fixed his eyes on the door.

"I'm getting my revolver," he said, almost inaudibly. "I'll shoot down the first one who breaks into my home! No one has the right to barge in like that."

He started to pass his wife and head to the bedroom.

"We'll see about that," he said. "We'll see about that . . ."

Fists again pounded the door and the bell was ringing shrilly.

"Well?" asked Findler, who had stepped into the hall when he heard the noise. "What's happening here? That's just great. If the brothers catch me here, in their excitement they might take me for a Jew and smash my teeth in."

He ran his hand tenderly over his mouth.

"Don't you have a back door?" he then asked Silbermann, who was standing there watching him, as though he were expecting help and advice. "And to hell with it, you can foist your damned building on somebody else," he added.

"I'm getting my revolver," Silbermann repeated mechanically, "and I'll shoot the first one who breaks into my house!"

"Now there," said Theo Findler, to calm him down. "Easy does it. Better you should go. I'll talk to them. See that you get out through the back door. And I'll take the place for ten thousand. Do we have a deal?"

"You are . . . All right, all right, it's a deal."

"So then get a move on! I need you alive so you can sign the deed."

"Go, go," his wife begged.

The doorbell rang again, and Silbermann wondered why no one was kicking in the door.

"And what will happen to my wife?" he asked helplessly.

"Just count on me," said Findler, full of confidence. "I'll take care of everything, but now see to it that you get out of here!"

"If anything happens to my wife . . . you won't get the building."

"Fine, fine," Findler reassured him, "but if you don't disappear, then you'll be putting both your wife and me in danger!"

He straightened his jacket, ran his right hand over his bristly hair, took a deep breath, and went to the door.

"Well?" he asked in a booming voice. "What's going on?"

"Open up, Jew!"

"Have you ever seen a party block leader who is a Jew?" Findler asked coarsely.

"Shut up, you filthy pig, open up!"

Findler turned around to make sure Silbermann had left the hall with his hat and coat, then signaled to Frau Silbermann that she should hide in one of the rooms, and then shouted, "I'm a member of the party!" He tore open the door. "There is no Jew here!" he announced.

Six or seven young men were standing in front of him. For a moment his forceful appearance intimidated them. He reached into his breast pocket to show them his party book.

"The Jews swindle everybody," said one of the men. "Silbermann a party member—of all the Jewish nerve!"

"I'm not Silber—" Theo Findler doubled over and fell to the floor. One of the men had kicked him in the crotch.

TWO

Silbermann hurried down the back stairs. They're probably lying in wait for me, he thought. Ach, I should have stayed. What's going to happen to Elfriede now? He wondered whether he shouldn't go back. But Findler's there, he reassured himself. A good thing that is, too. The man's a decent person despite everything. If I'd stayed upstairs I'm sure I would have done something out of desperation. Resisted, or actually fired the gun, after all you have to do something, you can't just let them do whatever they want to you. Not that it would have helped matters—on the contrary. Silbermann realized that if he had fired, it would have been out of fear. Fear, plain and simple. Fear of the concentration camp, fear of prison—and fear of being beaten.

Dignity, he thought, a person has his dignity and that's something you can't let anyone take away.

He stopped moving when he saw a man standing at the bottom of the stairwell, smoking a cigarette. Silbermann straightened up and approached the man with measured steps, calmly withstanding his gaze. As he came close, he asked the man for a light.

The man reached into his pocket, took out a pack of matches, lit one, and held it out to Silbermann.

"Here you go," the man said. Then he asked, "Tell me, do a lot of Jews live here?"

"No idea," Silbermann answered, amazed at how indifferent he sounded. "You should ask the doorman. I'm a stranger here myself." He raised his arm and said, "Heil Hitler."

The other man returned the greeting, and Silbermann walked past him without being stopped. Don't turn around, he told himself. Don't walk too fast or too slow. Because if you stick out precisely when you're trying so hard not to, if you look suspicious because you're trying to look as unsuspicious as you can . . . My God, what do these people want from me?

He had already left the hallway and crossed the courtyard. As he walked he reached up and felt his nose. How important you are, he thought. Now everything depends on what you look like, it's up to you whether a person is a free man or a prisoner, you determine how a person lives, or even if a person stays alive. And if a person wasn't lucky with how you happen to look, you just might get him killed.

Outside the entrance to the apartment building he ran into another shady character. "Well," he said in a forceful voice, instinctively imitating Theo Findler, "what are you hanging around here for?"

The man gave a start and automatically assumed what weak people consider a strong stance.

"Oh," he said, in a way that was both chummy and respectful, "just a little Jew-hunt."

"Ah," said Silbermann, with apparent disinterest. Then he walked on, casually raising his arm in the official greeting. Once more he was not stopped. When he reached the street he paused for a moment to take everything in. What's happening upstairs? he worried. If only I knew. Surely they won't . . . Yes they will. But Findler is there.

Suddenly he felt very afraid. The thugs could come down any minute and leave the building, or one of their lookouts might suddenly get suspicious and decide to stop him after all. So he again set off, quickening his pace.

It's strange, he mused, as he crossed the street, thinking he'd be safer on the other side. Ten minutes ago it was my house that was at stake, my property. Now it's my neck. Everything's happening so quickly. They have declared war on me, on me personally. That's what it is. War has just been declared on me once and for all and right now I'm completely on my own—in enemy territory.

If only Becker were here. Hopefully the business won't go to pieces. That's all I need. I absolutely have to have that money in easy reach. Hopefully Becker isn't gambling it away. Oh well, he's the only one I can count on after all. And what if he does lose a few hundred marks at cards, what does that matter? More important things are at stake.

But I do need that money. Money means life, especially in wartime. A Jew in Germany without money is like an unfed animal in a cage, something utterly hopeless.

He passed a phone booth, then turned around and went back. I'll just make a call, he thought, and then I'll know what's going on.

The idea cheered him up, but the phone was occupied, and he had to wait awhile. The lady's voice was too loud to be contained by the booth, and Silbermann learned all about a fur coat that needed mending, about the film *Love in the South*, and about some man named Hans who had a sore throat.

Silbermann paced nervously up and down. Finally he tapped on the glass pane to signal he was waiting. The lady turned her face toward him, and that made such an impression that he granted her another five minutes' conversation before deciding to give the glass another tap.

Finally the phone was free and he hastily dialed his apartment. No one answered. He tried twice more to connect, but without success.

Findler must be still dealing with them, he reassured himself, and hung up. Those boys are hard to get rid of. Calling was a dumb idea anyway, because as long as those people are there nobody can say anything to me. Silbermann then dialed his lawyer.

A tearful female voice answered. "Herr Doktor Löwenstein and his wife aren't here."

"Where is he then?" No answer.

"He isn't here . . ."

"I see, and who are you?"

"I'm the servant girl."

"Then please tell Herr Doktor Löwenstein that . . ."

"It would be better if you called another time," she interrupted. "There's no telling when he'll be back."

Silbermann hung up.

"No doubt they've rounded him up, too," he mumbled.

He dialed the number of a Jewish business friend, but no one answered there, either.

Silbermann grew more and more dismayed. Hilde was right, he concluded, all Jews have been arrested, and I may be the only one who's escaped.

He rang up his sister.

"It's Otto," he said. "I'm calling from a phone booth. They showed up at my . . ."

"I don't want to hear about it, Otto." She cut him off. "Our whole apartment is one big heap of ruins. I wish I'd been there when they came. As far as I'm concerned they could have taken me, too. Now I'm stuck here wondering what's happened to Günther. A fifty-six-year-old man, fifty-six. And he can't take getting upset like that. This is the end . . ."

"But surely they'll let him go." He tried to calm her down. "Can I help you somehow? Although I don't particularly want to come over." He heard a crackle on the line. "Good-bye," he called out, startled. "I hope things go well with you, very well. I'll be in touch."

They're tapping the lines, he thought. He quickly left the booth and looked around. The arresting officers will be here right away. Is it still even possible to telephone?

He climbed on one bus and rode to the Schlesischer Bahnhof, where he had to change for another. As he stood on the platform wedged between many other people, he noticed a young man and woman next to him pressed tightly together. He observed them closely, first examining the relaxed face of the girl and then that of the man.

Peace! he thought. They still have peace. Their small

world is shielded by millions of lives just like theirs . . . and together they love and together they hate—and always in the majority. Although in the end it won't do them much good, either.

He asked for a ticket, and after he had paid for it, he leafed through the bills in his pocketbook to see how much money he had on him.

One hundred eighty marks, he determined. Enough to leave the country—assuming that was possible. But even if it was, he thought, he wouldn't do it. He wanted to save his fortune. He wasn't about to let that get snatched away so quickly.

If everything goes well, he thought optimistically, Becker will bring eighty thousand marks tomorrow. Then—he calculated further—I'll get another ten thousand in cash for the house, and if I'm lucky I can sell the mortgage note with a discount. He smiled weakly. I'm still a pretty wealthy man, he concluded. And there are plenty of poor anti-Semites—if there still is such a thing as a genuinely poor anti-Semite—who despite everything would happily trade places with a rich Jew like me. There was something about the idea that cheered him up a bit. They really ought to take a poll to find out, he thought. But why should they trade anything at all? They'll simply take my money and then they'll be rich anti-Semites.

The bus stopped, and Silbermann bought a newspaper from one of the vendors who were mobbing the exiting passengers. He frowned at the headlines: "The Murder in Paris." "Jews Declare War on the German People." Shocked and angered, he crumpled the paper and threw it away.

I was fully aware that war had been declared, he thought.

But that I'm the one declaring it is news to me. It all sounds like a bad joke, like "Robbers Severely Wounded in Attack by Cash Courier" or "Patient Robs Doctor to Pay His Fee." As if the pike declared war on all carp and accused them of being accessories to attempted murder just because one he ate gave him a stomachache.

Silbermann lit a cigarette.

So a seventeen-year-old boy resists the suggestion he do away with himself and instead fires in the general direction of the source of such advice. And in so doing he, and therefore all of us, have attacked the German Reich.

Silbermann left the bus and pushed his way through the people thronging the streets until he reached the hotel where he had often stayed when he lived in a suburb that had no nighttime transport. To this day he always ate his midday meal there if he happened to be in the neighborhood.

He walked past the concierge, whom he'd known for years, and was annoyed at the unresponsive expression of the man, who had averted his eyes as soon as Silbermann had entered, undoubtedly to avoid having to greet him.

I remember a quite different welcome, Silbermann thought, and he felt a small, hollow twinge in his stomach.

He searched for a familiar face as he walked slowly through the lobby and entered the reading room. Only a few men were sitting there, mostly traveling businessmen who were leafing through the magazines, studying the stock prices on the last pages of the newspapers, or busying themselves with writing letters. Silbermann glanced around the comfortably furnished room, and for a moment he had a pleasant feeling of security.

Everything is just the same, he thought. Then, again

feeling anxious, he repeated the sentence: everything is just the same. And nevertheless I have the feeling that something must be different, and not only for me.

Morosely he looked over at the others.

There you sit, he thought. In your countries it isn't customary for law-abiding citizens to be attacked in their homes and hauled off to prisons or concentration camps. In your homelands the chair of the board of directors doesn't have a machine gun next to him when he asks for a vote of confidence. But when these things happen here in Germany, when all is said and done you find it rather novel and quaint. Because no one does anything to you, and the same hotel that for me has now become a jungle full of dangers is for you a peaceful abode where you can happily drift along according to your custom. And when you go back home, you will report that one can dine quite well there in the Third Reich.

Silbermann sat down, picked up an English newspaper, and began leafing through the pages, every so often casting a grim glance at the people he had decided were foreigners. Then he lit a cigarette and began to read an article.

Suddenly he felt someone nearby and looked up. Standing in front of him was Herr Rose, the hotel manager, whom he had known for years. Judging from the man's sheepish expression, Silbermann could guess what he was after. Nevertheless he greeted him with an unselfconscious "Guten Tag" and held out his hand.

Rose first tried to ignore the gesture but then whispered, "Please don't."

Silbermann quickly retracted his hand. His felt his face turn red and was ashamed of his shame.

"Herr Silbermann," Rose said as quietly and politely as could be expected from a man who had spent his whole life in the hotel business, no matter what the situation. "This is extraordinarily embarrassing for me. You are an old and dear guest of the hotel. But . . . you understand? It isn't my fault, and things surely won't stay this way, but . . ."

"What's going on?" asked Silbermann, who knew very well where Rose was heading but had no intention of letting him off the hook. Instead he felt he needed to hear a candid admission of what Silbermann saw as a lack of character. And the other man's embarrassment almost did him good, or at least helped him get past his own.

"So you wish to throw me out?" he finally asked, his voice dry, and looked at the hotel manager.

"Please don't put it that way," Herr Rose implored, straining to cope with the demands of the situation—the snubbing of a valued client with impeccable credit. "We were always very happy," he continued, hastily, "to have you here so often as our guest, and if in the present moment we are obliged to ask you, it is very much against our will, and we hope . . ."

"It's all right, Rose." Silbermann cut him off, realizing that the man's meek manner made him feel better than he wanted to admit. "I understand."

Silbermann brushed off any further explanation with a wave of his right hand, nodded to the manager, who bowed slightly in return, and left the reading room. He passed through the lobby and paused as if he wanted to say something to the concierge, who now also made a slight bow, but then went on his way. When he reached the revolving door that led outside, he stopped once again.

Where can I possibly go? he wondered. The Jewish guest-houses have undoubtedly been ransacked by the SA. And the small hotels are absolutely unsafe: many of them are storm trooper hangouts or the like. Should I simply find some flop-house and stay there? Those should still be open to us. But are they really? Even those aren't worth the risk, because if I show up at one by myself and ask for a room, I'll look suspicious. And whatever I do, I can't let that happen.

Nevertheless he decided to look up a small hotel he had sometimes used to host business friends from out of town, and after waiting awhile in vain for a streetcar, he decided to take a cab. When he pulled up to the hotel, he noticed a storm trooper standing by the entrance, but after a moment's hesitation Silbermann stepped calmly past him and entered the small lobby.

"I'd like a room," he told the waiter who was coming to meet him.

"Shall we have your luggage brought from the station?"

That's right, he thought: you need luggage if you're spending the night in a hotel, otherwise you might stick out.

"No, thanks," said Silbermann, trying to appear absent-minded. "May I first have a look at the room?"

The waiter, who was evidently also taking on the role of concierge, grabbed a key from the numbered board, led Silbermann to the elevator, and accompanied him upstairs.

"Bad weather," he said.

"That's for sure," Silbermann answered, reluctantly.

"Excuse me, sir," the waiter continued, "but is there something going on in town today?"

"Such as what?" asked Silbermann, at pains to keep calm. "What's supposed to be going on?"

"So many Jews are staying here. I wonder if we aren't making things difficult for ourselves."

"Really?" Silbermann muttered. "How so? Have they now declared it's illegal to host Jewish guests?"

"I don't exactly know," the waiter replied. "Anyway, I couldn't care less. After you."

The elevator had stopped at the fourth floor. As far as I'm concerned we can go right back down, Silbermann thought to himself, as he stepped into the corridor to let the waiter show him the room.

At first Silbermann couldn't make up his mind, so he paced up and down the room with the disgruntled expression of a disapproving guest. The waiter's remark had made him distinctly wary and had set off a chain of anxious thoughts. But in the end Silbermann took the room, having decided that other hotels would be no less dangerous.

He rode back down with the waiter and, as he had feared, the man handed him a registration form.

"Yes, yes," he said gruffly, as though preoccupied with other matters. "Later . . . what was the room number again? Forty-seven? . . . Ah, right . . . forty-seven."

As he left the hotel he bumped into someone on the street. He mumbled a brusque "Excuse me": recent experiences had convinced him that a rude and impolite demeanor offered the most effective protection.

"Excuse me," the other man apologized with an excessively polite, almost abject voice. But then he added in amazement, "Silbermann, thank God, Silbermann. You're the first real human I've met."

It was Fritz Stein, the former proprietor of Stein & Co., and an old business friend. They shook hands. Stein was so excited, he clung to Silbermann's hand and wouldn't let go, despite the latter's attempts to wrest it back.

"What do you think?" Stein asked. The short, chubby man was greatly distraught. "Have you already heard?" Silbermann finally managed to free his hand from Stein's grasp.

"I know everything," he explained. He found Stein's jumpiness disconcerting, even though he realized it was more than justified, given the circumstances.

"Then you know more than I do," Stein responded.

"Did they also pay you a visit?" Silbermann inquired with a smile.

"You might say that." Having found a companion in misery with whom he could speak openly, Stein's inner posture grew more erect and less cowering. "What are we going to do?" he asked. "I've often wanted to call you these last days about a business proposition. Actually now would be a very good time to talk about it. I think it could be extremely interesting for you."

"Listen," said Silbermann, somewhat taken aback by the other man's change of mood. "Do you really believe that at the moment I feel like making any kind of deal? Clearly my constitution isn't as hardy as yours, my friend."

"Let's just say it doesn't need to be. For months now bankruptcy has been circling over me like a vulture crowing 'seizure of assets.' I truly feel sorry for my creditors. Their things were all smashed up in my wife's apartment, as if it all still belonged to me."

After briefly pacing back and forth, they stopped in front of a shop window.

"I admire you," Silbermann said thoughtfully. "You're a brave fellow. If I had more of your optimism I wouldn't be so apprehensive." He laughed. "You'll even manage to make money off the rope they hang you with."

"I should hope so," Stein hurried to answer very cheerfully. "Otherwise how would my wife be able to pay for her widow's veil?"

"Are things really that bad, or are you just joking? You shouldn't do that."

"I'm not—I mean every word in earnest," said Stein. "As you know, I sold my business, and now the buyer isn't paying. What am I supposed to do? I have to chase up a living somehow. But to get to the point, if you're willing to risk putting up thirty thousand marks . . ."

"No, stop," Silbermann responded. "Forget about that. Right now I really do have other worries."

"I wish I were in your shoes," Stein answered slowly. "You're just unhappy. Whereas on top of everything else, I don't have anything to eat."

Silbermann looked at him in surprise, then took out his billfold.

"Would fifty marks be of help?" he asked. "Sadly, I don't have much on me."

"Of course it would be of help. I'll take it. I'll pay you back next week. Every now and then the man who took over my business gives me a small partial payment, but naturally that depends on his mood." He stashed the money in his pocket. "What are we going to do?" he asked again, and looked around, eager to do something.

"I have to call Becker. Unfortunately he's gone to Hamburg."

"And how are you coming along with your house? You better hurry and sell, if you want my advice."

Silbermann described the negotiations. Stein nodded his head at every sentence, as if he had expected that everything would turn out the way it did.

"I wish I were in your shoes," he finally said again, with that quiet note of envy that counts as a compliment for the person envied. "You look so Aryan. At least people aren't afraid of you, the way they are of me. There's no place to turn, and people avoid me as if I had the plague. I keep saying: people are afraid I might infect them with my Jewish nose." He gave an unhappy laugh.

"Admittedly I have two Aryan friends left," said Silbermann. "Becker and Theo Findler."

"Calling Findler a friend," said Stein, "strikes me as a bit rash. Friendship with that man isn't something anyone's ever been able to boast about."

"You may be right, but if you no longer have any real friends left, you sometimes just have to squint and pretend you do. At least that can be a little reassuring. But what are you planning to do now?"

"I've taken a room there," Stein pointed to the hotel that Silbermann had just left.

"In that case . . . perhaps we'll see each other again."

They said good-bye.

Silbermann watched the other man leave. There was something calming about Stein's gait, something confident and life-affirming. He didn't place his feet straight on the ground, but at an angle, and his body had an almost imperceptible sway as he walked. As usual, his bowler was tilted back on his neck, and as he watched, Silbermann forgot all about the time and circumstances. He felt as though they'd just made a deal after all, neither particularly good or bad, merely something to keep connected, to stay in business together.

And to think that once I backed him up for credit in the amount of fifty thousand marks, Silbermann recalled wistfully. Stein & Co., serious people, not a big firm, but solid. And now on the verge of ruin.

He stepped into a restaurant to have a bite for supper. I ought to have invited Stein, he thought, as he looked over the menu, but then I, too, was afraid of his Jewish nose.

He ate with relish. After supper he lit a cigar and spent a few peaceful moments thinking of nothing. Then he remembered what he had to do and hurried over to the telephone. He dialed his home number and grew increasingly anxious as the ring tone kept sounding in short intervals. Minutes passed. No one answered. Finally he hung up.

Maybe there's something wrong with the phone, he thought, searching for a benign explanation. That happens every now and then, so why not today? On the other hand, why should that happen precisely today? he then thought. That would be very strange indeed.

He tried again, but with the same result. He grew more and more worried, and wondered if it wouldn't be better to go there and see what was happening firsthand, despite the danger that would entail for him as well as for his wife. Then he had the comforting thought that his wife must have decided to play it safe and was spending the night with one of her female friends. This was all the more likely given the fact that under the present circumstances she would be in need of company as well as protection. Of course in that case the servant girl ought to have picked up the phone, but Silbermann simply assumed she must have taken advantage of the opportunity to go to the movies, for which she had a pronounced fondness.

So he was calmer, if not entirely reassured, when he dialed the number of one of his wife's good friends, thinking she might have gone there. And even when Fräulein Gersch informed him that she hadn't seen his wife in weeks, he wasn't too distraught, because this did not disprove his theory. Fräulein Gersch, he now learned, had had a falling out with his wife. But she did offer to go to the apartment right away to keep Elfriede company, if she was at home. Fräulein Gersch was probably even glad to have an excuse. She also assured Silbermann that as far as she knew, women had in no way been harmed in the events of the day.

Silbermann asked Fräulein Gersch for the names and telephone numbers of his wife's other friends, so that he could call them as well. For his part, he had always been much too caught up in his business dealings to know who his wife's current bridge partners were.

As it turned out, Fräulein Gersch didn't know all of his wife's friends, either, so after he had dialed the given numbers with no result, he still believed it was possible she was staying with a different acquaintance.

To distract himself from worries about his wife, he asked to be put through to Hamburg. After just a few minutes he was connected to the Vier Jahreszeiten hotel, where Becker, who had put on certain airs of late, was newly accustomed to staying. Silbermann had to wait on the phone for a long time, and he was annoyed that he hadn't booked a person-to-person call, because even now he was still opposed to unnecessary spending. Finally he was told that Herr Becker was not in.

He's out gambling, Silbermann concluded, appalled. At this very moment he's gambling away my money, my chance to survive. Silbermann left the restaurant and went back to his hotel.

I should have gotten hold of a suitcase somewhere, he thought as he entered. This is making a horrible impression. Hopefully they'll think I'm some husband whose wife has kicked him out. That's an acceptable kind of misfortune— one that isn't considered a crime.

Should I even sign the registry with my real name? Silbermann wondered. If there's an inspection they'll haul me in right away, but if I give a false name I'd be breaking the law. It's terrible. The state is practically forcing a person to commit an offense.

This time they didn't give him the registration form but simply handed him his room key and let him know that a Herr Stein was waiting for him in the vestibule. Stein really could show me a little more consideration, Silbermann thought, and was immediately ashamed of his reaction.

"Good news?" asked Stein, who was sitting with another gentleman with similarly Jewish features.

"None at all."

"No news is good news. But why don't you sit down?"

"I'm pretty worn out from all the commotion. All I really want to do is go to bed and sleep."

He said good-bye, went to the elevator, and rode up to his room. A waiter, who was holding a full tray in his hands, went with him.

"Did you do away with your concierge?" asked Silbermann on their way up.

"He was arrested this afternoon. He was a Jew, after all."

Silbermann was taken aback and said nothing.

Once in his room, he quickly locked the door and then threw himself on his bed to think. "He was a Jew, after all," he heard the waiter's sober explanation. "He was a Jew, after all . . ." Obviously the waiter found this explanation sufficient. As though he viewed the arresting of Jews as something utterly normal, as much part of the daily routine as collecting a tip from a guest. A Jew was arrested, but then again: he was a Jew. Was any further explanation necessary? Evidently not, as far as the waiter was concerned.

I'm not staying here, Silbermann decided. He jumped up and looked around the spacious room. It's absolutely impossible for me to sleep here. They might drag me out of bed in the middle of the night, and if that makes a racket and bothers the guests enough, they'll open their doors to ask a maid what's going on, and she'll say, "Oh, nothing. They've just arrested a Jew, that's all." And perhaps the guests will answer, "Oh, is that it? . . . But do they have to make so much noise in the process?" The only thing these people want is not to be disturbed, that's all they're concerned about.

Of course once I'm arrested it makes no difference what the other people say or how they say it. Only that's not true, because if they weren't so apathetic . . . In any case I'm not safe here. They're going to arrest me, possibly even kill me. If only so I won't protest and become a bother and disturb the good citizens who are entitled to their rest. Because what they care about more than everything else is their sleep.

Silbermann paced up and down his room.

It's a wonder I'm even still alive, he thought. I no longer believe they've merely forgotten about me. But perhaps they'll carefully undress us first and then kill us, so our clothes won't get bloody and our banknotes won't get damaged. These days murder is performed economically.

He straightened his tie in the mirror and ran a comb through his hair. Then he cautiously opened the door to his room and peered out into the broad corridor, without seeing a soul.

Look how spooked you're getting, he thought. Just now I imagined I heard steps. And to think I fought in a world war. But that was different. Many against many. Now I'm completely alone and have to wage my war all by myself. Am I a conspirator? That would be good—at least then I would know how to act. But I'm just a businessman, nothing else. I have no energy, no momentum, that's it. Even a thief on the run with his loot has a smirk on his face—whereas all I have is fear.

He sighed quietly and stepped into the corridor, then walked quickly to the elevator and rang to call it up. Once back in the lobby, he went over to Stein, who was still sitting with the other gentleman, discussing past or possibly future business dealings.

"Listen, Stein," Silbermann said quickly and quietly. "I'm leaving this hotel. The Jewish concierge was arrested today. I assume some member of the staff is in contact with the police, or even worse, with the party. And they might very well sic the SA on us."

"Where do you intend to go?" asked Stein, rather calmly taking in Silbermann's report.

"I don't know yet, but I'm not staying here under any circumstances."

"I'm staying," Stein declared. "After all, I won't be getting out of the German Reich tonight. Nor will you. What purpose does it serve to make yourself meshuga on top of that. Anyway, things always turn out differently than you think."

"If you want to be a fatalist, that's your business," Silbermann interrupted. "I intend to do what I can to avoid falling into their hands."

"But where do you want to go? It's the same in every hotel. All a matter of luck. Even in the cemetery a Jew isn't safe from getting shoved around. What are you going to do?" He shrugged his shoulders in a gesture of resignation.

"So are you coming or not?"

"Listen, Silbermann, if you take me along, with my nose, you might as well stay here," he said, dismissing the thought with an almost scornful laugh. "Flee, with my nose? Absurd."

"You could be a South American, or an Italian," Silbermann said to console him.

Stein brushed off the idea with a wave of his hand. "I could be, but I'm not. I have a German passport." He shook his head. "No," he said, "there's no help for me. I have to see to my business, that's all I can do. A rich Jew is still worth more than a poor one. So don't let me detain you. Farewell and take care. I'll call you in a few days, once the anti-Semites have calmed back down. I'd like to make this deal with you, you know? By which I mean that you'll make the deal and pay me a commission. I'm telling you, what you get off those scrapped ships is nothing by comparison. This is a positive gold mine."

"I don't think I'll be making any more deals," Silbermann said slowly, "but feel free to call me in the next few days."

He paid for his room and explained his sudden departure

more or less neatly with an unforeseen trip, gave the waiter who was filling in for the concierge a handsome tip, without really knowing why, and left the hotel.

I'll take a train to Hamburg, he decided when he was out on the street. That's the best thing. I have a fine man there, that Becker. I can talk things over with him and he can intercede, too. Surely today was a case of things getting out of hand. Tomorrow the government might well declare it all happened without their knowledge. Even if it is full of anti-Semites, it's still the government, and this is something they simply can't allow. On days like this the task is simply to survive with body and soul intact. Whoever gets hurt is always wrong. Whoever comes through unscathed is right. I want to be right.

He took a streetcar to Bahnhof Zoo. On the way he counted his cash: he had ninety-seven marks left.

He marveled at how quickly it went. From one hundred eighty to ninety-seven. From now on he had to be thrifty, at least until he caught up with Becker, since being short of money in this situation really would be the last straw.

Once at the train station he purchased a ticket to Hamburg and went straight to the platform, even though the train wasn't due to depart for another hour. He bought a pack of chewing gum from a vending machine, and, thinking that this could calm and distract him, he stuck one piece after the other into his mouth, slowly and meticulously chewing away as he had often seen others do, until the tough substance gradually released its peppermint flavor.

He chewed vigorously for some time, with the intended mindlessness, and without deriving any pleasure—he was merely following a self-imposed task. As he did so he paced up and down the platform. He tried thinking about something pleasant, and finally imagined that his wife was likely already in bed and sleeping. But this thought brought others in its wake and, instead of reassuring him, only made him more anxious and afraid.

She's bound to be worried, he thought. At least I ought to send her a card.

He went to the waiting room, approached the buffet, and asked for a postcard. Then he sat down, ordered a coffee, and began to write, careful not to interrupt his deliberate chewing:

Dear Elfriede.

I've gone to Hamburg for a business meeting. I'll be back tomorrow. Don't worry, I'm doing fine. I tried calling but unfortunately couldn't reach you. I very much hope you're doing well.

Many heartfelt greetings,
Otto.

He looked over the contents of the card and decided it was in no way suspect, though he couldn't imagine what he might have written that would have aroused suspicion. He left the waiting room, passed through the ticket barrier to mail the card, then returned to the platform and resumed his pacing. He was cold, and shivered as he rubbed his hands together. He had left his gloves at home. Suddenly he saw a Sicherheitsdienst officer appear next to him.

Bahnpolizei—railway police, he thought, startled. They're

going to search the train for Jews. Silbermann couldn't remember ever having been so nervous. And it was hardly an unfamiliar sight: after all, how many SS and SA men had he encountered every day without really thinking anything of it? But now he sensed that every uniform was out to get him, and whenever he caught sight of a party member he felt: "That man is my sworn mortal enemy," and "He has complete power over me." He had reacted the same just after the Nazi "takeover"—but now it was even worse.

Silbermann resumed his pacing. When he was twenty meters away from the SS man he again turned in his direction. Am I really more anxious than other people? he asked himself. How would an SS man feel if he were forced to move about inside a Bolshevik state? And what if he had some additional marking, some feature that made him stick out like poor Fritz Stein?

These thoughts allowed him to feel his fear was justified. It was also comforting to imagine his enemies encountering their own day of dread, and Silbermann, who had always viewed the party of expropriation with disapproval and disgust, now found himself almost sympathizing with it, as his possible avenger. The idea was tremendously satisfying, and he clung to it for some time.

From a safe distance, Silbermann darted a glance at the unsuspecting man in uniform, as though to say: just wait, this is a long way from being over.

The train pulled into the station hall, and Silbermann, who had positioned himself in front of the sign marked 2ND CLASS, got rid of the gum he had been faithfully chewing the entire time—which suddenly struck him as very silly. Then he boarded the train. He entered a smoking compartment, took a forward-facing seat by the window, and looked out at the platform, which was still quite empty. He yawned, checked his watch, and determined that it would be quite a while before the train departed. The idea of waiting was hardly a pleasant one, since he didn't think he would recover his inner peace until the train was moving.

In any case I'm looking forward to speaking with Becker, he thought. He felt a growing desire for that man's company—although more as his business partner than for the person himself.

Hopefully he'll still be awake, Silbermann thought, but even if he's already in bed it doesn't matter. I'll simply wake him. I absolutely have to speak with him today. How come he didn't warn me? Usually he always knows everything in advance.

Suddenly Silbermann had a horrifying suspicion.

Becker had known. And it suited him this way. Now he has me at his mercy. He can rob me of my entire fortune in one fell swoop. The truth is I never fully trusted him. Maybe he's just as much a scoundrel as Findler! Here he's already pocketing half the revenue, but that's not enough for him. He wants the capital. He's already hinted at that. What did he say recently? "I need something to build on, Otto. When I think about it, I realize I don't have anything at all that I can build on."

And he's a Nazi, too. He's never made any secret about that. Maybe he just wanted to wait for the right moment so he could grab everything at once. A gambler. How could I have ever trusted a gambler? But these days it takes a gambler to do business with a Jew—no one else dares.

Silbermann couldn't sit still any longer. He stepped into the corridor and leaned out a window. The fresh, cool air did him good.

How could I possibly have thought that Becker wanted to betray me? he now asked himself. He was always a decent fellow, and we've known each other half our lives. It's the times that make a person doubt everyone and everything. Still, you shouldn't let them throw you off track.

He stepped aside to make room for a married couple who, having checked several compartments, finally sat down in his. The man could easily be a Jew, Silbermann thought, and leaned back out the window. The train was sparsely occupied, and Silbermann was glad not to have any other travelers choose his compartment.

I'll be able to sleep, he thought, once again yawning. I'm certainly tired enough.

The train slowly started rolling, and Silbermann left the corridor. He settled comfortably in his seat, closed his eyes, and tried to fall asleep. But even though the rhythm of the wheels, which had always had a lulling effect on him, made him more tired than he already was, he stayed awake. Now and then he registered bits and pieces from his companions' conversation, which from what he could tell moved from a critique of shared acquaintances to the pros and cons of air travel.

After ten long minutes of trying unsuccessfully to fall asleep, Silbermann righted himself in his seat. Only now did he notice that the man was wearing the gold party badge on his coat lapel. Silbermann automatically furrowed his brow and cast a sullen glance in his direction, then he tilted his head back into the upholstery but kept his eyes open and stared sleepily ahead, without thinking anything in particular.

First thing tomorrow morning I'll call Elfriede and send her a telegram in addition to the postcard, he resolved. Maybe I should have called Fräulein Gersch again. And what about Becker—strange that I haven't heard a single word from him. I'm eager to know if he picked up the money. Also I ought to write Eduard one more time, the boy has no idea what's going on here . . . And what actually happened at home? I probably should have sent someone to check. Here I am sitting in this train and have no idea, they might have done something to her, my God. At least Findler was there—the man's uncouth but he's reliable. This display he puts on, this pretense of decency—that's what Findler has—a phony uprightness like all these scoundrels. Ten thousand marks down payment, how outrageous can you get! Thank God Elfriede has money. Where's it all going to lead? I'm as helpless as a little child. Who could have imagined anything like it? In the middle of Europe, in the twentieth century!

The conductor came and checked the tickets.

Silbermann felt a need to say something and asked when they were due to arrive in Hamburg, even though he knew.

Before the conductor could reply, the man with the gold party badge answered the question. Silbermann thanked him for the information, and a conversation developed. After a few remarks about the weather, the speed of express trains and automobiles, the man with the party badge asked if Silbermann played chess.

Silbermann nodded amenably, and the other man immediately pulled a small travel set out of his briefcase and began arranging the pieces. This was a novel situation for

Silbermann, but he didn't see any reason not to accept the challenge. Besides, he assumed the game would make him focus on other things, which would be helpful as well as relaxing. It would also occupy the other man enough to keep him from talking.

It soon became clear that Silbermann was by far the better player. For a moment he wondered whether he shouldn't let the other man win, just for the sake of caution, but in the end he couldn't bring himself to do it, and after an hour of silent combat he put the other man in checkmate.

"Very nice," acknowledged the man with the party badge, and began to explain to his wife, who had dozed off during the match but was once again awake and drowsily sizing up Silbermann, why he had lost his king's pawn and what other mistakes had led to his defeat.

"If I had moved my rook to a3 instead of g4, then you would have . . . no, I should have castled beforehand, but then you would have taken your knight and, no . . . obviously I should have first moved my queen back. I have no idea, normally I play much better. But I'm exhausted, that's what it is."

Silbermann nodded to everything.

"Your opening impressed me," the man said, with the authority of an expert. "Oh well, I just wanted . . . but shall we perhaps play another round?"

It was clear he desperately wanted to make up for his loss.

"I'm not sure we'll finish before we get to Hamburg," Silbermann pointed out.

"We can play a blitz game. Incidentally, if I may, my name is Turner."

"Pleased to meet you," Silbermann answered dryly.

He now expected the question: And with whom do I have the pleasure?

I'll just say Silb, he decided.

But the other man didn't ask, and so they began their second round. This time the man with the party badge tried very hard and managed to gain a slight advantage over Silbermann. But Silbermann also concentrated and played with a dogged earnestness and a fervent inner rage, as if something extraordinary depended on their game.

His opponent's face reddened, and the man blinked excitedly as he pressed his lips together and kept nudging his wife to call her attention to the various positions. At one point he wanted to take back a move but abandoned the idea when he caught sight of Silbermann's slightly raised eyebrow. Then he made two different moves than he had intended, and ultimately he lost this match as well.

"You're a very skillful player," he said, but this time his voice sounded more reproachful than respectful.

"I played poorly," Silbermann lied, aware of the arrogance implied by this self-belittlement. The hostile remark further humiliated the defeated man, who could at least claim to have made Silbermann exert himself.

The man shuffled about uncomfortably on the seat cushion, looked at his fingernails, then at the chess set next to him, and finally said, "All good things come in threes. Don't you want to beat me a third time?"

"I'm not at all that confident in my ability," Silbermann said by way of restraint, and so they began their third match.

I'm going to be reasonable, Silbermann decided. I'm

going to lose. But he won once again. They played a fourth and fifth match, and as the train pulled into Hamburg the man with the party badge had just lost his sixth. His regard for Silbermann was now practically boundless.

"I must see you again," he requested as they said goodbye. "It's been a long time since I encountered a player as good as you." He gave Silbermann his calling card.

Silbermann read: Hermann Turner, chief engineer, Kleiststraße 14, and glanced at the telephone number.

"I just might give you a ring in the near future," he said, good-humoredly.

"Yes, please do," the other said, with all the humility of a mediocre player trying to entice a grandmaster to a game.

They shook hands and parted company.

A real human being, Silbermann thought happily. That was a real human being despite his party badge. Maybe things aren't all that bad. People with whom you can play chess, and who can lose without being offended or insolent, are hardly robbers and killers.

His chess victories had given him quite a boost, and when he left the station, he no longer had the feeling he was fleeing, that he was weak and all alone. He had proven that he could still win. He wondered whether he should take a taxi, but then decided to go on foot, since the hotel wasn't all that far away. Few people were on the streets, and there were almost no cars. When he came to the Jungfernstieg, he looked out over the Alster and spent a while staring at the gray water. He studied the reflections of the streetlamps on the dark flowing surface and inhaled deeply the refreshing, moist, cool air.

"What actually is the matter?" he asked himself. Things are hard, and there's harassment, that's certain. But sooner or later they'll leave us alone again, and I'll just emigrate. Things aren't all that bad, when it comes down to it. Despite everything, I'm still alive.

THREE

Becker was sitting with two Sturmführers, clearly at ease and enjoying himself, dining and drinking champagne—as had become his custom in recent years after closing a business deal. When he caught sight of Silbermann taking a seat at the next table, his relaxed mood vanished and he seemed on edge, shooting reproachful glances at his friend. Don't even think of joining us, his eyes warned, while at the same time asking: Why did you come? Why did you follow me? What on earth are you thinking, anyway?

Silbermann acted as though he hadn't noticed his partner's admonishing gaze and chiding glances. He studied the menu for a long time and then ordered a steak and a half-bottle of red wine, in a natural if somewhat faltering voice. He had slept through the whole morning and by the time he woke up it was practically one in the afternoon. Now it was nearly 2:00.

The evening before had gotten very late. Becker hadn't

been in the hotel when Silbermann arrived, and after waiting a long time in vain, he went to look for a place to spend
the night. He hadn't dared to ask for a room in the Vier
Jahreszeiten—the doorman's "Heil Hitler" had sounded too
sincere. So he had gone to a guesthouse for foreigners that
he knew of, where he was able to sleep undisturbed. However, when he filled out the official registration just as he
was leaving, and they saw his name, he was told that in the
future he'd be better off staying in a guesthouse reserved
for Jews. The comment did not exactly improve his mood.

Silbermann cast sullen glances at Becker.

That man sitting there, he thought, that friend of
mine—at least I hope he's my friend—has my fortune in his
pocket. Then he wondered whether their Hamburg business
associates might have tried to change the terms of the deal. In
actuality everything had been clearly spelled out and agreed
to, he told himself. But nothing was so clear it couldn't
become murky again. On the other hand, Becker was a capable businessman and also a reliable one. Reliable, without a
doubt. Absolutely. Together they had netted seven thousand
marks from dismantling that ship: if they had taken on the
actual scrapping as well, they would have likely earned even
more. As it was, they'd put in a lot of work and had had their
share of troubles. In any case I'll be happy and content just
to get my money back, thought Silbermann.

He raised the wineglass to his mouth. That was my last
deal in Germany, he promised himself. To earn three thousand five hundred marks I risked seventy-eight thousand.
He shook his head. Never again. Was it a sure thing? He
was about to find out. He didn't want to consider it a sure
thing as long as Becker had the money. Then again, clearly

Becker was someone he could rely on. He gave his friend another anxious, distressed look. Why didn't the man come up with some pretext to leave the others and join him? And what on earth was he doing with two Sturmführers?

When you think about it, what reason do I actually have to trust him? Silbermann worried. Trust is something I really can't afford. Not that I have to be suspicious all the time, no—but I do have to be careful. Trust or caution? My brother Hans fell in the war, fighting for Germany. He had trust. But that's just nonsense—what does one thing have to do with the other?

Becker stood up.

Now he's going to sit down with me, Silbermann thought, and casually set his knife and fork down on his plate.

But Becker strode calmly past his table, followed by the men in uniform, without so much as a greeting. For a moment Silbermann was speechless. Then he called out, "Waiter!" He paid for his meal, jumped up, and hurried after Becker, pulling his coat on as he walked. Becker had just left the dining room and was already in the lobby when Silbermann again caught sight of him. He was paying his bill, still accompanied by the two Sturmführers. Then he said a noisy good-bye to the clerk and left the hotel without noticing Silbermann, who had stopped as soon as he saw his partner.

Now I'm done for, Silbermann thought, distraught. Becker's going to cheat me out of my money, and then what? Beyond that he couldn't say.

After a moment's reflection he followed Becker, who was flanked by the Sturmführers and chatting with them as he strolled leisurely toward a taxi stand. Suddenly he came to an abrupt halt, turned around, and saw Silbermann ten steps behind him, staring at him with wide eyes and a half-open mouth. Becker gave a reluctant grimace and touched his hat. Silbermann hastily returned the greeting, relieved.

This is when I ought to go up to him, he thought, and ask what he's done with my money, what does he think he's doing, has he gone mad . . .

Silbermann took a step forward, then stopped, propped his foot against a wall, and fiddled with his shoelace. All of a sudden he was afraid of Becker, afraid of the power the other man had over him.

Be careful you don't get yourself arrested, Silbermann told himself, or get yourself beaten up, that's the last thing you need!

When he stood back up he saw Becker climbing into a taxi with the Sturmführers.

"Well, it's off to Berlin," Becker shouted out to Silbermann and waved good-bye.

"Thank God," Silbermann sighed quietly to himself. He was moved. "Becker you good honest fellow you." Then he was ashamed of his emotion, just as he had been ashamed of his earlier suspicion of Becker, and he decided that neither feeling had actually occurred.

He hailed a cab and went to the station, hoping to meet Becker there or later in the train. After he paid the fare he realized that he had only two twenty-mark bills left. If it weren't for Becker, he consoled himself as he climbed up the stairs inside the station, I can only imagine how worried and scared I'd be.

Silbermann took care not to let Becker see him, and

ultimately boarded a third-class car, even though he'd purchased a second-class ticket.

I don't want him to feel I'm watching his every move,
he thought tactfully, but he had to admit that he was also
acting out of caution, since he wanted to avoid attracting
the attention of his friend's companions.

There was only one open seat in his compartment.
Indifferently he surveyed the faces of his fellow passengers.
Directly across from him was a man who was puffing away
on a cigar of inferior quality. Silbermann guessed he was
traveling on business. As the train left the station, the man
stood up and made his way to the window, though not to
say good-bye to someone, as Silbermann had thought, but
to close it.

After half an hour the air in the compartment was full
of caustic fumes that badly irritated Silbermann's sinuses.
When he could no longer stand it, he got up and took refuge
in the dining car. He was also very hungry, as he'd left most
of his steak on the plate in the restaurant, and so he treated
himself to a large meal, since he was feeling encouraged that
Becker was nearby and that he must have the money. After
finishing his meal, Silbermann stayed in the dining car, but
as he leafed halfheartedly through the *Mitropa* magazine, the
old thoughts and worries came back.

About twenty minutes before the train was due in Berlin,
he decided to fetch his hat and coat from the compartment,
where he became an unwilling witness to a highly political discussion. The presumed businessman, who had earlier
shut the window, was in the process of explaining the ins
and outs of grand politics to the other occupants of the
compartment.

Silbermann took his seat and tried to ignore the lecture, since he was already somewhat familiar with what was being said. He looked past the man sitting next to him, watched the rainy landscape rush by outside the window, and thought about his own affairs. More than anything else he was increasingly worried about the fate of his wife, whom he'd again tried calling from Hamburg, with no success. The last twenty minutes of the journey were a real torture.

What has happened to Elfriede? he asked himself anxiously. He didn't understand how he could have gone to Hamburg without knowing for certain. At the same time I can't let Becker get away, he thought, as his other problem again loomed oppressively large. To distract himself he finally started listening to the man expounding on politics, his voice hoarse from talking and smoking.

"Blood and iron," he proclaimed, "those are what *we* use to achieve our political goals." The way he stressed the "we" showed how glad he was of his affiliation, as if he were an important member of the government. "The Jews," he continued, with raised voice, "used to say 'Germany must become European.' But today we say: 'Europe must become German.'"

The others listened quietly, their faces registering either agreement or indifference.

"Don't we want to open a window?" a modest voice asked at last.

"No," said the man. "I have a bad cold."

Confessing such a human foible undermined his hold on the others, and a window was opened despite his forceful protests. This in turn seemed to exacerbate his underlying rancor, and he immediately launched into a broad, unsparing attack on the Jews.

Silbermann stood up, put on his coat, and left the compartment. I'll meet Becker in the office, he decided, and hurried through the corridors to the lead car, so he could be the first person out and avoid having to run into his friend.

As soon as the train came to a stop, he jumped down and hustled off the platform. On the lower level of the station hall he looked for a telephone booth in a renewed effort to reach his wife. As he had feared, the phone in his apartment again went unanswered.

He did reach Fräulein Gersch, however, who told him that an unexpected visit the previous evening had kept her from checking on Elfriede. So she had gone today around noon and had rung the doorbell and waited for ten minutes, but no one had answered.

Her report weighed heavily on Silbermann and he asked if she had inquired with the other tenants in the building.

No, unfortunately she hadn't thought to do that, but she'd be glad to stop by again.

"Thank you," said Silbermann, "I'll go myself. I can't stand this uncertainty. I absolutely have to find out what happened there."

"I can only imagine how you're feeling," she said. "It's a pity that my aunt chose to visit yesterday of all days. But call me again tonight at nine. Unfortunately I can't get away at the moment, but I could go again around seven. Incidentally I also heard today that nothing happened to the women, that only men were arrested. So you don't need to be worried. Just stay calm and wait until this evening. If you go there something unpleasant might happen to you. One of the tenants might report that you've come back . . ."

"Well, in any case many thanks," Silbermann interrupted her. "With your permission I'll ring again this evening. Good-bye." Her consoling words had done little to ease his anxiety.

He decided to give his sister another call. She was home, but so frightened she could barely speak. When he suggested they meet in spite of everything, she cried out in terror.

"But we can't meet in town, given the situation you're in. And I can't leave the apartment. I keep thinking they're going to let Günther go. Every time the doorbell rings I jump, thinking it's him. Because they can't hold him for long, a fifty-six-year-old man. And I absolutely have to be here when he comes back."

"But . . ." That's not going to happen so quickly, he wanted to say. Nevertheless he kept quiet. Why should he take away her hope?

"Do you have an Aryan lawyer who might be able to intercede on his behalf?" he asked instead.

Yes she did.

"And money?"

That wasn't a problem, either.

He said good-bye and hung up.

Where do I go now? he wondered. It would be more than careless to let Becker run around very long with over eighty thousand marks. It was already foolish of me to let him collect the payment, but then again, you have to show a partner and friend a little trust. Have to? Well, in any case, what's done is done. But now it's time to retrieve the money, otherwise he'll get so used to having that kind of cash he won't want to part with it. On the other hand, I really ought to go to our apartment right away, he then thought, before finally deciding that Becker was his first priority.

After all, he reassured himself, it's also in Elfriede's interest, and if she isn't at home and is staying with a friend—which is far more likely—my presence there will be of no use. Whereas in Becker's case if I don't show up it can be downright harmful. And if by chance Elfriede is at home, she'll still be there in an hour. I've worked myself into a dither for no reason.

He debated with himself like this for some time. Then a new thought occurred to him: Findler. He should have guessed he wouldn't find the number, but he leafed awkwardly through the latest supplement to the phone book anyway. It had been only six weeks since Findler moved out of the guesthouse where he'd been staying up to that point, and into his own apartment, where he could come and go as he pleased while keeping down the expenses required to maintain his comfortable lifestyle. Just two days earlier Silbermann had jotted down the new number with red ink in one of his many notebooks—which were always on hand when there was something to write down, but never when something needed to be looked up—only now he was unable to remember it, after failing to find it in the phone book.

Instead, he tried calling the Kraus & Söhne firm, with whom Findler shared an office to save on rent. The entire office was small, and Findler had rented the smallest room, where he could be found from ten to twelve in the morning, eager to accommodate people who needed to borrow money and who possessed collateral—and where he also managed his properties. But the line was busy, and after trying to get through for two more minutes, Silbermann hurried out of the booth, when the matter of Becker again crossed his mind.

I should have called Findler a long time ago, Silbermann thought, as he left the station and approached a taxi. Naturally I forgot his number. All misfortune stems from forgetfulness.

He told the driver to go as fast as possible, and within just ten minutes the car pulled up to the office building where Silbermann had his firm. He paid the fare and went inside, checking to make sure the sign BECKER SCRAP AND SALVAGE CO. was in its place, as he'd been doing ever since someone had once unscrewed and stolen it. He rang for the elevator even though he could see it was on its way down.

I wonder if Becker's already here, he thought.

The elevator stopped, and out stepped his employee Fräulein Windke, who evidently had something to attend to.

"Guten Tag, Fräulein Windke," he greeted. "Is Herr Becker already here?"

"No," she answered. Silbermann had the feeling she was very surprised to see him. "Herr Becker just called. He'll be here in twenty minutes."

Silbermann thanked her and stepped into the elevator. As he was about to close the door he thought of the astonishment on her face. What was the matter with her? he wondered. Aha, she's probably surprised that they still haven't arrested me. He watched her walk away.

Do I even dare set foot in my own firm, he asked himself. What if Windke is phoning her fiancé. He's an SA man, after all. As it is I have the feeling she has something against me. Ach—that's nonsense. What do I care? Ridiculous. Surely I can go to my own office!

He closed the door, punched the button, and headed upstairs. But then he stopped the elevator at the second floor.

Better not, he thought. It's more sensible if I wait for Becker in Café Hermann. You can never be sure . . . I really didn't like the look on Windke's face.

He rode back downstairs. "What times we live in," he sighed as he left the elevator. He went out of the building, once again reading the name on his company's sign: BECKER SCRAP AND SALVAGE CO.

Becker, he thought. Indeed! Pretty soon I won't have any business coming here. My lovely private office. And to think the desk I needed finally arrived just fourteen days ago. And I ordered a new switchboard as well. This year to date I've invested three thousand marks in office equipment and typewriters and all that kind of thing. And I have no doubt we would have pulled off the deal with Heppel, which I've been working on for five months. The real business is just starting to happen, and I would have easily gotten the loan from the Dresdner Bank. What a disaster! Now everything will go to Elmberg & Co. If only I'd sold a year ago. But no, I just sat comfortably in my office, year after year, thinking life would simply go on like that forever . . . I had no idea. And that's the truth!

In a gloomy mood he crossed the street and went into Café Hermann, where he often stopped for a bite in the morning and coffee in the afternoon. He ordered a beer and began keeping a close watch on the opposite side of the street—which made for an excruciating half hour.

If it hadn't meant giving up his seat by the window, he might have rung up Becker in his apartment, because it seemed likely that Becker had reconsidered the matter and instead of going into the office he might simply call to learn if there was anything new.

Silbermann was getting more and more worked up. Here I am sitting right across from my own company and I don't dare step inside. And I'm the owner! The sole owner! It took me years of hard work to build it up, and now—now every apprentice has more say-so than I do! I can't dismiss my employees when it suits me, but they can denounce their boss whenever it strikes their fancy and have me sent to a concentration camp. It's like I'm some kind of schnorrer, begging from the people whose wages I pay.

Soon I'll be forced to ask: How is Apprentice Werner feeling today? Did he have a good night's rest? Is he in a good mood? Or maybe he's just fed up with me in every respect—as a person, a Jew, and as his boss. Perhaps he's taking his cues from some seventeen-year-old Hitler Youth squad leader? Silbermann laughed angrily.

And this Fräulein Windke, he thought, prancing from one pay raise to the next, because her fiancé is also a little führer! Come to think of it, she has no real reason even to speak with me—after all, nobody expects her to—so the fact that she does just shows what a magnanimous person she is!

Klissnik the accountant, on the other hand, isn't inclined to make any effort whatsoever, no . . . The fellow permits himself to show up late every third day. And because he's an

Aryan he can get away with it! On top of that I'm sure he'll demand a raise and I'll have no choice but to give him one!

What am I supposed to do to gain the goodwill of my employees and keep them happy? I can hardly make each one a partner!

Silbermann angrily drummed his fingers against the window. "That's it," he snarled. "I'm shutting down the business. I've had enough!"

Just then his friend's familiar gabardine coat appeared on the opposite side of the street. Having already paid for his beer, Silbermann jumped up, hurried outside, and rushed across to Becker. Becker saw him coming and waited calmly for Silbermann to approach.

"I've spent hours wondering what happened!" Silbermann groaned when he reached his friend. "You have no idea! Did it all work out?"

They shook hands.

"Are you coming up?" Becker asked, and then right away answered his own question. "Better not."

They went into the café that Silbermann had just left. On the way Becker talked about his trip, how much they'd drunk, how great it had been, and what a pity it was that Silbermann couldn't have met the two Nazis, who were splendid fellows even if they were stinking anti-Semites. Then they sat down.

Becker crossed his arms, looked expectantly at Silbermann, and said, not without a trace of arrogance, "So, out with it! Why did you come chasing after me? Probably got scared, eh?"

"Do you have the money?" Silbermann asked, without answering the question.

"First tell me what's going on with you," Becker demanded aggressively.

"Haven't you heard what they're doing to Jews?"

"You mean these incidents . . ."

"They attacked us in our apartment. I was barely able to escape. Findler was there, he stopped them."

"Really?" Becker acknowledged with indifference. "The main thing is that nothing happened to you. By the way, did you sell that old shark your building?"

"Ten thousand marks down payment!"

Becker shook his head. "Ten thousand marks! What on earth got into you?"

"Just tell me: how did things go? Why didn't you speak to me in Hamburg, and why were you traveling with those Sturmführers?"

"One thing at a time." Becker began his report. "So, naturally those junk-dealing Jews caused trouble. You know how they wheel and deal. This time it was on account of the riots and so on. So I said to myself: Becker, you've never been a match for these people, and I quickly rang up a friend of mine in Berlin. Then he came to Hamburg along with another one. And when they showed up this morning wearing their uniforms, well, that was all it took, those Jews signed right away! Naturally I raised the price by five grand. You see how I do business? I'm counting the five thousand as travel expenses."

Becker gave a proud, contented laugh and placed his broad, heavy hand gently on Silbermann's shoulder. Silbermann brushed it angrily away.

"That was extortion!" he stated slowly.

"How else do you want to do business with Jews like

that?" asked Becker, offended. "They told me they wanted to get out of Germany. Their relatives had been arrested, and they kept going on and on. I took it all in very calmly, and finally I said: but you've already purchased the ship—and endorsed the transfer order from the Reichsbank!—you have to take it! 'Well,' said old man Levi—you know what a smooth talker he is—'I'm not sure we're still allowed to do business. And government intervention counts as a force majeure, we have no choice.' I don't give a damn about that, I answered, you have to take the ship! Then he started to fuss. 'First I need to make some inquiries.' Straightaway I had the boys come over, and lo and behold: everything went smooth as silk. Fool that I was, I should have asked for ten thousand marks more. They were so scared they gave me a cashier's check right on the spot, although I'm sure they would have preferred to have eked out another two days' interest. But we know those tricks. At first it's all brash talk, but once you take a swing there's nothing to back it up. A lot of whining, that's all."

"You didn't exactly behave decently," Silbermann said sharply.

"I'm not going to get ruined by some filthy Jew! What do I care if they're having difficulties? Why do they do these outrageous things, murdering diplomatic secretaries and so on. If they shoot at people they have to count on the fact that people are going to shoot back. And whoever sticks his stupid snout out is going to get hit. I'm telling you: I don't care if there are three pogroms happening at once! I'm not going to get taken in by any Jews because of that, not by a long shot. So don't be coming to me looking for sympathy!"

"You're completely forgetting," Silbermann said, agitated,

"that the person sitting across from you is a Jew. You spend two hours with these people from the party and you start behaving like a—swine."

"That's enough," said Becker, his eyes bulging the way they always did when he was mad. "You aren't my superior anymore, understand? The times have changed a bit. I've put up with a lot from you, more than from anyone else. But just because I've always been considerate, you get cocky, that's just like a Jew. What do you think you're living off, hm? Who closed the last deals? Where would you be if I hadn't been so decent as to take the lead? You think you can impress me with your big mouth? Mine is just as big. So, now I've said what I wanted to say!"

"Gustav, you have to send back the five thousand marks. That's extortion plain and simple!"

"And the way I saved your capital is completely on the up and up? Jews always stick together. I've said it before and I'll say it again. Because you're afraid that a Jew—and one worth millions at that—might lose his money, you want to take away mine! That's also typically Jewish!"

"But Gustav, be reasonable for a moment! Do you really want to turn into a criminal in your old age?"

"Spare me your lectures on morality. Other people do exactly what I'm doing. Everybody uses whatever advantage he has, but you expect me to be an idealist, is that right? As if you hadn't made a fortune off the bad luck of others. Now your own luck has turned bad, and we're the ones making money. But that's something completely different, is that right? No, my friend, it's only fair. You may have shrewder heads, but we have harder fists and we're in the majority. Actually you should be glad I don't blab on you! So don't be telling me things. You think I've forgotten how you used to take advantage of me? As your authorized representative all I ever earned was three hundred marks. And how much did you make? Because I happen to know!"

"You are the most ungrateful person I've ever met! I'd like to know what would have become of you if I hadn't hired you right after the war. And now you hold it against me that as the head of the company I earned more than you did? After all it was my money I was working with and not yours, wasn't it?"

"And where did you get your money from?"

"From my father and my own work. I can honestly say that I earned it!"

"And now I'm starting to earn money for myself. All these years I've watched how other people lived. Now it's my turn! I should have squeezed old Levi for fifty thousand marks! Oh was I ever dumb!" Becker was getting more and more worked up. "Too nice, I'm just too nice. We're simply no match for you Jews, that's what it is."

Faced with this spontaneous but not exactly blind hatred, it took a while for Silbermann to find the right response.

"You've known me for twenty-three years," he then said slowly, "through war and peacetime . . ."

"Don't come to me with that old song!"

"Gustav, if you weren't . . . the way things are now, if you were a man of character, then you would . . ."

"Stop with all this blathering. You think I'm that stupid? Now you've gone and shown your true colors! You'd be happy to rob your friends to help some lousy rich old Jew! People of your kind can't even have friends unless they're Jewish."

"Did you drink too much? Or did you lose money gambling? Gustav, what's gotten into you? Judging from all your moral outrage, I take it you have some other dirty tricks in mind."

"Dirty tricks? I don't give a damn how you see it. I just want to tell you point-blank that our friendship is over. From now on each of us is doing his own deals. We no longer have anything to do with each other!"

"Gustav, what on earth is the matter with you? You can't fool me. Do you think I can't tell how hard you're trying to sound enraged?"

Silbermann probably shouldn't have said that, because now Becker really became furious. His face turned alarmingly red before he regained control of himself.

"This is too much," he snapped, with feigned obstinacy. "You insulted me . . . you followed me . . . you mistrusted me . . . so now I'll give you a reason to do so! Because we're through, we're finished! You can have Becker Scrap and Salvage Co. I'm giving up my shares, I don't want to keep a single one, even though I lent my name. So kindly make sure it's removed immediately. That's right! And as for the eighty thousand marks, we're splitting that. That's the simplest thing. And in return you get all your shares back. And then we're done with each other."

He said that as harshly as he could, but his voice was trembling, and Silbermann, who was at first taken aback by the bold proposition, had the impression that the other man was practically desperate, forcing himself to utter each of his nasty proclamations. It seemed to him that Becker felt obliged to prove that he was equal to the times, rather than following his own volition, his own conviction.

"Gustav," Silbermann said quietly, "why are you so intent on becoming a scoundrel? It doesn't suit you at all."

"You tell me," Becker asked, switching to his normal voice, "am I not within my rights? A person only gets one chance in life. And I've never had one! So now I have to take advantage of it."

"You're mad," said Silbermann. "You sniveling swindler!"

"Shut up. If I were mean I could say: Jew! So, do you agree to the separation proposal? Because if you don't, then I'll go ahead and keep everything. Another person in my situation would certainly do that. But I'm just soft in the head."

"You want to steal my money that I entrusted you with?"

"The payment is written out in my name."

"I'm not talking about the payment, don't play dumb. I trusted you, Gustav. And I still do. Enough of these bad jokes."

"Jokes? I know how you can twist your tongue. That's why you're a Jew. But I've made up my mind and you're not going to talk me out of it!"

"There are laws!"

Becker laughed scornfully. "If threats are what you want," he said, "I'm in a far better position than you."

"Gustav, it's not the money I'm concerned about, well yes, I'm concerned about that as well, but there's more at stake. Please believe me! I simply can't bear to see a man like you become a miserable lowlife and blackmailer. There still have to be people who maintain their decency and humanity no matter what opportunities might come their way. Who don't turn into swine just because they see a puddle they might wallow in."

"I am a decent person," Becker said without conviction. "On that point I insist."

"Well, you were at one time. Tell me, do you find it easy to break your word?"

"What word? I don't know anything about any word. Stop talking so much. Either accept my proposal or don't."

"I don't! If someone robs you and then you agree to take back half of what he stole, that makes you an accomplice to the theft."

Becker jumped up. "I'm warning you," he growled, switching to the formal *Sie*. "That's enough of all this wheeling and dealing!"

"I'll get you sent to jail," Silbermann declared. He was so agitated he was no longer weighing his words. "And I'll tell everyone I know about your dirty extortion. I'll denounce you to your party. I have no doubt that they'll take the money away from you. Because when it comes to robbing Jews they claim exclusive rights. They don't tolerate unfair competition. You'll see who you're dealing with yet, you disgraceful crook!"

"I've always known you were a low-down shyster," Becker retorted. He had sat back down and was once again using the familiar *Du*. "Do you even know what you are? A nervous little Jew quivering over his money. If I were like you, I wouldn't give you a penny, I'd simply have you sent straight to the concentration camp. Where you could denounce me as much as you like."

"Do you remember what you said to me yesterday, Gustav? You spoke of friendship!"

"I've seen what kind of friend you are. Why do I always have to be the stupid nice guy?"

"You don't believe a word of what you're saying."

"But I'm supposed to believe you, is that right? You slick talker, you. Who sent in a false tax declaration, eh? Who bought the building on Kantstraße for a song during the inflation? Was it me? Do you remember how you were the only one to get leave in 1917? And why was that? Because you had purchased war bonds. Something the rest of us couldn't afford . . ."

"Are you telling me you wouldn't have done that if you could have? Are you trying to hold me responsible for the entire system? For the fact that there are social differences? Reproaching me for having money? So that you can justify robbing me? And for a few days of extra leave, for a minor instance of injustice, you want to pull off a major swindle? You're scolding me for being a capitalist? You? Who want to become one by any means including the slimiest? Don't be a fool, Gustav. It's enough that you've become a scoundrel."

"I'm just using my advantage, just as you've taken advantage of your situation. That's all," Becker said casually.

"There is egoism that is justified and egoism that is not. There are limits!"

"Now you want to tell me what's justified and what isn't? Everything you did was well and good, and everything I do is wrong? I'll say it again: I'm simply taking advantage of my situation!"

"There were times when my situation would have made it easy for me to steal another man's wallet. But I can honestly say I never did!"

"You were also always a rich man! That a wealthy merchant doesn't steal a silver spoon is no reason for him to flatter himself."

"Agreed. But I'm not talking about silver spoons. Don't try to be clever, Gustav, that's just too much. You know very well that all my business dealings were absolutely impeccable and that I've always acted properly."

"Meaning I haven't? More decently than you in any case. At least I haven't threatened to send you to jail!"

"You couldn't have. You wouldn't have had any reason."

"In 1930 you paid four thousand marks less than you should have in taxes, and in 1926 it was as much as nine thousand marks."

"In the first place that's not true, and in the second place everyone does that."

"Well, taxes were always taken out of my three hundred marks."

Silbermann lit a cigarette. "You're being a scoundrel and you know it," he said, exhausted. "And even if I really had dodged the tax, that by no means justifies your abusing my trust. After all, you're my friend, and I've never been friends with the tax office. And even the most decent person would rather pay too little taxes than too much. Only a criminal, like yourself . . ."

"I'm warning you, don't start up again. And now I'm asking you for the last time: do you agree to the proposal or not? If you refuse, then I'll leave the whole amount with a notary until the matter is decided, since I own fifty-one percent of the shares. I'll simply dissolve the company. And any remaining assets will be divided one way or the other."

Silbermann tried once again to change Becker's mind. "Gustav," he said slowly. "You can't possibly do that! Look, that would be . . ."

Becker stood up theatrically. "I consider our conversation

ended," he said formally. "I'm now going to the notary and will deposit the money there. I feel all the more compelled to do so because you, as I happen to know, intend to leave the country. Consequently there is a danger that if you get hold of the funds you might transfer them abroad. This way, however, your share of the company will be placed in a blocked account. Auf Wiedersehen, Herr Silbermann!"

He actually made a move to leave.

"I accept," said Silbermann. "But I will never understand how you"—here he corrected himself and switched to the formal *Sie*—"how you could do something like this. In stealing from me you are dirtying yourself. Disgusting!"

Becker was visibly on edge. "Would you finally shut up with all your dumb talk," he muttered gruffly. "Don't take me for such a sentimental fool. Money has no smell," he quipped. "Because if it smelled like you, I wouldn't take it at all."

Becker placed his briefcase on the table and Silbermann looked on without interrupting as he drafted a deed of partition. Now and then he glanced in his notebook, which led Silbermann to believe that Becker had previously had his lawyer spell out the various points, and had therefore been entertaining the idea for some time.

"Actually your portion would amount to only forty-one thousand marks," Becker said after a while, "since you only have forty-nine percent of the shares."

"Yes, and you have fifty-one, for which you didn't pay a penny. Which you are supposed to administer as trustee, according to our agreement."

Becker testily put down his pen. "Is there anything else you'd like to say?" he asked sharply.

"The only legally valid agreement is the partnership! As you are undoubtedly aware. Or would you like to declare in a court of law that the agreement was a fiction?"

"Stop talking this nonsense, you! Or else I might feel forced to . . ."

"To what?" asked Silbermann. "If it came to a trial, you would lose miserably. You can be sure of that. After all, there is our written correspondence. I still have your letter in which you affirm our oral agreement. I even have it . . . wait a moment . . . yes—I even have it on me."

Becker tossed down his pen. "It's good you're bringing this up now," he said. "That's fine with me. Let's take the matter to court. If you were to win—assuming that you really would win—what would that bring you? First you'd already be a guest in a concentration camp, you can bet your life on that. And as for your money? Everything would be in a blocked account, and by the time the matter made its way through the courts all Jewish property would have long been seized. And then there's the billion-mark atonement levy. So be my guest, let's take this to trial." He stood up once again.

"Idiot," Silbermann said, with disdain. "On top of everything else, you expect me to cheer you on, is that it?"

Becker sat down again. "What you should do is shut up," he said. Then he continued writing and muttered, "I won't put up with your taunting. You . . . you are far too common, too coarse for my taste!"

Despite his indignation and distress, Silbermann couldn't help laughing.

Becker finished his draft and handed it to Silbermann to look over.

Silbermann merely glanced through it and said, "I see you've mastered the technical side of theft as well as the theoretical. Should I sign this, or do we want to have it notarized?"

"It's already six thirty," Becker stated. "The notary will be closed, but if you sign the contract and the receipt—naturally you'll receive a counter-receipt from me—and if you hand me the letter, I'll pay you your share right away. You can keep the company shell, as long as my name is removed. There are hardly any liabilities, and in any case they'll be fully covered by what's in the postal checking and bank accounts. As far as the receivables are concerned, well, I'll let you have fun with that. I don't think you'll get Ollmann to pay, now that nothing's left . . . Apart from that there aren't any. You have methodically dismantled the business. If it were up to you, in half a year I would be penniless and you'd be in Paris. I'm not completely stupid."

"I didn't dismantle anything, we just took the entire capital in order to . . . but it's pointless to talk about it. Here is your letter."

Becker opened his briefcase, took out a few packets of bills, and began to count.

"Forty-one thousand five hundred marks," he said, when he was finally finished. "So there, I gave you fifty percent after all. Be so kind as to count it." Then he bent over the table and whispered confidentially, "See that you manage to get it over the border."

"Spare me your advice," Silbermann said dismissively.

After they finished the transaction, Becker sighed. "No offense, Otto," he said, suddenly lapsing back into the old, friendly tone. "Once I really start winning, you know my system, you'll get your money back with interest. Yesterday I lost nine thousand marks because I had to stop too early. But now I'm going to win back every penny I ever lost."

Silbermann stood up abruptly. "For a real villain," he said, "you're lacking in flair. And for a decent human being, but above all for a friend, you're decidedly too slimy for my taste."

He walked out of the café. Becker watched him, taken aback.

The Jew isn't all that wrong, he thought. But I have to pay my debts once and for all. I can't cheat the people out of their money. This last moral consideration calmed him once again. A pity, though, he went on thinking, as he left the café, we were friends for so long—I'll make up for it all eventually!

FOUR

Silbermann's coat pockets were bulging out from all the bills, so he went to a shop to buy a briefcase. After making the purchase he realized it was already 6:55, so he dashed to the nearest post office, where he took a form from the telegraph counter and sent a local telegram to his wife. Because he was worried about returning to his apartment, he asked her to meet him in a café closer to home.

When he left the post office he wondered what he should do with the forty-one thousand five hundred marks he had recovered. He decided not to dwell on the matter of Becker and how deeply his former friend had disappointed him, although that did little to stave off his painful, depressing reflections.

He took a streetcar to the place where he was expecting Elfriede. For some strange reason he was convinced that she would come. Once inside, he set his hat on a chair and went to the men's room to transfer the money to his briefcase. On his way back to his table he noticed that the place was full of men in uniform, and he instinctively hugged his briefcase close to his body. Half an hour passed. By then Silbermann had drunk his third cup of coffee and was becoming increasingly nervous.

Hopefully the telegram was delivered right away, he thought. How long does that usually take? I should have asked. If she had received it, she could be here in five minutes. Assuming she was at home. After all, she had to go back to the apartment sooner or later. I'm sure I've been waiting here at least an hour, he thought, but a glance at the clock told him it had been only thirty-five minutes.

Mulling over his situation, he wondered: what am I supposed to do now? Because they're still going after Jews. I can't stay a single night in my apartment—not with forty-one thousand marks!

We have to leave Germany, but no place will let us in. I have enough money to start a new life, but how to get it out of the country? I don't have the nerve to try to smuggle it across. Should I stay or go? What to do?

Should I risk ten years in prison for a currency offense? But what other choice is there? Without money I'd starve out there. Every road leads to ruin, every single one. How am I supposed to fight against the state?

"Waiter, please bring me a glass of water."

Other people were smarter. Other people are always smarter! If I'd realized in time what was going on, I could have saved my money. But everyone was constantly reassuring me, Becker more than anybody. And fool that I am, I let myself be reassured. Which is why I'm stranded here.

The devil take the hindmost. An old but true saying. And this time I happen to be the hindmost. But aren't there still six hundred thousand Jews living in Greater Germany? How do they manage? Oh, they'll know how to take care of themselves. Other people always know better. Just not me, even though I wasn't born yesterday, either!

Maybe things aren't half so bad, and the whole business is one big psychosis. But no, I should finally acknowledge the reality of the situation: things are going to get worse— much, much worse! Moreover, the fact that it takes someone like Becker to disabuse me shouldn't come as a surprise. The scoundrel. But what good does it do to get worked up? I have to get out of Germany! Only there's no place to go! To make it out of here you have to leave your money behind, and to be let in elsewhere you have to show you still have it. It's enough to drive a person mad! If you dare do anything, you risk getting punished, and if you do nothing you'll be punished all the more. It's just like in school. If you did the math problems completely on your own you'd get an "unsatisfactory," while if you copied off a better student you'd get a "good"—unless you were caught, and then you'd get a "fail." Which is what you would have gotten in the first place if you'd been entirely honest and hadn't even attempted to solve the problem: one way or the other, you always wind up with the same result.

He smiled sadly and lit a cigarette.

Nevertheless I have to try to make it out, he thought, and sighed. Except I know I'll wind up right inside the barbed wire. I see it coming.

He reached for his briefcase and placed it behind him, against the back of his chair, just to feel secure.

Forty-one thousand marks, he thought, that's still something! Even in the Third Reich. I count myself lucky that I recovered that much. If I'd been a little more sensible when I spoke with Becker, I probably could have salvaged even more. But when faced with such despicable behavior, who could avoid getting riled up, let alone be able to coolly assess the situation?

Silbermann only now realized that for some time he'd been looking a few tables away at an attractive woman of about thirty who was wearing a green dress. The woman smiled faintly—just enough to encourage him.

"Well," said Silbermann, then he looked away. My type, went through his head, and: she looks very charming, refreshing . . . He recalled days long gone when he had been somewhat of a "ladies' man," and without intending to, he once again observed her. I'm letting my guard down, he thought, relaxing my internal discipline. That's a bad sign! I get mesmerized by a pretty face and let myself be cheated by idiots. Am I starting to go senile? Is she actually smiling, or am I just imagining? That would have to be determined. Now she's turning away. And she's right to do so. Not only am I married, but I have plenty of other worries.

He turned serious again and let out another sigh, which attracted the woman's attention.

They always think everything is meant for them, he thought, with reproach as well as amusement. Naturally anytime a man sighs it must be because of a woman.

He looked at the clock.

What's keeping Elfriede? I'll try reaching Findler again, he decided.

He stood up and walked past the woman. She didn't smile at all, which was also fine as far as he was concerned.

Inside the booth he searched through the phone book to find the number of the guesthouse where Findler had been living. A maid answered who not only did not know Findler's new telephone number but had no idea he even existed. He asked her to check with the others, but the landlady, who might have been able to tell him, was absent, and the rest of the staff didn't know.

With all the back-and-forth, the phone conversation lasted about ten minutes, and afterward Silbermann hurried back into the café since he still hoped his wife might have turned up, but she hadn't.

Meanwhile the lady in green had left, a fact that he only noted in passing, but which further dampened his mood.

He had the impression that the place had emptied out, and soon the waiting became unbearable. Then he was horrified to realize that he'd left his briefcase on the chair when he went outside to phone. His absentmindedness worried him greatly, and he forgot all about the lady in green. Keeping an anxious eye on the other guests, he hurried to stash some of the money back in his suit pockets, so that at least he would avoid a total loss.

It was already eight o'clock. He ordered a meat platter and ate with good appetite. However, every time the door of the café opened, he gave a start and turned around, hopeful but also expecting another disappointment. By twenty minutes after eight he'd finished his meal and asked the waiter for the bill.

That's it, he decided, I'm going to go. I simply have to

know what's happening. Then he remembered that at nine o'clock he could call Fräulein Gersch, but after a moment's hesitation he decided to leave after all. He was so impatient that instead of going on foot he took a taxi.

The eighteen-year-old son of the doorman was standing in front of the building, dressed in the uniform of the SA. When he saw Silbermann climbing out of the cab, he turned around and hurried inside.

That's a bad sign, thought Silbermann, pausing for a moment to weigh his options. In any event I'll have to be very quick and leave the apartment right away, he concluded.

He rushed up the stairs. He rang several times and, since he didn't hear any footsteps, he unlocked the door. He was distraught to see glass splinters on the rug. Then he noticed that the large front-hall mirror had been shattered.

Calling card of the master race, he thought, incensed, and hurried into the dining room. Seeing that the furniture was still intact, he concluded that yesterday's visitors hadn't ventured into this room. And even though they must have posed a great temptation for such robust hands, the crystal bowls were also still intact.

"Elfriede!" Silbermann called, and rang immediately for the maid. Obviously they're not here—I knew it, he thought, and once again called out his wife's name. He opened the door of the parlor. Here the marks of heavy feet were evident. The floor was littered with shards of porcelain. Silbermann saw the étagère standing amid the shattered tea service.

He again called out, "Elfriede!" Then he sensed that was pointless. She isn't here, they've taken her away, it's possible they've done something to her. And meanwhile I took a train to Hamburg . . . I ate and I drank coffee and chattered away and saw to my business deals. I was everywhere but here, which is where I should have been.

He went to the back part of the apartment to look for the maid. He called out for her, checked in the kitchen and in her room, but of course she wasn't there. Of course! How on earth could he have thought that everything would be normal and exactly the way it had been except for the telephone being out of order?

"I made it too easy for myself," he groaned as he moved quickly to the bedroom and then the dressing room. "My optimism was nothing but cowardice! If only I'd come back sooner, but instead I chose to sit down with Becker—as if I couldn't just have easily waited until later to let myself be cheated. What use are the forty-one thousand marks to me now!"

He looked at the objects lying on the floor, the overturned tables and chairs, the slashed paintings and torn-down curtains. Then, in an act of hopeless, unrestrained fury, he kicked a pile of books that had been pulled off the bookcase, sending them flying in all directions, and collapsed onto a leather armchair that had withstood all attempts at destruction, and stared expressionless at the floor.

"The end of the song," he mumbled, "the end of the song." He didn't know exactly what he meant by that.

Something gleamed on the carpet. He picked it up. It was a party badge that one of the intruders must have lost. Silbermann studied the small swastika. "You murderer," he whispered, "you murderer . . ." He put it in his jacket pocket.

"This is evidence," he said out loud. "Sufficient evidence!"

He reached into his pocket and clasped the badge tightly, as though he wanted to crush it. Then he took it back out and studied it once again. Finally he stood up.

"I'm going to examine everything," he said. "I'm going to make sure everything is substantiated and then . . ." He didn't know how to go on. He saw that they'd broken into his desk and the money stored there was gone. "Yes indeed," he said, "yes indeed"—as if that gave him great satisfaction. But then he was overcome with despair.

If only I'd stayed, he thought. If only I'd stayed here! It would never have ended so badly. I would have talked to them, given them money. Because what else are they after? Nothing. I was never politically active. Never in my life. Only once did I buy a forbidden newspaper, but not a soul on earth knows about that.

Suddenly he had an idea. He hurried to the dining room and lifted the large Delft bowl off the credenza. Underneath he found her letter. He was so excited that when he tore open the envelope he damaged the contents. He pulled up one of the tall carved chairs, sat down, and read:

Dear Otto.

The people just now left the apartment, and they intend to come back. I called the doctor right away, because Herr Findler was badly hurt. Tonight I'm going to Ernst's in Küstrin. I have no idea what I should do, but I'm not staying here another hour. I took the money from the desk. I'm giving Frau Fellner the key to the apartment and in Küstrin I'll hire a carrier to retrieve the things. Please write *immediately* to Ernst's address, but it's better if you

don't come. Jews in the small towns are being treated
even worse. The best would be if you went to Eduard
right away!!! After all, I can come later. Please write
at once, because I'm terribly worried about you . . .

The ending was hardly decipherable.

"I ought to be glad now," Silbermann said to himself
quietly. "So why aren't I?"

So, she has the money, he then thought. Why didn't they
steal it? People break into houses in order to steal. He shook
his head and went on speaking his thoughts out loud. "I
don't understand. The whole thing is simply unreal. They
come, they break in, they chase people away—it doesn't
make sense for them not to have stolen things."

He stood up.

Still, it's all good, he forced himself to think. "Everything's fine," he then said. "It was just a false alarm. She's
safe—of course I'll go to Eduard. Actually I ought to be
dancing with joy, when I think about how lucky I've been."

He sat back down. I have to check again to see if they
really didn't steal anything, he then decided. That had to
have been their motive. What else could it be? Hate? They
don't even know me. And out of the blue like that. In one
day? Following orders? Strange.

He went through the apartment.

No, they hadn't stolen anything, as far as he could see,
only destroyed things. The government, he thought, knows
why it does what it's doing. The government needs money.
But why did these individual people do this? Why?

Then he remembered Findler. Poor man, he thought. It
turns out that transacting business in this particular milieu

isn't so simple after all. Silbermann couldn't help smiling, though at the same time he felt it wasn't very nice of him to do.

He had entered the bedroom and let himself drop onto his bed. I have to leave, he thought, as he closed his eyes. "Ach," he said to himself. "I'd really like to stay. To sleep . . . But instead now I have to head to the border . . . I've never been capable of that sort of thing, I simply don't know how. Secretly slipping past the guards . . ." He shuddered at the thought. "What do they want from me anyway," he asked quietly. "All I want is to live in peace and earn my bread . . . The border! Me, sneaking over the border—my God."

He jumped up.

It's no use, he thought. Now is no time to let myself go! I have to pull myself together!

Newly resolved to do whatever he must, Silbermann vigorously smoothed out his jacket. Then he started packing his suitcase, taking only what was absolutely essential for the journey, and his mood again became more hopeful. A quarter hour later he was finished and took one last walk through his apartment. We had such a beautiful, comfortable life here, he thought, and now I have to leave everything behind and run away from my old life, because . . . because . . .

Succumbing to his worries, Silbermann sighed and again sat down on the chair, until the bell of a passing streetcar startled him back to his plan of action.

From underneath a pile of magazines that were stacked in a side shelf of the bookcase, he retrieved some hidden papers, including his military service book, the membership cards of various Jewish organizations, as well as the land registry deed for his building.

He felt sad as he stared at the certificate. That once meant money, he thought: seven thousand marks in rent. And fool that I am, I had the whole building repainted last year. Another thing I could have done without.

In an attempt to shrug off his melancholy mood, he strived to discern a certain pathetic irony in the new circumstances. It's actually quite simple, he thought: I've been declared to be in the service of a hostile power, which means I'm back to being a soldier. Only now my mission is to smuggle myself and my briefcase through both German and French lines.

But no matter how emboldening his thoughts, his mood could not be lifted.

He stowed the papers in his briefcase and took out six thousand marks to put in his suitcase. Then he debated whether he shouldn't also quickly pack his suits, his wife's fur coat, and her evening dresses. In the end he decided not to, since he felt he'd already spent too long in the apartment.

We're losing so much, he consoled himself, that these things no longer matter. He contented himself with locking the cabinets and drawers and taking the keys. Of course I forgot the most important thing, he thought, as he carried his suitcase through the apartment for the fifth or sixth time. Did Elfriede at least take her jewelry? She should have written about that, now I have to ... Why didn't she—I don't understand!

He set down his suitcase in the front hall and went back into the bedroom. He opened the drawers of the nightstand but found nothing except a receipt for the milk delivery. Then he hurried into the dressing room, forced open the door of the small medicine cabinet, since he couldn't find the key, and looked for the small case that was usually stored there. When he didn't find it he sighed with relief. She had taken it with her. Of course, a woman never forgets her jewelry, not even if she's in mortal danger. Anyway, it's a very good thing she thought about that. She can live for a while off of that if something should happen to me—until I'm settled abroad.

He left his apartment. Slowly and very calmly he climbed down the stairs.

If only I were already downstairs, he wished. If only I were already in the taxi. Hopefully the doorman's son won't be standing outside.

He was.

Silbermann raised his hat, the other man raised his arm.

"I'm going away for a few days," Silbermann felt obliged to explain. "Would you please tell your mother that I'd be very grateful if she would look after the apartment?" His voice sounded hoarse and husky.

The young man didn't answer but eyed him brazenly, so it seemed to Silbermann—or downright insolently.

He reached in his pocket and pulled out a twenty-mark bill. "Would you give that to your mother? For her trouble?"

But the other man seemed to regard the gesture as attempted bribery. He turned around without saying a word and with excessively dignified bearing went inside the building, leaving Silbermann standing there.

Silbermann stared blankly as the young man walked away. Now there's someone who really is being guided by hate, he thought, taken aback. He shrugged his shoulders and hurried to the nearest taxi stand.

But where should I go? he wondered. After all, a person

ought to know where he wants to go. A person needs a destination. France? That would be the logical choice. But how do I get there? Perhaps through Switzerland? As if it were easy to get into Switzerland. Luxemburg? No, Goldberg tried that last week. And failed, and he's younger than I am. So if he didn't manage . . . Where shall I go? Where can I go?

For now I'm still free, I've managed to keep a portion of my wealth, and nevertheless I don't know what to do. Despite all that, I'm a prisoner. For a Jew the entire Reich is one big concentration camp.

If only I'd gotten a visa early on! But who could have foreseen any of this, and Eduard's certainly taking his time. I would have . . . Would have! What do I have? A passport with a big red *J* on the first page. But I also have money— thank God!

He took a cab to the Charlottenburg Station.

The first thing I'll do is get a timetable for the trains, he decided. Then I'll have to see. I'll simply take the first train that's leaving. No, that won't work. I really do have to figure out where to. So I'll head in the direction of France. First to the Rhineland. Then I'll be closer to my destination. And tonight I'll sleep on the train.

Anyway I can call Eduard again in the morning. Perhaps in the meantime he's . . . managed to . . . hard to imagine. But not impossible. Then everything would happen legally. Otherwise it won't work. I'm not a risk taker. I'm a businessman, I make deals. These times are demanding too much of me!

He was happy that for now at least his wife had escaped all trouble. She has her brother, he thought. A good thing that is! I wish I had someone, too.

He checked his suitcase at the baggage counter and then very carefully studied the departure times listed in the time-table. As he searched, he ran his finger down the columns. At last he believed to have found the right train.

"Aachen, eleven forty-eight, from the Potsdamer Station," he said quietly. Aachen, he thought, is near Belgium. I'll travel to Aachen! In any case it can't hurt. Once I'm in Belgium, I can get to France. And in Aachen I can still think things over and figure out which border is easiest.

He purchased a detective novel at a newsstand, bought a first-class ticket to Aachen, and retrieved his suitcase. Then he went to the platform for local service. In just two minutes one of the electric trains arrived, and Silbermann climbed aboard.

After he stowed his suitcase on the storage rack and placed his briefcase behind him, he opened the book he had just purchased and began reading, hoping this would distract him and bring some measure of calm. As a rule Silbermann enjoyed letting himself get entangled in literary crimes, and he found murders every bit as engaging as bank robberies. He also felt reassured by the ultimate arrests. But even though the prose read quite fluently and two corpses were discovered on London Bridge on the very first page, the book couldn't distract him from all his worries and problems. He kept reaching for his briefcase and checking to make sure his suitcase was still there. Finally he set the book aside.

I should have packed the silverware in a box, he thought. It now also occurred to him that he should have looked in the buffet for his wife's jewelry case, because he remembered that she was always searching for new hiding places where possible intruders wouldn't think to look. Once she'd even hidden the case under the plates on the lowest shelf. But then he figured that because she'd thought of the money in the desk, she must have remembered her jewelry as well, and felt relieved.

And what's going to happen to my company? he asked himself, and tried to calculate how much money he'd already lost. But then he broke off this unpleasant accounting and went back to the question of how he could get his money out of Germany. Even if they don't check anyone else at the border, they're bound to check me, because I'm much too agitated. And it's impossible to hide forty-one thousand marks on your person.

But of course—he was intending to cross the border illegally. Wasn't it old man Wurm who'd recently told a story about two Jews from Breslau who'd been shot attempting to do just that? No, it was Löwenstein. Why would he even say something like that? As if people didn't already know what's going on! Besides, getting shot was preferable to being stuck in this condition for the foreseeable future. But perhaps he'd get arrested, and then: concentration camp, confiscation of property, prison . . . And what would become of his wife?

He wondered how her brother had received her, considering that he, too, was a Nazi. Ernst was probably afraid of compromising himself because of her. But he was her brother, after all, and Silbermann had served as a guarantor when he settled with his creditors. Otherwise he would have gone bankrupt, plain and simple, reckless as he was. No matter. In any case, he's in my debt.

They arrived at Potsdamer Station and Silbermann

stepped off. Only when the train started moving again did he realize he'd left his book behind. The loss upset him. He was not so much irritated by the fact that he'd now likely never discover the circumstances surrounding the double murder on the Thames, because of course he'd also forgotten the novel's title—all he could remember was that it contained the word "secret." What he really found distressing was that he'd caught himself forgetting something for the second time that day, and he could only expect that his anxiety would cause additional and perhaps more sensitive losses.

As he was heading to the platform for the train to Aachen, he reflected on the fact that he really should have said goodbye to his wife. This is like a ship going down, he thought, or a volcano erupting, or an earthquake ordered from above. And the earth really is shaking, but only under us.

After he'd climbed the stairs and passed through the ticket barrier, he sat down on a bench to wait for his train. She'll be so worried and afraid, he then thought. I have to write her right away. What a good thing it is that she's a Christian—at least nothing can happen to her. I can hardly imagine if I had that worry on top of everything else, as it is I'm worried about something happening to her anyway. It also occurred to him that he hadn't said good-bye to his sister and that he hadn't found out anything certain about the fate of his brother-in-law, Günther. And to think I'm actually someone with a real feel for family, he wondered. But when all is said and done, people are simply hard-boiled egoists.

Nor did he now feel at all inclined to call his sister again. It's too depressing, he thought. We'll just talk back and forth, she can't help me and I can't help her, and all we'd do in the end is unnerve each other further. What's the point in that? Things are already hard enough! I'll write her tomorrow and send her some money. She'll need that before long, because Günther will soon stop receiving his pension, or else it will be assigned to cover his rations in the concentration camp. The truth is that I'm still relatively well off, he thought, and sighed.

Maybe I ought to divide the money and leave ten thousand marks for Elfriede. Who knows how long she'll still have to stay in the country. But then the Nazis will end up taking it away from her, or else Ernst will talk her out of it for some dubious business deal. Besides, she has to join me in the next few days, no question about it. As soon as I'm out of the country I'll get her the permit. As long as she's living in Germany I won't have any peace. People will help me. Everybody will understand! I'll manage in eight days what Eduard couldn't achieve in his entire life.

Besides, if I leave her the money, she'll try to smuggle it across the border herself, and she's far less capable of that than I am. Ach, whatever I do is a mistake. Everything is all wrong. Even if I do manage to get the money out of the country, it's entirely possible that they'd hold her hostage until I turned myself in along with the money. Maybe I'm dragging her down with me into misfortune. The best thing would be for me to wait and spend the next few days in Aachen or Dortmund or perhaps go back to Berlin later and try to get a visa. But there's no chance of that working out, either.

By this point he felt so hopeless that he didn't react at all when the train pulled up, but simply stayed slumped on the bench.

What do I want to do? he asked himself. Is there anything left for me to do at all? Every choice is an unwise one. But he couldn't simply stay on the platform, and more than anything else it was the hope of at least being able to sleep on the train that finally motivated him to climb on board.

He'd chosen first class because he believed that there he would be safest from suspicion and the ensuing harassment.

After looking into a few compartments that were partly occupied, he found one for smokers that was empty. He sat down and closed his eyes. Sleep, he thought, all I want is to sleep.

He hadn't dared purchase a berth in a sleeping car. Being deep asleep in bed puts you completely at the mercy of others, he had thought. A few minutes passed, then the door to his compartment was opened, and with great deference the conductor pointed out seats for two gentlemen.

A spirited "Heil Hitler" was proclaimed.

"Heil Hitler," Silbermann returned the greeting, starting up from his half-sleep and then resuming his position, while making an effort to maintain his composure. He quickly turned his face to the window so the others wouldn't notice how terrified he looked. But it turned out they weren't Gestapo men, as he had first suspected, but bona fide travelers.

"Did you notice," one was saying to the other, "that the whole first class is full of Jews. Half of Israel is on tour."

"No, really?" the other man seemed surprised. "I didn't notice at all."

Silbermann began feeling very uneasy.

"Then again maybe I'm just imagining things," the first

one continued. In any case, this morning in the train from Munich I easily counted about twenty head."

"What are the people supposed to do?" the other asked, disinterested. "Do you have the papers? I want to look them over one more time." The man who had first spoken rummaged through his coat pockets and ultimately fished out a manuscript. He handed it to the other man, who Silbermann guessed was his superior, based on each man's respective attitude, and who began reading contentedly.

"Is everything set?" the man asked as he leafed through the draft. "Are we being picked up from the station? Has the press been adequately informed? Do you have a decent photograph of me on hand? Because recently the *Köln Illustrierte* ran a picture of me that made me look ancient. Kindly make sure I'm not made into an old man ahead of my time."

The other man eagerly pulled some pictures from his pocketbook and handed them over. His superior looked through them.

"This photo is out of the question. It shows me with a mustache. Good grief . . . Here, this will work! Take this one."

"Yes of course," the other agreed. "That's the one I wanted to use as well. First simply on account of the SA uniform."

His boss read further in the manuscript. "This needs to be re-transcribed," he said after a while, during which the train had started moving. "Here, instead of 'the new Reich's mission vis-à-vis Europe,' it should say 'concerning Europe.' All such foreign expressions should be deleted. And instead of the word 'culture' you should, wait a minute . . . I had found a better expression—what was it?"

"Nobility of mind?" the other hurried to interject.

"Nonsense. Think for a moment!"

"National advancement?"

"No!"

"Community spirit?"

"I didn't say that! I had come up with a new expression. Make an effort!"

Silbermann stood up and left the compartment, making sure he took his briefcase with him.

I recognize the gaunt one, he thought, believing he had seen pictures of him, but he couldn't remember the man's name. He now regretted having followed his impulse to step out. I should have stayed and listened, he thought, wondering what new word the gentleman had come up with for "culture." He went back inside the compartment.

But either they had found the lost word, or the supposed author had given up the search. Perhaps he'd solved the dilemma by simply leaving out the concept of culture altogether. Whatever the case, both men were now silent.

After about ten minutes the conductor came back, opened the door, and said, with the same deference, "Everything is all fixed up and ready!" Both men stood up, collected their belongings, and left the compartment, having amiably taken their leave of Silbermann. They'd probably just been waiting for their beds to be made.

Silbermann was very contented to be alone. He drew the curtain, spread a newspaper on the seat cushion where he wanted to place his feet, and stretched out. The whole first class is full of Jews, he thought as he fell asleep. If only it goes well . . . He didn't sleep very deeply, and frequently woke with a start, frightened and bewildered. Then he would glance around the compartment, where he'd left the light on, before falling back asleep.

The train stopped and soon started up again. The door was shoved aside, and a man peered into the compartment. His attire was very run-of-the-mill, as Silbermann, who had woken up when the train resumed its movement, immediately noticed. He also sensed there was something distraught about the new arrival, and he had the impression that the man was not accustomed to traveling first class. The newcomer politely removed his hat and took the window seat opposite Silbermann.

"Excuse me," he said, almost meekly. "I'm afraid I may have woken you. Please go on sleeping. I'm going to make myself comfortable as well."

He took off his jacket, hung it carefully on a hook, and once again took off his hat, which he had put back on after greeting Silbermann, and placed it on the luggage rack.

Silbermann yawned. "I'm already feeling a little refreshed," he said. He pulled his cigarettes out of his pocket. "Do you smoke?"

The other thanked him and reached into the case. Silbermann couldn't help noticing the man's hand. It was red and chapped, and several nails had been split and hadn't grown back properly. Suddenly Silbermann realized that the other man had no suitcase.

Perhaps he's running from the law, he thought for a moment. But then he observed the man's ruddy cheeks and anxious expression, and when he noticed his brown eyes Silbermann decided instead that he was sharing the compartment with a Jewish tradesman trying to escape. He considered it unlikely that the man was a con artist, given his staid, petit-bourgeois demeanor, but Silbermann nevertheless decided he needed to make sure.

"Hard times," he said, quite slowly.

The other man eyed him suspiciously.

"Indeed," he concurred, with a serious tone, but then quickly added, probably to be on the safe side and neutralize his agreement, "depending on how you look at it."

"Are you traveling on business?" asked Silbermann with polite interest.

The other man reached below his ankle to scratch, bending so low that his face could no longer be seen. "Yes," he muttered. Then he sat up and said, without looking at Silbermann, "Well then, good night."

"Good night," Silbermann replied.

"Shall I turn off the light?" the man asked.

"It can stay on as far as I'm concerned."

"That's fine with me, too."

For a few minutes both men were silent, but then the newcomer asked, very quietly, as if he were afraid Silbermann might already be asleep, "When do you think the train will be in Aachen?"

"Sometime around twelve, I think," answered Silbermann, also instinctively whispering.

"Thank you."

More minutes passed. Then Silbermann asked if the other man would mind if he opened the door to the corridor, to let the smoke out.

As if he'd been given an order, the other man leapt to

his feet. "Not at all," he said, and slid the door about ten centimeters to the side. He sat back down and asked, now more bravely, "Are you traveling abroad?"

"No," said Silbermann, "and you?"

"Me neither," the other was quick to reply. "I'm traveling on business," he then quickly added, as if he'd already forgotten Silbermann's earlier question and his own answer, and as though traveling on business necessarily meant staying in the country.

"That's right, of course," said Silbermann. The other man had turned to face him, but when Silbermann tried to look him in the eye he averted his gaze. "What line of business are you in, if I might ask?"

I'm making him afraid, thought Silbermann. But I have to know! If he's not trying to get out of the country, then he must be a criminal. And I don't want to fall asleep in the same compartment as a criminal. After all, I have my entire fortune in my briefcase.

"I deal in furniture," said the other man quickly. Too quickly, it seemed to Silbermann, who had now grown suspicious.

"Do you have good sales agents?" he asked.

"They're all right," said the man, and looked out the window.

"I was guessing that you're the head of a firm . . ."

The man gave Silbermann an anxious look. "What made you guess that?" he asked.

"Well, I thought that since you were traveling first class. Not many agents can afford that. You must do very well."

I'm behaving like a perfect inquisitor, Silbermann thought. And how easily the situation could be reversed. But now he felt that he was the stronger person, and he was resolved to be merciless in his quest for information.

"I usually travel second class," the man answered, as though he had to explain himself. "But they told me there were no seats available in second class. That's why I'm traveling first class."

This is exactly how people get trapped in lies, Silbermann thought to himself. If the man had any imagination he surely wouldn't try to make me believe something as ridiculous as that. There are more open seats in second class than anyone could ask for. And why did he even answer my question? Why is he lying? Why is he taking something that requires no justification whatsoever and offering up an improbable explanation? He isn't a crook, he's far too clumsy for that. Only people who are used to speaking the truth give themselves away like that when they're forced to lie. A Jewish tradesman, of course, my first impression was right!

Silbermann fixed his gaze on the man and quietly asked, "Are you Jewish?"

"What makes you think that?" the other asked back, distraught, and it was clear how much he wanted to get up and escape the interrogation. But he probably lacked the courage to do so.

"So, I take it you are Jewish! Do you know where you want to go? Do you have a particular destination in mind?"

For a moment, the other man was silent, then he again asked, "What leads you to think that I'm a Jew? Do I look like one?"

"Not necessarily," said Silbermann, who was now fully confident and secretly proud of his psychological prowess.

He was so convinced of the validity of his premise that he returned to his sleeping position.

The other man seemed emboldened by this movement, which was clearly not directed against him. "They stormed my store," he began whispering. Then he jumped up and shut the door, even though the corridor was empty. "I had a cabinetmaking shop." He resumed his report, then stopped and asked, "But please tell me what led you to believe I'm Jewish? You aren't Jewish yourself?" The return question was inevitable, and his voice betrayed hope as well as fear.

"I had the impression you were agitated," said Silbermann.

"Are you an Aryan?" the other asked, rephrasing the question. Silbermann's lack of response to his first question had probably led the man to conclude that he was dealing with a comrade in misfortune.

"I'm also Jewish," Silbermann declared.

"Thank God," the other man said, relieved.

"So where do you plan to go?" asked Silbermann.

Now it was the other man's turn to be suspicious.

"I'm not planning to go anywhere," he said evasively. "I'm just traveling. I was advised to travel first class because that was safer, but it wasn't good advice. I can see how badly I stick out here. Tomorrow I'll take a train back to Magdeburg. Things are bound to have calmed down by then."

"You don't want to leave the country?" asked Silbermann.

"No, no," the other was quick to reply. "I'm staying in Germany. Despite everything I am a German!"

"Good night," said Silbermann.

For a moment he had hoped his companion might give

him a useful tip, but he realized that he couldn't expect such confidence unless he himself was willing to open up, which he was not inclined to do. He tried to fall asleep, but after a few minutes the other man started talking again.

"Did you manage to save your money?" he asked quietly.

Silbermann muttered something incomprehensible.

"Because if you had money," the other man continued, "it would be easier . . ."

"What would be easier?" Silbermann sat up, now interested, and lit another cigarette.

"Well . . . you know . . ." the other man hesitated.

"I'm not sure I understand," said Silbermann, who thought he understood quite well and felt a new sense of hope.

"I only kept a hundred marks. That's not enough to get out of the country—assuming that's what a person wanted to do."

"Do you want to get out?"

"Do you?"

"Perhaps. Do you know a way?"

"We don't know each other at all. I mean, even if I did know something . . . You understand what I mean?"

Silbermann flicked the ash off his cigarette. "First I'd have to have a clear idea of what we're talking about," he said, businesslike. "The rest can all be sorted out."

The other man thought for a moment and looked at Silbermann, unable to decide. He had his doubts, but he realized that Silbermann would only show his cards after he did.

"I was given an address. Supposedly it's someone who

can arrange something. From what I've heard he asks for a lot of money. And in addition to that he's a Nazi."

"But basically you think he might be able to get someone out of the country? I'm not necessarily speaking for myself, of course, but in general the matter interests me."

"They say that he takes anything of value at the border. You're completely at his mercy, but he'll see that you get across!"

"Who is this he?"

"I don't know exactly, and even if I did, as I said before, I don't know you at all . . ."

Silbermann nodded. "Of course," he admitted. "Of course I could easily prove to you who I am and that I'm Jewish, but I don't know . . ."

"What don't you know?"

"If there's any point."

"Oh," the other said eagerly, and it was clear that he, who had disclosed so much, was now also asking for some show of trust. "Surely we could help each other out somehow. You obviously have money, and I have a way out, but not the money it requires. We could complement each other."

"But if, as you say, your man robs people at the border, I don't find the prospect very enticing."

"So is it a lot of money you're carrying around?"

"No, definitely not."

"I've told you everything. But you're not telling me anything! Don't you trust me?"

"I do, but as you rightly pointed out earlier: we don't know each other, and it's also debatable if we'd be of any benefit to each other even if we did."

"My name is Lilienfeld, Robert Lilienfeld."

"Silbermann."

"So, Herr Silbermann," said Lilienfeld, now grown bolder. "I trust you, even if just because I very much need you. Listen: we could get off together in Dortmund and look up the man together. I would introduce you, and in exchange you would pay my way."

"We could do that. And I'm happy to give you the money. But you'll have to pay him yourself."

"Agreed."

"And assuming a person had a little more money that he needed to have sent on very quickly, do you also know how that can be arranged?"

"You're not allowed to take anything," Lilienfeld insisted. "In no case are you permitted to have more than ten marks on you. Otherwise if we get caught we might be accused of smuggling currency. Besides, I already told you that you have to expect the man to pat you down at the border. If you're lucky, all he'll do is take your money."

"You don't know any other way to . . . ?"

"I have no idea! Just don't tell the man that you have money, and under no circumstances should you hide the money on your person. Or any valuables!"

"But . . ."

"We simply have to be glad if we manage to make it across with our bare lives."

"Even out of the country you need more than a bare life to survive. You need money! Or do you think they feed Jews there for free?"

"I'll find some work," Lilienfeld assured him hopefully.

"As far as I know, immigrants aren't allowed to work

without a special permit, and by the time you get one of those you'll have long died of starvation."

"That remains to be seen!"

"No," said Silbermann emphatically. "For me it's out of the question."

Lilienfeld jumped up. "And how am I supposed to pay the man?" he asked, agitated. "I'm short two hundred marks. My life depends on two hundred marks! If I'd only traveled third class . . ."

"Calm down." Silbermann interrupted him. "You'll get your two hundred marks! And in exchange you'll give me the address of the man. I may come back to the idea."

Lilienfeld tore a page from his notebook and wrote out the name and address in large, clumsy letters. He genuinely seemed to have come to trust Silbermann. In any case, he handed Silbermann the paper even though he hadn't received any money for providing it.

"Hermann Dinkelberg, Bismarckstraße 23," Silbermann read in a low voice. "Is that enough?" he asked. "Or do I have to refer to someone?"

"That isn't necessary. Just tell him that you want to leave the country, and if he asks how much money you have, say: two hundred marks. You can give that to him right away, because he'll get you over the border!"

Silbermann stuck the note in his pocketbook and handed Lilienfeld three hundred-mark bills. "You might need a little extra after all," he said. "If you like you can give me back the hundred marks at some later date."

"No, no." The cabinetmaker declined. "All I need is two hundred marks exactly! What am I supposed to do with the rest? Tomorrow afternoon I'm leaving Germany. Then

I won't be able to get rid of the money and that will be my downfall. I know you mean well, that's very generous, and I thank you, but please just keep it!"

He handed the extra hundred marks back to Silbermann.

"That's never happened to me before in my life," said Silbermann, shaking his head.

"Me neither! But now let's really try to get some sleep. Tomorrow I have a pretty strenuous hike ahead of me. I'm just happy that I met you. It looks like there really is such a thing as a silver lining."

"Only because the cloud is as dark as it is," said Silbermann pessimistically.

"You shouldn't despair," Lilienfeld replied, gently running his hand over his billfold. "You see how things are going with me . . ."

"You're also in an enviable position! You can move about freely. But I have to haul my money wherever I go. Under the circumstances, that's a real millstone around my neck."

"Just leave it in Germany."

"And what am I to live off abroad?"

"You'll have to work!"

"I've worked my entire life, my friend. I'm a merchant, and a merchant has to have capital. These days a tradesman is a lot better off."

"Then you just have to start all over again once you're there."

"That's easy to say. I'm no longer young, and I also have my wife and son to take care of!"

"You're right," sighed Lilienfeld, almost with a note of contentment, "it's a bad situation . . ."

Silbermann realized he wasn't going to fall asleep again so soon. He pulled aside the window curtain and for a while looked out at the pale dawn, gazing at the landscape, the bare fields, small forests, isolated houses, the monotonous autumn tableau of the flat countryside. He stretched a bit, then turned out the light since it was already bright enough.

"What time is it?" he asked his companion, who had also not yet fallen asleep and who'd been watching Silbermann with his big brown eyes, following every movement with drowsy interest.

"Six thirty," said Lilienfeld.

"I'm dead tired but I can't fall asleep," Silbermann explained. "I feel a sense of looming catastrophe in my stomach."

"That's because you haven't had any coffee yet," Lilienfeld said, and turned around to go back to sleep.

Silbermann continued looking out the window. I've passed this way before, he thought. On our honeymoon. To distract himself, he tried recalling the time and circumstances. He'd just been promoted to corporal and had received eight days' leave to get married. Five days were taken up with wedding preparations, and they hadn't been able to leave until the evening of the sixth day. He still remembered all the details fairly exactly, down to what his wife was wearing and how she looked. Elfriede had been very excited. Never again did he see her laugh and cry as much as she had on that trip. They had held on to each other in a way that now seemed to him more clenching than clinging. But the conditions hadn't been favorable for a simple, innocent honeymoon, because the country was at war.

And then there were the fantastic plans she'd concocted! She suggested they flee to Switzerland because she didn't want to let him return to the front. Deep down she probably realized this was impossible, but she refused to accept that and had to be consoled. He promised her that the war wouldn't last much longer, and then she sighed and said: yes it will. Which prompted him to explain why the enemies of Germany were on the verge of collapse and how life in a dugout was relatively safe.

In the end she believed him, and then everything was wonderful once more, although the fear of separation gnawed away at every happy minute. Finally, as if by mutual agreement, they only spoke about the two days they had left, about what they had planned to do but wound up not doing because the wedding had been more important than the honeymoon.

We were so happy and so unhappy at the same time that we couldn't even tell the difference, Silbermann reflected—that was how jumbled all their feelings and sensations had become.

Of course the last day had been a terrible ordeal, and ultimately all they ended up doing was waiting for the moment when they had to part. Looking back, Silbermann didn't think it was all that bad, since they'd been young and could believe in the future, and despite everything they'd been able to live in the moment.

How happy I was, Silbermann thought, with a quiet feeling of self-envy.

He stepped out of the compartment and walked down the corridor, then came back, sat down, and observed the cabinetmaker, who had fallen asleep and was shifting fretfully as Silbermann watched until he finally woke up. Before he opened his eyes, he felt for his breast pocket, where he'd hidden the money and most likely his passport as well.

"Are we close to Dortmund?" he asked quietly.

"You still have a long time," Silbermann replied. "Get some sleep."

But Lilienfeld sat up. "I don't know," he said. "I'm so restless. I have such a strange feeling. I need a glass of brandy. I don't think I can take being hounded like this. Normally by this time I would have already swept out my shop and rolled up the shutters. I had to let go of my journeyman assistant, the business was doing so poorly, and my apprentice never showed up before eight. There's someone for you—completely inept!"

He looked at Silbermann. "I talk too much, don't I?"

"Not at all," Silbermann replied. "Keep going. It does me good to listen to you."

"I told the boy a hundred times," Lilienfeld continued, "not to hold the board with his hand when he's using the plane. But no matter how often you say it, he doesn't hear it. And as you can guess, one day the thing slipped and then the lout couldn't work. So for a whole month all he did was stand around. Apart from that he was a good kid! I wonder if he's found a new apprenticeship. I still have to send him his certificate. When I told him I was leaving, he wanted to come with me. He's Jewish, too, you see . . . I'm so anxious. I dreamed about the war for the first time in years. I was just hanging there, stuck in the barbed wire and freezing. That's a feeling, let me tell you!"

"I turned off the heat earlier," Silbermann explained. "You know, I've been thinking about the war too for the past few days. It's no wonder."

"Do you think we should move to second class?" Lilienfeld asked. "That might be safer."

"And when the conductor comes and sees you have a ticket for first class, that will really look fishy!"

"But it's always less nerve-racking to be around a lot of people. At least for me. Do you think there are Gestapo officers on the train?"

"I don't know."

"Maybe we should get off and take third-class seats on the next train?"

"What do you think that will do? You won't be any safer there. You might get involved in a conversation that I wouldn't wish for you, and besides . . ."

". . . and besides, I chose to pay for first class, too, you were going to say," Lilienfeld interrupted, finishing Silbermann's sentence. "Except I've never traveled first class in my life. If only I'd been able to go on traveling third class in peace for the rest of my days!" He looked around admiringly at the compartment. "All very finely done," he concluded. "But it's plenty expensive! Probably nothing new for you, am I right?"

"I usually travel second class," said Silbermann. But listening to Lilienfeld about traveling third class made him wonder exactly why he had done so all those years. Then he added, almost apologetically, "Also on account of my business associates." He wrinkled his forehead, surprised at his own explanation.

"Well, you wealthy people have it easy," Lilienfeld said

wistfully. "You always manage to wriggle out of everything. Tell me, are you a millionaire?"

Silbermann smiled. "No, I'm really not," he said.

"I thought you might be. You look like one. So calm. I think as a rule rich people have smooth faces without a lot of wrinkles, right?"

"There are as many different types of faces as there are types of worry. If you don't have one kind you have another. Is my situation any better than yours?"

"Maybe not at the moment, but otherwise it is! I don't begrudge you, either. I don't envy anybody! At most my brother, he's in South America. He managed to get out of Germany and he's earning good money there. But he's also been through a lot. We all have. You, too. I'm really happy that you're a rich man. Because otherwise how else would I have managed to come up with the two hundred marks?"

"They stole two hundred thousand marks from me, if I include the apartment house!" said Silbermann, more to himself than to the other.

"Two hundred thousand marks," Lilienfeld sighed reverently. "And here I thought I shouldn't have asked for two hundred in exchange for nothing more than an address. But two hundred thousand! How does that make you feel? I can only imagine. I lost five or six thousand marks myself— that's how much my shop was worth. But this. It must be absolutely horrible. It would be better if you'd never had it, I think. And here you wanted to give me an extra hundred! That shows that you're a noble soul. But maybe you're also thinking it no longer matters."

"Maybe," said Silbermann, holding back his smile with effort.

"Still, you meant it very well," Lilienfeld decided. "You must be in complete despair, losing two hundred thousand marks—I think I'd do something to myself!"

Silbermann shook his head. "The amount itself doesn't matter," he said. "After all, losing your business was . . ."

"Yes, my wonderful shop," Lilienfeld interrupted, wistfully. "I had two display windows, you know? Sure they were small all right, but they brought in a lot of business! I even fashioned pews for the church, despite the fact that I'm a Jew! Incidentally, the Jewish community still owes me three hundred marks!" For a moment Lilienfeld seemed lost in thought. "And now it's all gone, everything, just like that! The windows smashed, and the landlord gave me notice. Then they wanted to arrest me on top of that. If only I'd been able to pack my tools! All gone, everything . . ." He propped his elbows on his knees and buried his head between his hands. "I wasn't even able to take my Sunday suit!" he said gloomily.

"You see, I'm no worse off than you," Silbermann said, picking back up the thread of the conversation. "Whether you lose two hundred thousand marks or your shop, it's not that big a difference. As it is, I managed to save some money."

Lilienfeld looked up. "Which is getting in the way of your own safety and security," he said, as if to insist that Silbermann was more unfortunate than he himself.

"Security," said Silbermann. "There's no security without money."

"But right now your money isn't making you secure. On the contrary, it is putting you in danger."

"There are always two sides to everything," Silbermann

admitted. Then he laughed. "I find it amusing how we're both pitying each other and how each of us is trying to prove that the other is worse off, as though that were some kind of consolation."

"I don't pity you at all," Lilienfeld contested. "Not in the least! You were always well off, but not me. I've been through a lot, but because of that it's easier for me now!"

"Exactly," said Silbermann, laughing. "It's easier for you!"

"You don't need to laugh about it. That's just the way it is. I haven't lost two hundred thousand marks, and I don't need to sneak any money over the border. I'm happy as a clam!"

"You're a nice person." Silbermann grinned. "Really!"

"You've always had it pretty good, am I right?"

"That's not a question for which there's a simple answer. In one sense you're right, but then again, I was in the war."

"The war wasn't good," Lilienfeld admitted. "But it wasn't all that bad, either. We were always just one of many, part of a group. And now we're alone. There's no longer someone giving commands, there's no order you can stick to. You have to run and there's no one telling you where to. The pressure's a lot worse now than it was under the Prussian officers. The war wasn't pleasant, by any means! But we were soldiers. Soldiers among soldiers. And now we're filthy Jews and the others are Aryans! They're living in peace, and we're being hounded, only us. That's the worst thing! The other carpenters are doing their business and getting on with their lives. While I have to get out, go away! That's the thing! The war was also a unique situation, but not just for us, not just for me! There was a community. Everybody was affected."

"Be glad you don't belong to the new community! It's

hard to imagine one that's worse or more stupid and brutal. A good minority is still better than a bad majority."

"So you say! But I had to sit in my shop and watch them march past, with flags and music. At times I could practically scream, let me tell you. They were all people I knew. The veteran's association, the skat club, the guild. All former friends, and suddenly you're sitting there completely alone. No one wants to have anything more to do with you, and if they do happen to run into you, then you wind up being the one who looks away just so you don't have to see them doing it. That's why I didn't dare set foot outside. I kept thinking: you'll end up bumping into someone and then get worked up all over again. This person was in your class at school, that person trained alongside you or was one of the regulars at your table in the pub. And now? Now you're just air, and bad air at that!"

"But all of that only reflects on the others!"

"It doesn't matter who it reflects on! The fact is that I've been through hell. They smeared the word 'Jew' all over my shop windows, and then I had to wipe it all off while the whole street was watching. The thing is that it was mostly the work of Willi Schröder, whose father I once had to take to court because he didn't want to pay. But this wasn't just some silly boy's prank, either. And it's not something you can really get over. What can I do about that, tell me. It's not a feeling you can ever get rid of, once it's there. If I were a pious Jew, I would say none of that matters. But I'm not. I was in the war, and I've seen it all!"

Lilienfeld paused a moment before continuing.

"And then you become so sensitive. You start smelling meanness everywhere. Whereas all you want is to be able to work in peace, have a glass of beer in the evening, play a nice game of skat, just like everybody else. And you can tell me all about the chosen people and how God is testing them. I couldn't care less about that. I'm perfectly happy being a tradesman. And now I have to put up with being treated like a robber and murderer! The only thing missing is for them to start spitting on us."

Lilienfeld stared dully ahead.

"So, it all just comes because I have a better head on my shoulders," he then said, convinced and relieved. He now looked as though he expected Silbermann to pat him on the shoulder and say, "Cheer up, Lilienfeld!"

Silbermann, who had been quite gripped by Lilienfeld's story, had to smile at his companion's naive conclusion.

"I'm thirsty for some coffee!" Lilienfeld declared, now that he had said his piece and was probably also afraid of falling into too melancholy a mood. "At the next station I'm definitely hopping off for a coffee and some brandy, that's my usual routine. Do you know when the dining car is open?"

"I'm not sure if there is one yet: it might get added at Dortmund. We can go through the train and check."

They both got up and went into the corridor. A man was standing at the window in front of the neighboring compartment. He politely stepped back to let them pass, and they went on.

"I hope he didn't hear our conversation," said Lilienfeld, after they were out of earshot. "You were speaking so loudly. One has to be very careful. I've heard these trains are full of informers."

They made their way to the next car, which was second

class, and where the corridor was completely empty. As they passed through two sleeping cars they ran into a member of the staff but no one else. Finally they wound up in a third-class car, where the corridor was full of people smoking, chatting, and looking out the window.

Lilienfeld stood on the coupling that was swaying back and forth under their feet and grabbed Silbermann by the arm.

"I'm not going any further," he whispered. "There are too many Christians here for my taste!"

"But why are you so afraid?" asked Silbermann.

"Why? Yesterday they attacked my shop. Once you've been through everything I have, you'll start thinking differently!"

"Come on, you just have to stay calm and keep going. No one can tell by looking that you're Jewish."

"Except you noticed right away!"

"Only because you were so uneasy."

"Well, in any case I'm turning around," Lilienfeld announced. "I don't have to prove how brave I am for a cup of coffee. Having the nerve to do something is all well and good, but having your peace is even better."

"What do you think might happen to you?"

"I don't know. All it takes is running into a single acquaintance and there you have it. Sure, that's not going to happen—but what if it does?"

They turned around.

"I don't understand you," said Silbermann on their way back. "Earlier you wanted to be in third class so you'd be surrounded by people."

"Call it paranoia," said Lilienfeld, enlightened. "I feel as if I were somehow branded. Besides, I don't think Jews are allowed in the dining car."

"Jews aren't allowed to live their lives," Silbermann answered. "Do you want to be ruled by that?"

Lilienfeld didn't speak again until they had reached their compartment. "Sometimes I feel utterly discouraged and fainthearted," he said, a little ashamed of his explanation. "It took me days before I was willing to leave my shop. Because I was afraid that someone might start shoving me around or insult me. Even though business was bad, I didn't chase after any new orders. You know sometimes I have the sense that nothing's going right anymore, nothing at all!"

"Come on," said Silbermann encouragingly. "I much preferred that nice optimism you had before. Don't give up on yourself like that! I'm sure you lived through far more dangerous situations in the war. And there you were lucky and came out of it safe and sound. Maybe in eight days you'll have already found work abroad, and then all of this will be behind you. Just don't give in, my friend! Don't break down. Keep your eye on the goal, and you'll be sure to reach it! Weltschmerz isn't something you can afford! That can come later, when you're digesting a good meal—then you're allowed to be melancholic."

"You're right," said Lilienfeld, noticeably brighter. "If you want we can go again!"

How great is the power of words, Silbermann marveled, not at all feeling the same encouragement he had talked his companion into.

"No, no," he said. "Let's leave it. You aren't completely wrong, either. A waiter is likely to show up soon, and if not we'll share a cup of coffee at the next station."

"I wonder if I'll make it," asked Lilienfeld, once again very downcast.

"Make what?"

"I mean, if I'll make it over the border. If I won't get caught. I could just as easily run right into the guards on the other side and get sent back. In which case I'd do myself in."

"Man!" said Silbermann with feigned jauntiness. "Stop all that shilly-shallying! And don't even think such crazy thoughts. If it doesn't work out the first time, then it will the second. I don't understand you!"

"Aren't you at all afraid?" Lilienfeld defended himself.

"I am. Of course. But I refuse to give in to my fear!" said Silbermann, nice and firmly.

FIVE

Inside the post office, Silbermann paced uneasily back and forth, waiting to be told the telephone call he had requested was being put through. So as not to arouse suspicion, he went out of his way to look relaxed and cheerful.

He'd arrived in Aachen an hour earlier and left his suitcase at the baggage check, while holding on to his valuable briefcase, which he was now carrying under his arm. After Silbermann had seen Lilienfeld off in Dortmund, accompanied by his strongest words of encouragement, he'd had time to write a long, detailed letter to his wife as well as another one to his sister that communicated only what was most essential. He'd also sent Elfriede a reassuring telegram.

If nothing else, I've put my affairs in some degree of order, he thought as he paced. He found it was pleasant and calming at least to have addressed things in writing, even if none of his problems had actually been solved.

But after he'd waited ten minutes and his call still hadn't

gone through, he gradually began to have misgivings. He wondered if his son might not be in, or whether a new regulation had been passed concerning long-distance calls, perhaps requiring the police to be notified whenever a number was requested for abroad. What if they stop me and ask me for the purpose of the call? Maybe they'll search me, too, and find the money. Especially in a border town they'd think I was up to something. What do you need these forty thousand marks for? they'll ask, and next they'll confiscate my money and haul me off to the concentration camp!

He was annoyed by these fearful thoughts, which he blamed on Lilienfeld. To ease his nerves he started humming to himself.

The clerk waved him over. That was very nice of him. After all, even though Silbermann was standing just across from the counter, the man could have conspicuously called out "Connection to Paris!" and many eyes would have turned in his direction.

Silbermann stepped inside the booth, stuck a cigarette in his mouth, and was about to light it when he remembered that he'd have to open the door during the call to let out the smoke. The burning match singed his finger before he managed to toss it away.

"Hello," Eduard answered. "Father?"

"Yes, good morning. How are you? I just burned my finger on a match."

"How are you and Mother doing? I've been worried sick!"

"I'm here in Aachen," Silbermann said pointedly. "Mother's in Küstrin with your uncle. Have you finally managed to get the permit?"

"No! I haven't—things don't happen that quickly. And it's unlikely I'll get anything very soon. I've already tried every possible approach, but . . . I'm very glad that you both . . . that you managed . . . I'm happy to hear your voice."

"You might not hear it so often much longer." He grimaced in pain as he rubbed his burnt finger on the cool metal of the telephone box.

"Can't you get to Belgium, Father? Or Holland? You could wait there."

"There's no chance. My only hope was that you could somehow make it possible. But you aren't the French government. I understand that. I'm sure you've done everything you could."

"I'm still trying and will keep doing what I can. It might come through yet. I'm just glad that you're in Aachen."

"That's no reason to be glad." Silbermann examined his burned finger, which hurt so badly he had a hard time concentrating on anything else, despite his urgent circumstances. "Yes, ma'am, we're still talking," he said to the operator who had cut in to ask. "So Eduard, see to it, all right? Be well . . . and I'll send on a few patterns."

"What kind of patterns?"

"You know, patterns," Silbermann said, in a forceful voice.

"Don't worry, Father. It will work out somehow."

"Let's hope so. Meanwhile I'm getting burned in more ways than one. My finger really hurts."

"Aha! I guess if you're able to quip about it, you're a little less worried about everything else."

"Rubbish. Just because you have worries doesn't mean

you can't feel pain at the same time. So you think the prospects are pretty dim, right?"

"For what?"

"The permit. Don't be so dense!"

"They're not completely hopeless, but . . ."

"That's all right. I see there's really no point in hoping! Nevertheless for me everything depends on getting it! So then, good-bye!"

"I'll see you soon, Father. I will . . ."

"Good-bye."

Silbermann left the phone booth. The pain in his finger had let up. Suddenly a man appeared out of nowhere a few meters away from him. Aha, he thought, with a calm that bordered on indifference: so now it's come to this, I'm going to be arrested!

"Where is the exit?" asked the man.

"To the right," answered Silbermann, without giving it a moment's thought, and without really knowing. But he had sensed the man's beady eyes had been sizing him up, and he felt he needed to shake him off right away.

Silbermann sat down on a bench, overcome with despair. Of course it's all going to end badly. What possessed me to think I could ever pull this off? He leaned back and stared with dull disinterest at the people around him. So here we are in Aachen, he thought. In Aachen with forty thousand marks, or more precisely forty-one thousand—loaded, as they say—but with no clear path or destination.

He now wondered why he'd expected anything from the phone call. If at least I'd given Eduard a little push, he thought, but then I had to go and burn my finger. How could I have possibly imagined he would have taken care of things? I should have just let myself get arrested like all the others. Life is probably calmer in jail than it is outside. At least you can get some decent sleep. But living like this means constantly tensing up and then collapsing, you run this way and that without getting a single step ahead.

He stood up and left the post office, found a newsstand, and bought four different newspapers. Then he walked to a small pub, ordered a glass of beer, and went to the toilet. There he unfolded the papers, took four thousand-mark bills out of his briefcase, and placed one inside each of the papers. Then he carefully folded them back together, put them in his briefcase, and returned to his seat. He called the waiter, paid for his beer, and went to a stationery shop, where he purchased some tape and packaged up the papers for mailing. He then addressed them to Eduard's landlord, returned to the post office, and mailed the parcels at the counter.

He had wanted to get at least some money out of the country and had concocted this scheme during his conversation with his son, and now that he had carried it out with great care and cunning, he hurried from the post office back to the train station. He decided to go to Dortmund and try his luck there with Dinkelberg, the human smuggler Lilienfeld had mentioned. This time he bought a second-class ticket, thinking he would be safer and less conspicuous there, because he was now practically obsessed with the thought that he might stand out. He also tried to identify which expressions and gestures were the most inconspicuous and innocent-looking, since he felt his inner unrest was somehow showing.

His train left just minutes after he bought the ticket. A

few officers were sitting in the same compartment. Silbermann didn't pay any attention to them and didn't listen to their conversation, and very quickly dozed off. But every time the train stopped he would give a start, ask for the name of the station, and go back to sleep.

Ultimately the captain sitting next to him asked, "Where are you headed?"

"Dortmund," said Silbermann.

"Then go ahead and get some sleep. We'll wake you up once we're there."

"That's very kind of you," Silbermann said by way of thanks.

Very kind, he thought, as he fell asleep.

When they woke him he cried out, clearly distressed: "My briefcase! Where is my briefcase?"

The men laughed.

"It's right next to you," said the captain, a well-nourished, contented-looking man. "You must be lugging around your entire fortune, eh?"

"Not at all," Silbermann replied hastily. "Just some papers. But important ones."

"The sleeping secret courier," a lieutenant joked.

"Ha ha." Silbermann gave an enthusiastic laugh. "Then again, even a secret courier could sleep in peace surrounded by German officers. But I'm just a businessman. Thank you, gentlemen. Heil Hitler."

He left the compartment. When he was on the platform he heard a voice calling, "Hello, hello, Herr Courier!"

Startled, he turned around.

"You left your suitcase," said the lieutenant, laughing, and passed it through the window.

Silbermann thanked him as he took the suitcase. "I'm so absentminded," he offered as an excuse.

"Not a bad cover for a secret courier," answered the lieutenant.

A nice man, thought Silbermann, as he watched the train depart. So, they're still out there: unbiased, normal, benign people. I had forgotten. One thing's for sure: he probably didn't think I was Jewish.

He picked up his suitcase. I really have to pull myself together, he thought. He was gripping the handles of his bags so tightly it cramped his fingers. I feel so weak, so flabby. It's enough to drive a person mad.

He stepped into the third-class waiting room, and although he stood out enough to draw some attention, he went to the buffet and ordered a glass of beer. He drank it all in one swig, spilling a little on his coat. He took out his handkerchief and first wiped his mouth and then tried to dry the beer on his coat. Next he ordered a second glass, drank it, then slapped his hand on the counter and said, "It's all going to work out," loudly and confidently.

"What will?" asked the barkeep.

"Pour me another, young man," Silbermann demanded energetically.

He looked around, eager for action. He jutted his chin out a little bit and thought: I should have gone straight to that Dinkelberg. The man will be of use. No doubt about it. The beer was placed in front of him. He raised his glass, took a swallow, and then set it back down, with some aversion.

"What do I owe you?" he asked.

"One mark twenty."

He paid and left. His confidence was gone. He had a sour

taste in his mouth, and he felt nauseated. He remembered that he hadn't eaten lunch and chided himself for being so foolish as to drink beer on an empty stomach. In the station hall he automatically went to the baggage check to deposit his suitcase.

If I could only go to a hotel and get a good ten hours' sleep, he wished as he left the station. I could stay in bed for days if they'd let me. He was convinced of that.

He stopped in front of a hotel and considered going inside. No, he thought, that won't work! I can't weaken, not when I'm this close to the goal, because not only am I trying to escape, I'm also running a race against despair.

A little while later he was standing in front of the address on Bismarckstraße where Dinkelberg lived, according to Lilienfeld's information. He rang the bell.

It would have been smarter to come here together with that little Lilienfeld, he thought.

The door opened.

"Does Herr Dinkelberg live here?" he asked the old lady who opened the door.

She shook her head.

"He used to live here!" she said. "Yesterday he was arrested." She scrutinized him as if she thought he were an accomplice.

Silbermann felt very uneasy.

"Ahh," he said, "well, well! Arrested! Who would have thought?"

Silbermann was distraught. How should I behave in a case like this? he wondered. I might end up making myself look suspicious.

"I knew something was going on," said the old lady. "It

couldn't end well the way he carried on. Every day taking a different woman up to his den, and all that drinking. Four officials were here, four of them! I always wondered where the man got his money, because he doesn't have a job. Such a young man. He was probably stealing!"

"You don't know why he was arrested?" asked Silbermann, and thought: a young man, I had imagined someone around fifty, how strange.

She eyed him distrustfully. "How should I know that? Go to the police and ask there!" She slammed the door.

Embarrassed, Silbermann doffed his hat and then hastened away, turned three or four corners, and finally stopped. And for this I came to Dortmund, he thought. It seems that everything is jinxed. No sooner is there a bit of hope, and . . . I wonder what happened to Lilienfeld? The poor man must be desperate. Now he's no better off than I am.

Silbermann felt dizzy and sensed a slight buzzing in his ears. I've been walking too fast, he thought. I need to catch my breath.

He went into a restaurant, sat down at a table, ordered something to eat, and, succumbing to a mad hope, placed another call to Paris. Perhaps there's been some development in the meantime, he told himself.

When the soup arrived he literally dove into it, but after a few spoonfuls he felt he couldn't get any more down. He lit a cigarette, then let it go out in the ashtray and forced himself to finish eating.

When the waiter informed him that the call to Paris had gone through, he jumped up and hurried to the telephone, rubbing his hands and busily wrinkling his forehead.

I'll call him three times every day if I have to, he decided.

Once he has as little rest as I'm getting, he'll start really making an effort. It's a well-known fact that people who live in times of peace have no idea about war. I'll see he gets moving!

"Hello," he called out. "What's new?"

"How could anything have happened since we last talked? It's only been a few hours! Although I did just speak with someone who's very influential, who said he would sponsor your application, and I went back to the ministry of foreign affairs, but we have to be patient. You have to bear in mind that they're dealing with thousands of applications. Everyone else has to wait as well. There's simply nothing more that can be done."

Silbermann didn't say anything else and hung up.

"Of course," he said to himself, "all talk and no action." He shrugged his shoulders, tired and resigned.

After he finished eating, Silbermann set off to look for a room. He'd gotten it into his head that it would be easier to lie low in a private room than in a hotel. He believed he could put off the official registration longer with some lady who takes roomers.

He stopped in front of an apartment building that had a notice in front saying FURNISHED ROOMS TO LET. He went inside, where the woman at the door directed him to the fourth floor, and with some difficulty he climbed up the stairs. The name on the door read SUSIG. Silbermann rang, and an old man wearing felt slippers and a robe with braid trim answered.

He eyed Silbermann closely, then took his pipe out of his mouth and asked, "Well now, what are you looking for?"

"You have furnished rooms to let?" Silbermann asked.

"Not me," said the old man in a dignified voice. "My wife handles all that."

He put his pipe back in his mouth, turned around, and left Silbermann standing in the open door, as if he wanted to leave it up to the visitor whether to stay outside or step in. Silbermann chose the first option. He watched the old man shuffle across the hall and disappear into a room. Silbermann waited. But one minute after another passed and nobody came. Finally he rang once again.

The door to the room where the old man had disappeared opened, and the old man came shuffling back up.

"Is your wife not in?" asked Silbermann, annoyed. "Or has the room already been rented out?"

The old man cleared his throat. "Honestly I have no idea," he retorted in a melodious bass voice.

"Can't you call her?" asked Silbermann, more forcefully.

"We don't speak to each other," the old man confided. "All the same . . . maybe she'll come herself if you ring one more time. Assuming she's here, of course!"

He turned around and walked calmly back into the room.

"Herr Susig," Silbermann called out. He was beginning to question the old man's mental state.

The man turned around. "All the same . . ." he said.

Silbermann shook his head. He was now convinced he was dealing with a mentally disturbed individual. "I'm going," he said. "Perhaps I'll come back."

"However I do think it's possible," Herr Susig explained, now more willingly, "that my wife will be back soon. She may have just gone to do the shopping. Still . . . if you'd like to come back?"

"Can't you just show me the room?"

"I don't deal with that kind of thing," the man answered tentatively. "All the same . . . if you'd like to accompany me?"

Silbermann followed the man inside. They passed through a large dining room, which Silbermann felt looked very bare, as it had no buffet or sideboard. Then they came to a back hall and finally stopped in front of a small room.

"It's not a big room," warned Herr Susig. "No matter . . ." He opened the door.

"But this is a maid's room," Silbermann declared somewhat indignantly.

Although he was clearly familiar with the room, the old man examined it carefully. "Yes, well," he pronounced. "All the same . . ."

"I'll take the room," Silbermann replied.

The old man nodded in agreement. "That's something you'd have to discuss with my wife," he said. "If you want to stay here right away it will be forty marks a month. You could pay in advance. That's how she usually does it."

Given the size of the room, Silbermann thought that was disproportionately expensive, but he didn't object and picked up his briefcase. "Can you change a hundred marks?" he asked.

The old man took the bill, scrutinized it, and then answered, "Not now." He slid the bill into a pocket of his robe and left the room.

Silbermann lay down on the hard, narrow bed that took up half the space.

Well he's an odd coot, Silbermann thought. All the same . . . He laughed. Will I ever see those sixty marks again? he wondered. He wasn't so interested in the money, which no longer had nearly as much value for him as it had had before, as he was curious about the old man. After a few minutes he fell asleep.

He dreamed that an old man was sitting across from him in a train compartment and observing him so fixedly that he eventually feared the man might know something bad about him. Then the old man grew bigger and bigger until he suddenly transformed into Becker, who made threatening gestures in his direction.

There was a knock on the door. Dazed from sleep and fright, Silbermann stayed in bed.

"Who's there?" he finally asked in a quiet voice.

"Frau Susig."

He got up and opened the door. A very plainly dressed old woman apologized profusely for having evidently disturbed him, and then stepped inside.

"I wanted to return your sixty marks," she said. "And then I wanted to ask you to fill out the registration form. You can do it later, whenever it's convenient. I hope you like it here. The neighborhood is very quiet, and so are all our renters."

"It's just too bad," said Silbermann, "that you don't have a larger room available. This one's actually a little too cramped for me."

"If you'd come the day before yesterday, you could have had a nice room in front, with a balcony. But now that's been rented to a gentleman from the party."

Silbermann said nothing.

"Are you from Berlin?" she asked.

"Yes," he answered.

"That's clear from your accent. Incidentally my husband can fetch your suitcase from the station, I see . . ."

"I really wouldn't want to impose on him," Silbermann said quickly.

"It's no imposition."

"Thank you anyway. I'll go myself."

She looked around the room. "I'll bring you some fresh hand towels," she promised. "When would you prefer to have breakfast? The other gentlemen have theirs at seven thirty."

"I'll do the same. How much does breakfast cost?" he then asked, to seem like a normal lodger.

"It's included. Didn't my husband tell you?"

"I can't remember. Perhaps I just didn't catch that. In any case, I'll take my breakfast at seven thirty with the others."

She left the room. Silbermann plopped onto the bed. At least just once I'd like to get some decent sleep for my money, he thought. And also: a gentleman from the party. Of course!

He got up again and took the registration form, scanned the individual line items, and started to tear up the paper, but then stopped himself and placed it back on the little table. He lay back down on the bed, closed his eyes, and tried to fall asleep, but now he couldn't. He had a headache and was unable to shake his thoughts.

Then he heard chairs scraping across the dining room floor, where there was no rug, as he had noticed earlier. Someone turned on the radio and he could hear dance music. He tossed back and forth, then tried counting, but stopped after reaching two hundred. Eventually, however, he did fall asleep, though only to wake up half an hour later. He had dreamt of his mother.

How strange, he thought, puzzled. I've been thinking about her a lot lately. Am I already so old I'm starting to unreel all these ancient memories?

He stepped up to the little mirror and studied his face, slowly running his hand across his unshaved cheeks.

I look absolutely horrid, he sighed, and sat down on the bed. How long has it been? he wondered. Father died in 1932—and she died in 1926, 1926! That's twelve years ago. She was an odd woman, he now thought. Without deep emotions. I don't think she was able to truly laugh or cry.

In the meantime someone had evidently turned off the radio, since he no longer heard any noise coming from the dining room. He lay back down on the bed and closed his eyes.

What had Mother really been like? he strained to recollect, partly to distract from his worries, but also to connect to his earlier life. He sifted through his memories, which were unusually lucid and took him further and further into the past.

Eventually he saw himself as a child of about seven years old, lying in bed and counting the tall brass rails designed to keep him from rolling out. After counting eight or nine he would stop and count them again, and then he would sit up and stare at the floral pattern in the wallpaper, which was dissolving in the half-dark but still visible. Insects were buzzing outside his window, and Otto tried to imitate their sounds as they flew into his room where they darted about for a while before disappearing once again. It was too hot to stay asleep, so he hitched his nightshirt up under his arms and lay down on the pillows. Then, half-speaking and half-dreaming, he began telling himself a story.

It was a story about cake and gooseberries, about Philipp the dachshund that belonged to his older brother, and about the spanking his father had given him that morning, which he hadn't deserved and which his father would come to feel sorry about. It was about Hilde, who kept bursting into tears and who was still very little and with whom he didn't want to speak anymore, and about Senta the cook, who always had compote on hand for him but whom he didn't like all that much because she kept telling him he was still just a little boy. Then he drifted into sleep.

Still half-asleep, he felt someone bending over and covering him up and watching him. Without moving, he blinked a little at the light coming from the lit candle and opened his eyes just a tiny bit. He was sure no one would notice, and the thought made him smile, but he pretended he was smiling in his sleep. That's how clever he was.

You ought to go to sleep, his mother said, also smiling.

Since he could no longer hide the fact that he was awake, he tried to sit up and hug her. But she pushed him gently back into the pillows and kissed his forehead so lightly that her kiss faded before he could really feel it. At the door she turned around and said, "It's time to sleep."

How soft her voice was, the way she said that! Now he actually did have to go to sleep, and besides, he really was tired.

All of a sudden he burst into tears.

His father had punctuated every slap with the words, "This will teach you!" The blows were methodical and evenly spaced. And although they weren't hard, they did sting quite a bit because his pants were stretched tight since he was bent over his father's knee, and the pain took quite a while to subside.

However, his tears were due less to the pain than to

the inherent injustice. To the fact that he had no way of defending himself just because he was younger and smaller. And the idea that it would always be that way weighed on him. He was convinced that he would never grow up. And even though all the adults insisted that once upon a time they, too, had been little boys and girls, he found that hard to believe, seeing how big they were now. He was afraid he'd have to go through life as a little boy, with a bearded tyrant of a father who was incapable of understanding.

As usual, he had Hilde to thank for his spanking. She always took advantage of their father's protection. He had no doubt she was the favorite, and the tears he was shedding came from the deep despair of feeling unloved. And now he couldn't even count on Senta the cook, who usually stood up for him. Senta, who made the best pancakes and who always let him taste her fruit preserves. She clearly liked him. So maybe he should simply marry her and move away. Of course that would make his family upset and they would worry about him . . . and he felt somewhat comforted imagining how troubled they would be by his leaving. He also considered the possibility that he might just suddenly die, and felt some delight picturing everybody's tears.

At that point even getting sick would have been of some help. Six months earlier he had come down with the measles, and he remembered very well how tender and caring his father had been, in contrast to his usual rough manner: for once he had finally allowed Otto onto the center of the stage, where he clearly belonged. So if he fell ill now his father would spend hours sitting by his bed, reading a book and constantly checking on him. It would do Otto good, and his mother would also come and stay with him, and then he would be given medicine, and his father would always take it first and when he swallowed it himself his mother would sit him up and he would smile, in pain but brave, and everyone would love and appreciate him.

By then he had stopped sobbing except for an occasional spasm. That's how it would be if he were sick. But what should he do now?

He started crying again, but the tears didn't come as easily as before. His misery had shrunk, and he tried in vain to draw it out a little longer, to plunge back into it. But he couldn't. His tears could no longer wash away his anguish, which was now hardened, and that was even worse.

If he went to Hilde and gave her a good shove, she would run back to their father, and he would get another spanking, and then he'd push her once again. What other choice did he have? Maybe he should just run away and never come back? Hilde was bound to be enjoying the fact that he'd gotten spanked. He was sure of that.

He stood up, filled with bitterness, and went into the next room, where Hilde was on the floor playing with his building blocks—the ones he'd just used to construct a Tower of Babel.

"Go away," he said, and stamped his foot. "Go away!"

"I'm telling Papa," she said, in a whiny voice, and stayed.

"Go and tattle," he challenged. "Go to Papa, you little crybaby."

But Hilde stayed where she was since she saw he wasn't doing anything to her, and went on calmly playing with his blocks!

"Those are my blocks!" he explained, and stepped closer.

"Oh . . ." she said, with confident indifference.

"You're not supposed to play with my blocks," he declared and sat down as well, still only watching, to see how far she would push things.

The spanking he'd been forced to endure had given Hilde a great sense of confidence and power, and she quickly stuck out her tongue at him.

He was so outraged he was speechless.

There she was playing with his blocks, after she had knocked down his tower, and on top of that she was sticking her tongue out at him! And there was nothing he could do. She had their father on her side. Now she would always be able to stick her tongue out at him.

He was so angry and indignant he started shaking. More than anything he would have liked to cry, and now he probably would have been able to since he felt so humiliated. But that was exactly what Hilde wanted, to see her older brother cry! After all, he was her big brother, because she was only five. So the only thing he could do was sneer at her.

"You stupid cow," he said, taking a superior tone, and kicked the silly tower she had built.

Now Hilde started to cry. "I'm telling Papa," she threatened, but stayed where she was. Perhaps she wasn't fully confident of what a second complaint might bring. That's why she was crying, and now he even felt a tiny bit sorry for her—after all, she was his little sister.

He let her cry a little longer and then suggested: let's build a Tower of Babel together. His tone was sullen and grumpy, but she accepted the offer of peace.

Ten minutes later, after they had constructed bridges, houses, and entire cities and then, like moody gods, destroyed them, she said with a snippy voice, "I'm still going to tell

Papa! You called me a stupid cow and you're not supposed to!"

"You knocked down my Tower of Babel," he said, outraged. "You played with my blocks, you blabbed to Papa, and yesterday you stole raisins from the pantry!"

"So did you!"

"I was allowed to. Senta said I could."

"She said I could, too."

"No she didn't."

"Yes she did."

They both went silent as they each searched for words that would seal a victory.

"I'm going to Papa," Hilde threatened, after a while. But it sounded a bit weak.

"Go ahead!"

"I will," she said, but even she didn't seem to fully believe she would. Perhaps his accounting had made her a little more reflective.

"Stupid cow," he said once more, decisively, to prove to himself that he had won.

Then they played some more. The door opened, and their mother came in.

"You're being so loud," she said, without reproach. "Please talk a little more quietly. I'd like to lie down."

She walked past them, and they both cringed a bit out of guilt. When she was almost out of the room, Hilde said quietly, as though just to herself, "I'm not a stupid cow!" She tossed her head back and looked at their mother as if expecting her to ask who had claimed she was.

"Don't quarrel" was all she said.

He couldn't simply let Hilde get away with such a sneaky

betrayal. "She stole raisins!" he called out, full of genuine indignation. "She stole . . ."

But their mother had already left the room. He couldn't count on her to help him much, either.

Hilde once again stuck out her little pink tongue.

He stood up and left her and the blocks and went to the kitchen to talk everything over with Senta once and for all.

Hilde also stopped playing with his blocks. Without him there it was no longer fun for her. She stood outside the kitchen and waited for him.

But when he came back he walked right past her without paying her any attention, because now he had definitively promised himself to Senta. They would get married and move away, and Hilde could stick her tongue out as long as she wanted, it no longer affected him . . .

Silbermann had probably slept an hour when he was wakened by steps in the corridor. For a moment they stopped in front of his door.

He listened anxiously.

But then they went on.

He jumped out of bed.

"There's no point," he mumbled. "I have to leave. I have to get out of the country. I can't stand it any longer. The anxiety is driving me mad. I'll go back to Aachen and try crossing the border there."

He stepped up to the mirror, washed his face, combed his hair, and left the room. In the doorway he thought: What nonsense. I really should stay here. Who knows when I'll have a bed again.

In addition to the Susigs, two gentlemen were sitting in the dining room, reading the newspaper. Silbermann knocked quickly and went in, and was met with a resounding chorus of "Heil Hitler."

Without returning the greeting he simply nodded his head and turned to Frau Susig: "I'm going to the station to pick up my suitcase."

"But my husband can take care of that. He'd be happy to."

"Go ahead," said the old man.

His wife looked at him severely.

"All the same . . ." he added, and nodded encouragingly to Silbermann.

"Thank you anyway," said Silbermann. "The fact is I have other business in town." And with that he left the room.

What strange people, he thought, as he climbed down the stairs, but he immediately forgot all about the Susigs and focused on his own affairs. He was surprised to find himself at the station after just five minutes, since he hadn't really paid attention to where he was going.

What a pity I don't have Lilienfeld with me, he regretted, since he's a man with practical experience. Two heads are stronger than one. You strengthen each other. I encouraged Lilienfeld and he did the same for me. Basically each of us was encouraging himself, but it did boost our spirits. Tremendously.

He asked for a third-class ticket for Aachen.

Is that Lilienfeld speaking out of me? he wondered when he heard himself ask for third class. But then he decided that was the right choice, since in second class he would have to be decently shaved in order not to attract attention.

He fetched his suitcase, then asked when the train was scheduled to depart and stepped into the third-class waiting room. Without ordering anything, he sat down at one of the wooden tables. For a few minutes he brooded without specific thoughts.

"All the same . . ." he said quietly, mimicking Herr Susig. "All the same . . ."

Those words seemed to best capture his mood. He said them out loud to himself three or four times.

Now I'm ready for adventure, he determined. I'll make it over the border yet, it's all manageable . . .

But he couldn't rid himself of the conviction that something would once again get in the way, that he simply wasn't up to the demands of the situation and would ultimately have to give in.

"Ach," he growled. "Other people are doing the same thing. And they manage to make it!"

He propped both elbows on the table and took his head between his hands. There's absolutely nothing more I can do, he thought, devoid of hope. The only thing I can do is think . . .

He stared dully at the tabletop.

How dirty it is, and how scratched, he thought. Why don't they refinish it? Probably because third class isn't worth the trouble.

He looked around the waiting room. A few workers were standing at the bar, drinking beer and making a lot of noise, which Silbermann noted with disapproval.

If I were to give each of them a hundred marks, he wondered, would I then have friends? For a few days perhaps—a hundred marks doesn't go very far.

He stood up and headed to the platform, trudging rather than walking.

More and more train rides, he thought, farther and farther

away, and meanwhile I'm already dog tired. Back and forth and forth and back. I'm so fed up with it all already.

He sat down on his suitcase and waited for the train.

Who or rather what am I now anyway? he asked himself. Am I still Silbermann, Otto Silbermann the merchant? Undoubtedly, but how did he wind up in such a situation?

He took a deep breath. "I'm living with loss," he said quietly. Then he made a clumsy movement, and the suitcase he was sitting on began to totter. With difficulty he regained his balance and got on his feet. He heard the train approaching and picked up his suitcase.

Actually all I have to do is jump in front, simply drop right in front of the train, he thought. Then everything would be over and nothing would matter anymore.

The train came nearer.

Silbermann stepped close to the edge of the platform.

Just fall, he thought, just let yourself fall . . .

"Stand back," a voice beside him thundered.

He gave a start and took three steps back. Then the train was there.

Have I completely lost my wits? he worried, surprised by his own weakness. To the point I would take my own life? I, Otto Silbermann? On account of the Nazis? The idea is laughable. I have thirty-six thousand marks on me. What reasonable human being takes his life with thirty-six thousand marks in his pocket? For fear of difficulties, for fear of the border, on account of a ridiculous border, which can be crossed in two minutes if a person can pluck up the courage? Impossible! A person simply can't do a thing like that! Why should a person commit suicide when he's carrying a briefcase full of life?

No, that's it—no more weakness! Twenty-four hours from now I may be saved, and if not, then I'll travel on, I'll crisscross all of Germany until I make it. As long as I have money in my wallet and even if it's a single thousand-mark bill, I'll have both the strength and spirit to live, and I can subsist for a long time off the energy I have stored.

And so, in a smoke-filled third-class compartment on the train from Dortmund to Aachen, Silbermann swore that he would go on living, under—and despite—all circumstances.

He repeated this vow in silence over and over and felt much calmer. He now sensed he'd gotten a grip on himself, that he was ready for all contingencies. He opened his suitcase and, after some cumbersome rummaging, managed to retrieve his razor. Then he went to the toilet to shave his beard, which was showing a handsome growth. When he sat back down his travel companions noticed the transformation.

"Made yourself pretty?" an older worker sitting across from Silbermann jibed. The disdain in his voice was obvious: being an unpretentious sort himself, he clearly didn't think much of such procedures.

"I merely made myself human," Silbermann joked.

His travel companions laughed. Silbermann now observed them: a young worker, a rather stout man who Silbermann thought was very intent on playing the important gentleman, as he cast commanding glances around the room, and a young, rather plain-looking girl of about twenty-two, who was knitting.

Silbermann's gaze returned to the young worker. He was struck by the man's sunken face and drooping shoulders. Undoubtedly a miner, he thought. They age quickly.

Those people don't get much out of life, although they go through a great deal—they probably don't even realize how much. They keep fighting for work, for better wages, for their bare lives—without noticing how time goes slipping through their fingers. They don't have any youth, these people. The struggle starts when they're fourteen years old and from then on it's a fight for sheer survival, with everything at stake.

It's the same with me. I can sense how closely death is nipping at my heels. It's just a matter of being faster. If I stop I'll go under, I'll sink into the mire. I simply have to run, run, run. When I think about it I've been running all my life. But then why is it so difficult all of a sudden, now that it's more necessary than before? Greater danger ought to bring greater strength, but instead it's paralyzing, if the first attempts to save yourself fall through.

He shook his head at the thought. I'd be better off talking! he decided, instead of just sitting here thinking and brooding.

"The weather seems to have taken another turn for the better," he remarked to all his companions.

At the same time he was telling himself: You're in a comfortable place, you can relax. Being around people is almost always nice, almost always . . . In any case he felt warmly reassured by the companionship, even if it was that of a train compartment, haphazard and unintended.

"It's going to rain again," the worker across from him said sullenly. He nodded his head as thanks for the cigarette Silbermann offered.

"On the contrary," declared the stout man, addressing Silbermann as his social equal: "In my opinion, and I believe

I have a feel for weather like very few people. In my opinion"—to Silbermann's ears this "in my opinion" sounded pompous—"tomorrow we're going to have a truly beautiful day, unless I'm very much mistaken." No, listening to him speak, it would be hard to imagine he could possibly be mistaken.

"No thank you," he said, declining Silbermann's offer of a cigarette. "I prefer cigars. They're easier to digest."

"Yes, well let's hope the weather will be good," said Silbermann flatly.

"Are you in sales, a commercial traveler?" the man was interested to know.

"Merchant," Silbermann answered, absentmindedly.

"I was a salesman in my youth," said the man, "then I took over the shop from my sister."

"I see," said Silbermann politely.

The man unfolded a newspaper and began reading.

"Do you have a lot of work?" Silbermann asked the older worker.

"Enough," the other man answered, not keen to share more. He, too, took a newspaper from his bag.

I want a conversation, Silbermann thought. I'd like to keep talking, without stopping. He rested his head against his coat, which was hanging on the hook and closed his eyes. He listened to the rattle of the wheels.

Berlin—Hamburg, he thought.
Hamburg—Berlin.
Berlin—Aachen.
Aachen—Dortmund.
Dortmund—Aachen.

And it may go on that way forever. Now I really am like a traveling salesman, and the route I've been assigned has more and more miles.

The fact is that I have already emigrated . . . to the Deutsche Reichsbahn.

I am no longer in Germany.

I am in trains that run through Germany. That's a big difference. Once again he listened to the wheels rumbling over the rails, the music of travel.

I am safe, he thought, I am in motion.

And on top of that I feel practically cozy.

Wheels rattle, doors open, it could almost be pleasant, if it weren't for the fact that I think too much.

Then he smiled. The Reichsbahn used to offer mystery tours, so-called Journeys into the Blue. Now he had been awarded such a journey, but this time it was sponsored by the government. There were periods in history when people had practically suffocated from a sense of ennui, and so they plunged into adventurous affairs, deliberately wobbling the chairs on which they sat so comfortably, simply for their own exhilaration. They turned to the stock exchange to experience some emotion. But these days citizens are more than adequately provided with emotional experiences. As a child I used to dream about trains. How gladly I would have traveled on one, farther and farther away.

Now I am on a train. Now I'm traveling.

Other trains shot past. A distant, piercing whistle came blaring inside and unfamiliar voices laughed in the neighboring compartment. But the wheels kept grinding the same song over the tracks: utility poles look exactly alike, utility poles look exactly alike, when one is in flight . . . when one is in flight.

Am I traveling? No! I'm stuck in the same place, like a person who takes refuge in a cinema where he sits in his seat without moving as the films flicker away—and all the while his worries are lurking just outside the exit.

There was more travel in the express train game we used to play as children, when we placed three chairs one behind the other, closed our eyes, and pretended to go racing across the country at a furious speed. Back then we traveled in our minds. We were everywhere and nowhere—and still inside our room. Now I'm not really traveling, I'm merely moving.

He gave a start.

I'm sinking back into melancholy, letting myself drift off into fantasies, he thought, annoyed at himself. Meanwhile what I need to do is cling to reality, which is what it is, unreal though it may be.

"Will we be in Aachen soon?" he asked.

This time the young girl answered. "There's still time," she said, looking at him thoughtfully with serious brown eyes.

Silbermann thanked her. Then he asked whether she, too, was traveling there.

She nodded.

"I'm meeting my fiancé," she volunteered, since Silbermann had evidently made a trustworthy impression. "I actually live in Dortmund, but the couple Franz works for, he's a chauffeur, they've been in Aachen for three days."

"I see," said Silbermann.

"It's so rare we get to see each other. He works for

the director of a company from Berlin, and I work in Dortmund."

"Why don't you move to Berlin?" Silbermann asked sympathetically.

"I'd like to, but that won't work. And it'll be some time before we can get married, too."

"And why is that?" asked the stout man, curious, setting the paper on his knee.

"Franz doesn't earn enough for two, and on top of that we'd need to furnish a whole apartment, which would cost at least a thousand marks. And where are we supposed to come up with that?"

"But you could get a marriage loan." Silbermann rejoined the conversation.

She shook her head vigorously.

"No," she said, "we don't want to start by borrowing."

"But that's better than nothing," the other man said, shaking his head at such an irrational attitude.

"Besides, it's not that simple," she explained. "I'm not sure we'd even qualify."

Silbermann leaned forward, interested, but before he could say anything, the other man asked, "And why wouldn't you?" He peered inquisitively at the girl.

"Franz isn't in the party."

"That has nothing to do with it," the man declared. "He would still get the loan. Just give it a try."

The girl shook her head. "It's no use," she said.

"And so you'll keep living in Dortmund while he's in Berlin?" Silbermann asked.

"I'd gladly move to Berlin, but you can't get work there

if you're from out of town," the girl said. Her voice sounded displeased.

"What type of work do you do?" asked Silbermann.

"I'm a stenotypist."

Silbermann looked at her closely. She doesn't exactly seem to be an enthusiastic supporter of National Socialism, he thought, and an idea began taking shape—though for the moment it was still quite vague.

"So you'd be quite happy if you could get married?" he asked.

"Ach," she said, sadly, "for now that's out of the question."

"Do you really have to have a whole apartment right away?" asked the stout man, astounded to hear such lofty aspirations given such limited resources.

"Yes," she said, firmly. "We need an apartment and a typewriter. That way I could make copies and earn extra money."

"You're absolutely right," Silbermann agreed. "You'd probably need a thousand marks."

"Yes," she said. "Then it would all work out. We've already saved two hundred fifty marks. We just need another seven hundred fifty."

"And how long have you been saving up?" the other man felt comfortable enough to ask.

"Oh God," she said, again becoming sad. "It could well take another two years before we manage all that."

"And in the meantime a war might break out," the man said, smiling. "The other countries won't leave us in peace," he added quickly. "And then what? Then you'll be sorry!

You're making life unnecessarily difficult for yourselves! Instead of going and asking for a marriage loan . . ." He shook his head and went back to his newspaper. "There's no helping you people," he said ruefully.

"But Franz was in a concentration camp," the girl said quietly.

They looked at her in shock.

The stout man cleared his throat and disappeared completely behind his newspaper. The old worker mumbled something unintelligible and lit a cigarette. And the young worker stared at the girl to the point that she turned away.

"And did he learn from the experience?" asked Silbermann, who was having more and more hope that he had discovered an ally.

The girl looked at him warily. "In any case he's had it up to here with politics," she said at last.

"He's right about that," said the old worker. "People like us, we're just . . ." He made a gesture of tossing something away and was silent.

The girl stared out the window for a few minutes and then packaged up her knitting and stowed it in her purse. Then she took out the breakfast she had packed, carefully unfolded the paper, and began eating a sandwich.

"Is your fiancé also from Dortmund?" asked Silbermann. The sight of her food made him hungry.

"No, he's from Aachen."

"Then he must be happy to be back home again?"

"Yes," was all the girl replied. She probably felt she'd said too much already.

Silbermann went into the corridor to see if there was a vending machine with chocolate. He didn't find one, but on his way to look and also on his way back, he passed a young boy with dark hair, about fourteen years old, who Silbermann thought had been watching him very cautiously. Each time the boy had squeezed so close to the wall it seemed he might be afraid of something. Silbermann went back into the compartment and tried to resume the conversation.

"Do you have a good position?" he asked the girl, just to keep her talking to him.

She shook her head. "There's plenty of work," she said, "but it doesn't pay well."

The old worker looked up, as though he wanted to say something, but contented himself with spitting on the floor.

The stout man wrinkled his forehead.

"We always have to complain, don't we!" he said, looking at Silbermann for approval.

"Who's complaining here?" the girl asked aggressively.

What a resolute young woman, Silbermann was happy to observe.

"You'd be well advised to watch your words," the man said, sounding serious.

"Now, now," said Silbermann soothingly. "What's all this about?" He smiled at the girl. "You don't have to scowl like that. It doesn't suit you."

Then he turned to the man. "Listening in on someone else's conversation makes one prone to mishear things, and then it's easy to create ill will."

The man's face turned red. He probably realized he was dealing with a man from a higher social status than his own, and even if he wasn't sure Silbermann really did have something important to say, he decided not to argue, just to be on the safe side.

"I simply can't stand hearing phrases like 'So much work, so little pay' anymore," he explained, now sounding noticeably milder.

"Those aren't just phrases," said the old worker. "That's how it is."

"Are you implying that things were better before?" the man asked tensely.

"I'm not implying anything," said the worker. "Besides, I'm in the party." He cast a disparaging glance at the man.

"I'm in the party as well," the latter hastened to explain.

"Since when, then?" the worker asked, snidely.

"That's nobody's business!" said the man, refusing to answer.

"But you're quick to butt into conversations that aren't your business," the young girl declared.

"If there's complaining going on, then yes."

"Don't sound so high and mighty," growled the old worker. "You act as though you're pushing the whole cart by yourself."

The man looked at him sternly. "You say you're in the party?" he asked.

"And for longer than you!"

Both men were silent. Silbermann noted a thankful glance from the girl. Then the two party members continued their argument.

"So how can you say," the stout man asked, "that one shouldn't concern oneself with politics? That's out and out defeatism!"

"I never said anything of the sort. Who knows what you might have heard? The gentleman is absolutely right: if you listen in on other people's conversations you're bound to mishear things. I have no idea what makes you think that . . ."

"You said . . ."

"First prove to me that you really are a member. Anyone can say that, and anyone can play detective. But whether he has the right to snoop around is another matter!"

"I'm not snooping. I'm simply fulfilling my duty, as every German should."

"Are you saying it's your duty to listen in? What kind of strange profession is that? I thought you ran a shop, or am I mistaken?"

"I don't owe you any explanation."

"But I owe you one, eh?"

"Indeed you do," said the portly gentleman. "And now show me your party card!"

This last sentence came as a sharp command. Reluctantly, the worker pulled his membership card out of his pocket and handed it to the other man.

He examined the document carefully. "It's good," he said then, and stood up, "but in the future you should control yourself better, my friend! And I would give you the same advice!" he said to the girl. Then he took his briefcase and left the compartment.

For a moment everyone was uneasily silent.

By a hair, thought Silbermann, just by a hair. His heart was pounding. And always when you least expect it . . .

The old worker stared sullenly ahead for a while and then said, "I'd like to open the window. The air in here is a bit . . ."

The young girl said nothing. She had turned pale and kept running her hands nervously over her sandwich paper.

"Some people are simply overzealous," Silbermann said, in a distinctly calm voice.

"Just anyone try and tell me what's what," said the worker. "I've been in the party for ten years. Just let them try!"

"See what happens when you go and open your mouth," said the young worker who had kept quiet until then. "You wind up having to deal with an ass like that!"

Silbermann stepped back out into the corridor. He gazed out the window for a few minutes, then went to the toilet to wash his hands. He hadn't shut the door properly and all of a sudden he heard the stout man's voice saying: "Let's see your papers."

Silbermann spun around. But the words couldn't be addressed to him. The man was probably speaking to someone just outside the toilet.

"Why should I show you my papers?" asked a nervous young voice. "I haven't done anything."

"Police. You see the badge? Let's go, show your ID."

"I don't have it on me."

"Of course not! Where are you heading?"

"I'm heading . . . to Aachen."

"What's your name? Out with it! Just don't lie. I'm warning you!"

"My name is Leo Cohn."

"Of course! What are you doing here on this train? Well, little Jew boy? Out with it! Or do you expect me to have to beg for half an hour?"

"My father was arrested and . . ."

"Serves him right. What's in your backpack? Money? To smuggle it across the border, right?"

"No. You can look for yourself. All I have is a suit and some underwear."

"You bet I'll have a look! And woe to you if you've deceived me. So now, let's go."

"But . . ." Silbermann heard the boy swallow.

"Let's go, boy, get a move on," said the voice of the portly man.

"Am I going to be sent to a concentration camp?" asked the boy.

"We'll have to see about all that. Come on, Cohn, forward march, Cohn."

"But I haven't done anything . . ."

"Are you trying to play one of your little Jew-tricks on me? You can still manage that, eh? Come on, I'm not going to eat you, you little garlic-head . . . come on, hop to it."

The steps faded. Silbermann opened the door and just managed to see the stout man pushing the dark-haired boy he had noticed earlier around the corner into the next corridor.

SIX

The headlamps cut a large swath of white light through the darkness, and the forest, which reached right up to the road, seemed full of shadows. Trees suddenly loomed tall, then merged with the darkness and disappeared.

Franz was driving at near maximum speed. He was nervous and agitated. I definitely have to be back within the hour, he thought. This is the first time I've taken the car on my own and it's going to be the last time, too. I've never even had Gertrud out for a spin. But a thousand marks . . . a thousand marks!

A car came from the other direction and he quickly lowered his beam.

He was worried. I'm risking everything, he thought. All on account of a rich Jew. But a thousand marks. Besides, Gertrud would have considered me a coward, and God knows I've already been through enough. If everything works out we'll be in good shape. That girl has more courage than a lot of men. And the poor fellow in back? He may be a rich Jew, but these days things aren't exactly rosy for him, either. I might even feel sorry for him if I had the time. For now the thing to do is take the thousand marks and marry Gertrud. It's almost enough to make me want to take a rich Jew to the border every week! For a thousand marks!

And if I get caught? Then it's all over. They're not going to let me off a second time. Still, I've risked my neck so often for nothing except the cause, so why shouldn't I dare to do something for myself, just once?

He stopped the car. Then he turned to Silbermann, who was sitting in back: "Here's the best place to get out. I know the area a little. Earlier I helped some comrades get across. I didn't take money for that."

"Naturally," said Silbermann as he got out.

"That's right," said Franz. "Frankly, I'm not so keen on the Jews myself. I had a Jewish boss earlier on. And he didn't exactly make me jump for joy, let me tell you. Believe me, this is the first time that I'm taking money for helping someone. And if it hadn't been for Gertrud and if she hadn't twisted my arm, we wouldn't be here . . ."

"It's all right," said Silbermann. "You don't have to hold it against me that you're helping me."

"I don't hold it against you. But Gertrud, she has a way of getting you to do things . . ."

"Franz," Silbermann said, trying to calm him down, "just be glad. Here's your money. And give your fiancée my greetings and tell her I wish her all good luck."

"You better wish that for yourself," said Franz sullenly, as he pocketed the money without counting the bills. "Because frankly this isn't going to be easy! Just keep heading straight. You'll come across a fire lane, but keep going until you reach the forest path. That's where the border is, but you have to keep going! Eventually you'll come to a road, but just keep on going straight ahead across the fields! If you hurry you'll be in Belgium in half an hour.

"Watch out for the Belgian gendarmes, and be sure you get to the nearest larger town as fast as you can. If they call out to you while you're still on German soil then stop, otherwise they'll shoot, you can bet your suitcase on that. Speaking of which, you really should have left it at home. Who on earth tries to cross the border with a suitcase—I've never seen anything like it. I'm surprised you're not hauling a furniture van as well!"

After carefully absorbing his grumpy driver's observations, Silbermann asked, "Do you think I'll make it?"

"That's a question I can't answer," said Franz. "I've already told you how things are. One person gets through and another doesn't. But if you're going to piss your pants right here there's no way you're going to make it. I've heard that they've beefed up the border patrols on the Belgian side. If they catch you you'll get sent right back, that's for dead sure! Now hurry up and good luck! And if you get caught please say you came all this way on foot. But I bet you'll rat me out first thing, am I right! You upstanding citizens are all alike."

"Have you ever crossed the border?"

"Have I ever crossed it?" Franz laughed.

"I'll give you another thousand marks if you take me across. I'm afraid I'll lose my way. I don't have any experience . . ."

"I see. And what did you promise my fiancée?"

Silbermann nodded. "You're right," he said uneasily. "I'll have to manage on my own." He held out his hand. "Good-bye."

"I can see it coming," Franz answered, now sounding angry. "You're going to run smack into the arms of the first border guard. Why did I ever let myself be talked into this! Now I'm really in for it!"

He got out of the car.

"What are you doing?" Silbermann asked hopefully.

"I'm not starting something and then leaving it half-done now am I?" Franz said, disgruntled. "Come on."

"Do you really want to . . . ?"

"No! I don't want to! But what choice do I have?"

"And you can leave the car here like that?"

"I took the key. All on account of these stupid thousand marks. It's not like both of us don't have paying jobs, too—bloody hell."

"I'll give you another thousand marks," said Silbermann, happy. "No, I'll even give you . . ."

"Just get your suitcase," Franz growled, and set off.

He seemed to know the way well, but he was in such a hurry that he ran more than walked. Silbermann tripped over roots, banged into rocks, and bumped into tree trunks. He was panting from exertion. His suitcase felt like it was made of lead.

After ten minutes of rushing like that without a break—Franz looked back from time to time to make sure Silbermann was following—Silbermann was exhausted and said: "I can't keep up. I need to rest a moment."

Franz stopped. "That's more or less what I imagined," he whispered. "Do you know what's going to happen if I get home and discover that the boss asked for the car while I was away? He sometimes goes out at night and he's also a real swine. He'd hand me over to the police straightaway simply for taking his car for a joyride. Of course it's just like you to peter out now, too. Hand me the suitcase."

He went on ahead.

"What's your guess as to the time?" Silbermann whispered after a while.

"Two o'clock, I think. Early enough to get caught."

Now Franz was feeling the weight of the suitcase. He set it down and cursed quietly.

"I'd like to know how it is that I wound up being your pack mule? Incredible! If someone had told me I'd be risking my neck for a bourgeois . . ."

"You're a decent person," Silbermann said quietly, pleased to be able to take off his hat and wipe his brow.

"There are no decent people," Franz replied. "Not according to the materialist concept of history. But what would you know about that?"

"Not much," Silbermann admitted.

"You see," said Franz, more graciously. "But I'm sure even you realize that one person's saint is another person's devil. And the devil for the working class is . . . But let's go. If I start thinking about it, I'll end up ditching you right here!"

Silbermann laughed.

"Psst!" said Franz, angry. They had reached the clearing.

"Is it much farther?" asked Silbermann.

"Ten minutes, but now be still!"

Franz listened in the darkness. Then he moved quietly ahead, making sure his footsteps made no noise.

Silbermann tiptoed behind him. Franz's company had

given him so much courage that he almost forgot the danger he was in.

At last they came to the forest path.

"I'd take you farther, to Lambert's—that's a friend of mine who runs an inn, but I have to beat it back to the car. Just keep going straight ahead until you come to the field I told you about, and then march directly across. Be sure to make as little noise as possible. After that you'll come to a little forest. Cross through that, and then you'll be in the village. The fourth house is Lambert's inn. Go inside but of course leave your suitcase in the woods. I'm assuming you're not dumb enough to walk into the village carrying a suitcase? So, tell Lambert that Franz sends his greetings, and he'll help you. He'll definitely want to make some money, but he'll take you farther. His stepson has a car. You speak French, don't you?"

"Yes, of course," said Silbermann.

"Of course—exactly like the lot of you! So, then, good-bye."

"Wait, I still want to give you the money."

"I'll take money for risking my boss's car, but not for risking my neck!"

"But . . ."

Franz had already turned around, and for a few minutes Silbermann watched his haggard, bony figure as it disappeared into the darkness. Then he picked up his suitcase. "I'm lucky after all," he mumbled.

A light rain began to fall. The drops splashed against Silbermann's face. He hurried ahead as fast as the suitcase allowed. He still felt some of the security that being close to Franz had provided.

It's going to work out, he hoped. If only I'd left this crazy suitcase at home. He thought about leaving it in the woods, but opening it and unpacking the money seemed too dangerous. I've lugged it this far, so I'll go on lugging it some more, he thought, when he had to set it down again. Otherwise the whole slog would have been for nothing.

He felt so exhausted that he had to rest for a moment.

I wonder if Franz is going to get into trouble, he asked himself. I don't even know his last name. I'll never be able to thank him. But what a stroke of luck. Actually I have that fat police spy to thank for meeting him.

Belgium, he then thought. I'm now in Belgium. And it doesn't look any different. I ought to be mad with joy but instead I'm afraid. And it's the same fear I had five minutes ago when I was still in Germany. If only I . . .

He thought he heard a noise and strained to listen. Weren't those twigs snapping somewhere? He jumped up, lifted his suitcase, and looked around, wide-eyed.

"No," he whispered, "no, no, no! It's over. I quit! I'm staying right here! I'm staying here even if they . . ."

But there was no noise—he'd been mistaken. The rain dripped down on him and calmed him somewhat. He picked up his suitcase and set off again. The blister on his index finger had burst from carrying the suitcase, and the pain refused to let up. He switched the suitcase to the other hand.

What if I get caught now, he thought. And sent back to Germany! But that simply can't happen!

To make as little noise as possible he went exceedingly slowly, testing the ground with his feet to avoid any missteps.

At least I'm in Belgium, he then thought. I managed after all!

The forest began to clear and through the darkness he

could make out something lighter colored. The road, he thought. He started to walk more quickly, without paying attention to the noise made by the snapping twigs. When he was out of the woods he looked around. He felt an almost celebratory sensation.

My shadow existence is over, he thought. Now I'll become a human again!

After he had carefully scanned the area and failed to see anything suspicious, he crossed the road. Before him was an open field.

Keep going straight ahead, he remembered. He jumped over a small ditch and felt the soft, damp tilled earth beneath his feet. If only I hadn't taken this damn suitcase with me, he again wished.

All of a sudden he heard sounds coming from the forest. Twigs crackled, first one flashlight switched on, then a second, and two figures emerged from the darkness about twenty meters from the place he had just passed, and headed in his direction.

At the first suspicious sound Silbermann had instantly thrown himself down and was now dragging his suitcase behind him, which thudded on the ground. His heart was pounding, and he opened his mouth wide to breathe. He pushed his face as close to the ground as his increasingly urgent need for air allowed.

Only the blurred outlines of the men were visible. They were standing in the middle of the road, pointing their flashlights this way and that. They conferred in whispers and seemed to disagree as to which direction he had taken, and then they separated. One stayed in place while the other walked over to the ditch, where he shined his light up and down before setting off in the opposite direction from Silbermann.

Meanwhile the man who had stayed put lit a cigarette and started walking very deliberately right toward Silbermann. He seemed utterly sure of himself—almost as though he were mocking both his colleague, who had doggedly continued in the wrong direction and was now fifty paces away, as well as the man who thought he could remain hidden.

This can't be. Silbermann prayed that it not be true. This simply cannot be! He can't have seen me, no!

At the same time he knew that the man who was now only ten paces away could surely hear his fitful breathing. Silbermann pressed his hand against his mouth.

"Eh bien," a calm voice now said. "Voulez-vous rester là?"

The man shone the light in Silbermann's face.

"Je l'ai trouvé," the guard now called out to his companion, who came hurrying over.

Silbermann had a hard time getting up. "Je suis . . ." he began.

"Vous avez traversé la frontière," the guard interrupted him and once again shone the light in Silbermann's face. "Il faut retourner!"

"Je suis un refugié," Silbermann continued, his voice hoarse. "Je suis juif."

"Tiens, tiens," the guard replied. "Mais quand-même. Vous n'avez pas le droit de passer la frontière. Il faut venir avec un visa. Alors, venez!"

In the meantime the other guard had arrived. "You have to go back to Germany."

"But I'm a refugee—I'm Jewish. They wanted to arrest me. They'll lock me up in a concentration camp."

"We're not allowed to let you through. Come with us!" The man grabbed him by the arm and started leading him back to the forest.

The guard who had discovered him carried Silbermann's suitcase and left the talking to his colleague.

When they reached the road Silbermann stopped. "I protest!" he said. "I'm staying here! You don't have the right, you're not allowed to do this! I'm in a free country!"

"You crossed the border illegally."

"I had no choice—I was persecuted."

"But everybody can't just come to Belgium!"

"I have papers. I have money. Wait, let me show you . . ."

"Come on!" the guard shoved him ahead.

But Silbermann resisted. "You have to understand," he said. "I can no longer go back. I only intended to stay one day in Belgium. My son lives in Paris. I want to go to Paris to join him!"

"Explain that to the Belgian consul in Germany! We have orders . . ."

"But I'm not going back! I demand to be taken to the guardhouse! It's not my fault I had to cross the border illegally. I'm being persecuted."

"It's not Belgium's fault. We're sorry . . ."

They had crossed the road. Silbermann stopped again.

"I can't go back!" he said. "It's impossible!" He turned to the guard who was carrying his suitcase.

"Mais oui, mon ami, that's completely possible," the man calmly replied.

Silbermann suddenly tore himself away from them. "Do what you want," he cried. "I'm staying . . . je reste . . . je reste!"

"If you don't go back voluntarily we'll have to put you on a train in Herbesthal. The next station is in Germany, and there the German authorities will . . ."

"You can't do that!"

"Mais oui!"

For a moment all three were silent. Then the two guards grabbed him vigorously by the arms and shoved him ahead.

"You know the way!" said the man who had discovered him. "Just don't come back!"

"Or else we'll have to put you on that train to Germany!" the other added.

They had reached the edge of the forest, but Silbermann was mistaken if he thought the guards would then leave him alone. They continued to escort him. Once again he stopped.

"I'm not going," he declared with desperate energy. "I won't stay longer than one day. I promise you I'll travel on immediately. I have everything. Money, papers. I'm not a poor man. You have to understand, they'll arrest me. If I can't stay here I'll have to kill myself. Belgium is my last hope. Gentlemen, I beg you, I've never broken the law in my life!"

"You have to go back. There's no point in talking. You have to go back!"

"Écoutez," Silbermann began again, turning to the first guard. "I'll give you five thousand marks! That's a fortune . . ."

"You must be crazy. Allez." the man answered calmly.

"Listen, it's a good opportunity for you, and for me it

would mean my life. I'll give you ten thousand—five for each!"

His shoulder felt a shove.

"Shut your mouth," said a rough voice, though Silbermann thought he detected a slight hesitation.

"Fifteen thousand," he raised his offer. "And I assure you I'll never say a word about it—that's in my own interest. Be reasonable, and be human! There are two of you, I'll give each of you the money right away. Think about it, seven thousand five hundred marks . . ."

"We're in Belgium here," the guard said, and Silbermann wasn't sure whether he was referring to a higher value placed on morals or a lower value of Germany currency.

"Ten thousand apiece . . ." Silbermann raised the offer. "That's enough to retire on and buy a house if you want." Since he was now discussing the business aspect of the negotiation, his voice was noticeably calmer and more self-assured.

The guards said nothing. If only they don't distrust each other . . . Silbermann was afraid. They can't see each other's face, and therein lies the danger.

"We can arrange it very quickly," he said. "I leave Belgium, and you can look out for each other, because you're both . . ."

"Be quiet," said the second guard curtly. Perhaps he wanted to make clear to his colleague that he was no less principled than the one who had first refused.

A misunderstanding between these two is going to be the end of me, thought Silbermann, despairing. He tried again: "Gentlemen, you are . . ."

But now the guard on his right shook his arm. "Will you finally shut up!" he snarled.

"If you keep on like that we'll hand you over to the German guards," added the one to his left.

"But we have to trust each other!" Silbermann implored, thinking that he understood things very clearly. "Ten thousand for each, right away. I'm guessing that's about fifty thousand francs . . ."

If they could only see each other's face, he thought. Then they would surely come to an agreement.

"That's enough," said the guard on his right. "One more word and we're taking you to Herbesthal."

Silbermann was silent. They had reached the forest path and stopped.

"Eh bien, Monsieur," the guard with the suitcase said very crossly as he put it down. "You're back in your fatherland. Don't come back under any circumstances! That would be very dangerous for you!"

"Gentlemen," Silbermann begged them once more. "I didn't mean to offend you. I assure you. But think about it . . ."

"If you show up here again . . ." the guard growled.

Silbermann turned around, cut through the forest, and tripped over a root as he stumbled back into the German Reich.

SEVEN

Silbermann stopped his ears with his thumbs. Utility poles look exactly alike, utility poles look exactly alike, when one is in flight. Utility poles look exactly alike . . . I'm starting to lose my wits, he feared. The monotonous singsong of the rails was more than agonizing.

How am I supposed to get any sleep? he wondered, and reached with his left hand to move his briefcase, which he had wedged between his back and the cushion, so that its lock kept digging into his spine. After his failed attempt to cross the border, Silbermann had stowed all the money in his briefcase and left his suitcase on the country road. He was in no shape to haul it around any longer.

That night he had hiked for another hour and a half before flagging down a large truck, which took him to Mönchengladbach. The two disgruntled drivers reminded him of Franz, and their occasional wry remarks, and their overall grumpy-but-positive outlook had done him good and lifted his spirits a little.

Now he was once again sitting in a train on his way back to Berlin. His unsuccessful venture had depressed him so much that he no longer wanted to try crossing into Belgium. He lacked the strength of purpose such an undertaking would require.

Having the whole compartment to himself, he opened the window and leaned out to get some fresh air. The sharp wind did him good. Then a bit of dust flew into his right eye and it took him nearly five minutes to get it out. By the time he closed the window the compartment had become cold. He ate a piece of chocolate and made another attempt to fall asleep. But the rattling of the wheels and the gentle swaying and rocking of the train brought him to the brink of despair.

He paced up and down the compartment several times, making a point of reading all the policies and regulations. Then he sat back in his seat, but immediately got up again and stepped into the corridor with the idea of walking through the train. He observed the people coming in the other direction with indifference, except when he encountered a man he thought looked Jewish, and involuntarily wrinkled his forehead. As he made his way down the aisle in a third-class car he ran into another person with similarly suspect features.

There are too many Jews on the train, Silbermann thought. And that puts every one of us in danger. As it is I have all of you to thank for this: if you didn't exist I could live in peace. But because you do, I'm forced to share your misfortune! I'm no different from anybody else, but maybe you truly are different and I don't belong in your group. I'm not one of you. Indeed, if it weren't for you, they wouldn't be persecuting me. I could remain a normal citizen. But because you exist, I will be annihilated along with you. And yet we really have nothing to do with one another!

He considered such thoughts undignified but couldn't help thinking them. If people are constantly saying: You're a good man, but your family is completely worthless. Or: You're nothing at all like your cousins, they really are a nasty lot—then it's easy to get infected with the general opinion.

And that was exactly what was happening to Otto Silbermann, who in his normal state was not one of those tragicomic figures known as Jewish anti-Semites. But at the moment he was so worked up he wasn't thinking clearly, and he viewed the sheer existence of his coreligionists as an insult.

You have all gotten me into this mess, he thought angrily, and glared at a man standing by the window whose appearance had led Silbermann to believe he was a fellow Jew. The man noticed and testily returned the scowl, then strode right up to Silbermann.

"Do you have some score to settle with me?" he fumed.

Silbermann was surprised and said nothing.

"So why are you staring at me like that?" asked the man, who struck Silbermann as a low-level clerk.

Silbermann didn't answer.

"Hey"—the man tapped his shoulder—"I'm talking to you!"

"I refuse to be spoken to like that," said Silbermann sharply.

"Listen, if we weren't stuck here on a train . . ." the other man answered, giving Silbermann a threatening glance.

"Then what?" Silbermann asked coolly.

"Then you would see!"

A third person, evidently a friend of the offended party, mixed in. "Are you picking another fight, Max?" he asked, shaking his head.

"That's none of your business."

The other man put his hand on Max's shoulder. "Just leave it be," he said.

"I have no idea what the gentleman wants from me," Silbermann now explained.

"Perhaps you said he was Jewish?"

"I didn't say anything," Silbermann answered, bewildered.

"If you had he probably would have clobbered you. Because he isn't, you see."

"I won't have people staring at me as if I were squinty eyed and had moneybags strapped on in front and back," said the man, now more conciliatory. "I'm in the party just like everybody else!"

"I had no intention of offending you," Silbermann assured the man. Then he turned around and went into the dining car where he ate his midday meal, which brightened his mood considerably. After much deliberation he finally resolved to go to Küstrin, to consult with his wife about the immediate future.

Maybe I can stay there a few days, until the worst is over, he hoped. He also planned to call his son again.

I'm never again going to try crossing the border illegally, he determined. It's clear I'm only suited for an ordinary life and not cut out for extraordinary adventures. He recalled the scene in the forest near the border and the return march that followed. Then again, maybe I should have made one more attempt, he thought. Maybe it would have succeeded. Will I ever again make it out of German territory? he asked himself. Even though it had proven futile, he now recalled the previous day's exploit with amazement that bordered on admiration.

Viewed from the dining car, his adventure lost much of its drama, and what in the moment seemed like a fierce life-or-death struggle now became a memory that while it still weighed on him, was less tragic—to the point of being comical. Which made the defeat somewhat less dispiriting.

It could have turned out a lot worse, he thought. I could have been caught by German guards. Besides, I'm not the only one hurt by how things turned out. Because now it's daytime again, and the Belgian officials can see each other's faces.

This was very satisfying to imagine, and he dwelled on the idea for quite some time. Twenty thousand marks I offered them, he thought. I must have been out of my mind. What was I supposed to give the next official who stopped me, and the one after that, and the one after that one? He smiled. In any case, he mused, I'm a lot tougher than I realize.

He paid and left. He very much hoped not to run into the man who had stood up to Silbermann's "anti-Semitism," and he didn't.

The copious, tasty meal had put Silbermann in a better mood, and once he was back in his compartment he sat down by the window and soon fell asleep. He slept for several hours and didn't wake up until the train stopped in

Hanover. He ordered a coffee from the dining car waiter who was passing by his compartment, then opened his window and stuck his head outside. He waved a newsboy over, purchased a few magazines, tossed them behind him onto his seat, and observed the travelers bustling around on the platform.

An elegantly dressed lady, who was standing outside his window talking with an older lady, attracted his attention. Without meaning to listen in, he caught a few scraps of their conversation.

"Don't say too much," said the older lady. "The less you speak, the better it is for you! After all, you have your lawyer, don't you? Remember it makes a much better impression on the judge if you simply take the slanderous remarks in stride and refuse to let them bother you . . . And there's no reason they should! After all he's the one at fault! . . . And be polite! . . . Calm and polite, that always makes the best impression . . . Don't let yourself get drawn into anything. Any settlement will invariably mean giving up your rights . . . And be sure to tell your lawyer that I'm prepared to testify on your behalf at any time. Just say the word and I'll come right away! . . . I know how he's treated you. It's perfectly . . . Where's the porter? Did you make a note of the number? I didn't either . . . You should always do that, you never know when you might need it. Oh there he is . . . Hopefully you have a decent seat. Don't smoke too much, it's not good for your complexion . . . And like I said, I'm ready to come at a moment's notice, you just have to write . . . And be sure and tell your lawyer everything. Otherwise he has no way of knowing . . . You've paid too little attention to the trial . . . And keep having him watched, by all means!

The more you . . . The conductor is waving. You have to get on . . . Just send me word and I promise I'll be there on the next train!"

Silbermann stepped back from the window.

So, those types of worries are still out there as well, he thought to himself, somewhat astonished. One should be wary of women with quarrelsome or malcontent girlfriends. Elfriede always only listened to me. He sighed.

The door to his compartment slid open, a porter entered and stowed two suitcases on the luggage rack, then went back into the corridor and stood there waiting. Silbermann lit a cigarette and leafed through one of the magazines he had acquired.

Now I'm curious, he thought.

He heard the porter say thank you, and someone stepped inside.

"Heil Hitler," said a high female voice, by way of greeting.

Silbermann looked up. "Heil," he said in an unfriendly tone.

He already knew quite a bit about the lady and at first observed her with only moderate interest. "Shall I close the window?" he asked.

"Oh, just leave it open," she replied, her gray-blue eyes flitting about in a very attractive way. As they met his gaze, Silbermann felt they registered and simultaneously affirmed his existence.

Her face was striking, though not beautiful in the classical sense. Even so, Silbermann found her eyes so lively and absorbing it was difficult not to be influenced by them, and to cast a coolly critical verdict based on purely aesthetic criteria. Perhaps a woman might have ascertained that her mouth was a bit too large and her nose a bit too short, but Silbermann was no longer able to muster true objectivity. Her eyes had transferred to him something of the electricity that he suspected resided inside her, releasing a gentle wave of warmth, which made it difficult for him to form a calm opinion.

The woman lit a cigarette and straightened her skirt. Then she opened her handbag to take out a lipstick and a compact mirror, stubbed her cigarette in the ashtray, after only a few puffs, and began applying her lipstick with intense concentration.

Silbermann recalled having earlier disapproved of such public touch-ups, but now he found that the sight of a woman tending to herself so lovingly could have something heartwarming. The associated coquetry was not objectionable in all circumstances. Moreover, in certain exceptional cases it was not without a certain charm, and he was convinced he was sitting across from precisely such a case.

He also found that he had done well to shave before leaving Mönchengladbach, even if he couldn't come up with any direct connection between his grooming operation and his new companion. He paged through his magazines, happy for the pleasant company, without entertaining further thoughts.

Little by little, however, his worries began to return, and they were so oppressive that when she asked him a question ten minutes later, he had to get her to repeat it, as he hadn't been listening.

"I was just wondering," she said, and her voice definitely

had a kind of warm brightness, "whether the train makes another stop or if it goes straight through to Berlin."

"I believe it stops in Magdeburg and Oebisfelde," Silbermann answered, putting down his magazine.

"Thank you," she said, her eyes as expressive as before. "You see, I forgot to pick up any reading material."

"Perhaps I might offer to share some of mine?" asked Silbermann.

"That's very kind, but surely you wish to read them yourself?"

"Certainly not all of them. As you see I have several. Please." He handed her two magazines. Meeting her eyes, Silbermann felt an enormous release of tension. "Is this your first time taking this route?" he asked.

She sighed in the practiced manner of those whom experience has taught to maintain discipline even while sighing, and to stay within accepted convention.

Silbermann was tactfully silent.

"Unfortunately not," she said at last.

"Do you so dislike traveling?" he asked sympathetically.

"On the contrary, but there are some occasions . . ." was all she said.

"Of course," said Silbermann, and sighed in a not-so-conventional manner. "There are some occasions . . ."

She looked at him.

Eyes like will-o'-the-wisps, he thought, dancing little lights.

Then he said, "One can travel to escape calm. But one can also travel to find calm."

Her eyes smiled, he was convinced of that.

"Frankly I'm just traveling to get to Berlin," she said.

Silbermann laughed.

I'm married, he thought. I am a person in flight. I don't have time to think about anything except my sad affairs, and I cannot and will not let myself be led astray.

"Nevertheless I'm very glad," he said, bending forward slightly to come closer to her, "that I took this train. It is so—pleasantly occupied."

Without answering him she took a magazine and began leafing through it.

Silbermann felt unusually foolish. He stared at the drab landscape passing by outside the window and suspected that his face had turned red. Am I looking for some kind of romantic adventure? he asked himself. No, nothing could be further. Of course perhaps that might be a . . . but that's nonsense.

"Would you happen to have some matches?" she asked.

"Of course," he answered, and quickly searched his pockets. Eventually he found some and gave her a light.

"Thank you," she said, examining him quietly. Then all of a sudden she asked, "Would you happen to be a lawyer?"

"Unfortunately I can't say I am," he said, surprised.

"The thought just occurred to me." She went back to the magazine she had been reading.

"I see," he said. "Actually there was a time when I wanted to become a lawyer. I even studied law for a few semesters. That proved helpful later on. Some degree of legal knowledge isn't a bad thing for a businessman. Perhaps I can help you with something in particular?"

"That's not why I asked," she replied.

"So, do I look like a lawyer? Like documents and trials and default decrees and fee schedules?" he asked, smiling.

"No," she said. "I mean, I don't know. I can never guess a person's profession just by looking."

"May I then ask why you thought I might be one?"

"Isn't that unimportant?"

"I'd be interested to learn the reason, but of course I don't want to insist."

"You reminded me of someone," she explained.

"Hopefully to my advantage," he joked.

She laughed, and once again scrutinized him freely. "Comparisons are difficult," she said, finally.

"I guess I don't come out so well in the balance?"

They both laughed.

There's something about the woman that might be called easy, Silbermann thought. Perhaps I'm only imagining it, since I know more about her than I ought to. In any case I've met people dead set on showing how proper they are whom I found less pleasant. He looked at her. A beautiful fever, he thought, without knowing exactly why that image had occurred to him.

"May I permit myself a question?" he inquired.

"Why not?" she said. "After all, it's up to me if I choose to answer."

"I wanted to ask you who it is I resemble."

"That's unimportant," she said, now cooler.

"But it's somehow on my mind."

"Let's just leave it at that," she said, and went back to her magazine.

At what? he asked himself.

Silbermann noticed she was holding the magazine close to her face. She's nearsighted but too vain to wear glasses. He found this minor double foible very endearing, almost touching. He pretended to be deep in thought, while in reality he continued to study her face, which relaxed as she read. Her forehead wasn't very high, he decided. In fact, it might almost be called low. He concluded that she couldn't be a very difficult or overly complicated person. On the other hand . . . In any case I'll never find out, he thought, with regret, and let out another sigh.

"Are things that bad?" she asked him, part ironically, part sympathetically. Silbermann sensed kindness in her voice: a genuine, womanly kindness.

"Things are even worse," he answered. That was supposed to sound self-ironic, but his smile seemed forced.

"Worries?" she asked, in a tone that was both interested and accommodating, but not without distance. "No doubt to do with your business."

She shook her head gracefully, to indicate how little she understood about the world of transactions, meetings, company foundings, and bankruptcies.

"No," was all he said.

This clearly piqued her interest. She was probably more familiar with personal worries, and now undoubtedly relegated his to the realm of emotions. While the merger of two firms might be foreign to her, she clearly knew something about disagreements between two people.

"What kind of worries can a businessman possibly have if not about business?" she asked.

Her question wasn't crude curiosity. All Silbermann heard was interest, pure human interest.

"Not everything is always about money," he replied, "although I'm the last man in the world who would deny its importance."

"That's not what I meant," she said.

He was silent. Finally he made a visible effort and asked, "Madam, would you say that I resemble a human being?"

She gave a perplexed smile and then grew very serious as she took in the tone of the strange question.

"I would say so," she said, emphasizing her answer with a firm nod of the head.

"I would say so as well," he replied. "Certainly I don't suffer from so-called inferiority complexes on that score."

"But why should you?"

Her question did him good.

"I'm Jewish," he explained, and looked at her almost threateningly.

"Ahh . . ." she registered calmly.

"That's right! Perhaps you're putting yourself at risk by talking to me?"

"Why would that be?" she asked, and looked at him, unruffled.

"I just thought perhaps. After all, not only have I been declared an outlaw, somehow I've also been made into a pariah. Isn't that so?"

"Why would that be so?"

"I have no idea why I'm telling you all this. When a person hasn't had a real conversation for several days the words just come blurting out all on their own. You see, I'm on the run. I haven't committed any crime, and not once in my life have I had anything to do with politics. Nevertheless they came to arrest me and they smashed up my apartment. Not entirely, but to a great extent. They're arresting Jews, as you know. Well, that's beside the point. Please forgive me!"

He had talked himself into an agitated state. She kept looking at his face.

"What is there for me to forgive?" she asked. "You're the one who's far more deserving of an apology."

"I accosted you with my story. A completely uninteresting tale. But the fact is I'm nervous because I'm being hunted. I'm not used to that. Somewhere inside I'm still living my old life, my normal life. After all, I used to be a free man! I don't know how to come to terms with it."

"Couldn't you get out of the country?"

"Where would I go?" he almost shouted but then regained control. "No place will let me in. I waited too long, far too long. I also never thought they'd push things to the extreme. And imagine, I served on the front! I was a citizen like everybody else. Besides, my one attempt was foiled at the Belgian border. They caught me and took me back to German territory. So I've been traveling ever since. Second class, even though I'm still well off. When they finally arrest me they'll get enough to furnish the state with a cannon or a torpedo. I don't know exactly."

"Is it that bad?" she asked, her voice faltering some.

He took pains to speak more calmly. "I may be exaggerating somewhat," he said. "But when one is about to be guillotined and has no idea why, it's hard to maintain one's composure."

"Where are you intending to go now?" she asked compassionately.

"All I can say is I'll just keep moving," he answered. "Beyond that I don't know. I'll keep traveling, keep going farther until they pounce, until I get stopped by some SA man. They're the ones who set me in motion and they'll be the ones who bring me to a halt."

"That's horrible," she said, and her eyes lit up more than ever. "How can you possibly stand it?"

She leaned forward a little and observed him with great interest. It seemed to Silbermann that her facial expressions alternated between compassion and curiosity, sympathy and a tension that verged on excitement.

"That's a question to ask someone who's decided to be a hunger artist by choice," he retorted, somewhat gruffly.

Now that he had aired all his troubles he felt over-whelmed by them, and his situation appeared more hope-less than ever. He struggled to regain his equilibrium.

"I beg your pardon," she said. "I didn't mean to offend you with my question."

"I know I'm being impolite, just that it's been three days . . ."

"I understand," she replied quietly, and he detected a flash of warmth in her eyes.

A hope began to grow in him. Don't let go, he thought, hold on to this woman, escape with her, break away. The only way to be rid of all the besetting circumstances is to ignore them.

He observed her searchingly and solicitously at the same time, without having any specific intentions.

"Isn't anybody helping you?" she asked. "Don't you have some contacts who could offer protection? Connec-tions can still do quite a lot."

"My so-called friends didn't leave me with the kind of money I'd need to acquire new ones," he said, immediately ashamed of how that sounded. I'm still trying to impress, he thought.

"Did they extort money from you?"

"They fleeced me! But that hardly matters anymore. Corpses get eaten by worms, that's the rule." He laughed harshly.

"My husband's a lawyer," she said eagerly. "He's also a member of the party and well regarded, but unfortunately we're not on speaking terms. Otherwise he would do something for you right away."

"Unfortunately," Silbermann interrupted, having recovered his calm, "I have to confess that I know the reasons better than I ought to. Without intending to, I overheard your conversation."

This unsettled her, and for a moment she was silent. "I see," she said. "Well . . . my friend has the worthy habit of lecturing me every time we part, which winds up benefiting others more than it does me."

"In any case I am sorry I had to learn I'm not the only person with worries," he hastened to counter.

"You feel sorry?"

"In your case, madam, I truly do. Although presumably I owe the privilege of your presence to those same worries."

"If at least I could help you." She steered the conversation back from her affairs to his.

"Please believe me that being able to speak with you is already a great help."

"Do you mean that?" She seemed prepared to believe him.

"Absolutely," he assured her.

"I don't understand why the members of your faith are

being attacked like that," she said, and her words showed a measure of kindness toward him. "Earlier I used to have a Jewish friend. If I'm not mistaken she emigrated to Palestine. But that's not at all what I wanted to say. You look so Aryan. Doesn't that help?"

"My last name is Silbermann!"

"I see. These days that's not a very fortunate name to have, is it?"

"No. Incidentally even if I were named Meier it wouldn't help. My passport is stamped with a big red *J*."

"That can't be!" she said, indignant. "I don't understand why. It may sound strange, and people don't usually say things like this, but I find you quite likeable."

He bowed slightly in her direction, then laughed. "Unfortunately the government doesn't share your opinion. It does not find me at all—likeable. It simply says: You, Silbermann, are a Jew! And with that it's declaring that my character and my qualities are entirely unimportant. It all boils down to either you are a Jew or you're not a Jew, not whether you're likeable or not likeable. The headline decides. The content doesn't matter."

"That's terrible." She sighed, and Silbermann thought she was growing somewhat tired of the topic.

He was surprised and annoyed at himself for having been so open. How is it, he wondered, that I'm telling so much about myself to a woman I have nothing to do with, who has nothing to do with me, and who at best might have a passing interest in the peculiar fate of a chance travel companion? Does it help me in any way to bemoan my situation to her? And even if I considered her curiosity a sign of genuine interest, what good does it do me? A woman will say "That's terrible" to everything. She'd say the same thing if she heard about a train wreck, or if an acquaintance sprained his ankle, or if she didn't make the streetcar on time. "That's terrible!"

My fate is turning into a figure of speech, that's all.

He felt an immediate urge to tell her that he could happily forgo her pity and that he had only said as much as he had because he wanted to talk, to hear his own voice, to gain some clarity, but certainly not to elicit from her a "that's terrible." He had no interest in that and could very well do without it.

"Why such a fierce look?" she asked, smiling.

"What's that?"

"You looked irritated. I can easily understand why you might be, but surely you realize I don't have anything to do with all that. I mean personally. I am not an anti-Semite."

"And if you were?" he asked sharply. "What difference would that make?"

She shot him an angry glance. "You may be on edge," she answered, offended, "but I have to insist . . ." She didn't know how she ought to continue and was silent for a moment. Then she said, no longer angry, but with a smile that seemed oddly naive, "If I were an anti-Semite, I could make things pretty difficult for you, couldn't I?"

"I'm not afraid," Silbermann declared, almost scornfully. "I'm really not. I am no longer afraid!" he repeated, as if he wanted to convince himself.

"Really?" she asked, and her smile didn't strike him as completely harmless.

"Are you trying to make me afraid?" he asked, also smiling.

"No," she said quietly. Her glistening eyes seemed almost moist.

"It doesn't take much these days," he added ironically, "to play the beast of prey when it comes to Jews."

Beast of prey? He had the feeling she was trying to appear harmless in the most dangerous way she was capable of.

"I see I have to apologize once again," he said, while at the same time thinking: and yet you're actually feeling somewhat flattered.

"But no—why? How come? Was your remark meant for me?"

He shook his head.

"It would never occur to me!" he assured her. "That is to say, the beauty of the predator, the dangerous elegance, which . . ." He sighed. "I can't even make a proper compliment anymore!" he said, and he sounded so pathetic she couldn't help laughing.

"But tell me, why do the Jews put up with all of this?" she asked in earnest. "I mean, why don't they defend themselves? Why don't they do something other than run away?"

"If we were such romantics," he answered, proud of his reasoning, "we would have hardly survived the last two thousand years."

"Is survival so important?"

"Absolutely! To survive is to overcome. It doesn't take a lot of skill to fall into the first crevasse, but it takes quite a bit to cross the mountains. It takes courage to live. For suicide all that's needed is despair." He paused and looked for other analogies. "It's a lot harder to push the cart than simply leave it sitting there," he then finished.

"And should one only live to push some cart? Isn't that a little too little? I for one am far more impressed by people who make their lives a shooting match. Who do what they feel like, and not what other people expect of them."

He laughed in a tone that was both condescending and benign. "Charming," he said, "that's absolutely charming! What would you do if you were in my place? Imagine you were Jewish, and that you still had a bit of wealth, but were trying to escape. What would you do?"

"Honestly I would enjoy myself enormously," she asserted, beaming. "I would simply start living as though each day were my last, and I would get more out of a single day than everyone else gets out of a whole year. I would—but you're laughing at me. Why are you laughing?" She wrinkled her brow, annoyed.

"How do you picture that exactly?" he asked, once again serious. "Do you think you could enjoy yourself if they'd stormed into your apartment three days earlier? If you knew where your relatives were staying but couldn't visit them? If you had to be afraid of every SA man because he could arrest you on a whim?"

"Are you married?" she asked, without countering his objections.

"I am . . ." He was silent. Perhaps that's no longer true, he thought. Perhaps I only used to be married. Certainly I'm on my own right now. Now I am completely alone!

"And your wife?"

"She escaped to her brother's. He's Aryan," he answered mechanically.

"That's terrible," she said, taking a small bar of chocolate from her purse. She peeled off the silver paper, studied the chocolate thoughtfully, offered him some, then broke off a little piece, which she put in her mouth and began to chew slowly.

"But isn't there any way to defend yourself?" she asked again, after chewing awhile in silence.

"Yes, I could throw myself in front of the train. Then it would stop for two minutes while they shoved my corpse off to the side. Do you really think that I, Otto Silbermann, could intervene in world history? You really are a romantic."

Now the conversation really was beginning to tire her.

"You ought to look at the humorous side of the matter," she suggested.

He looked at her bewildered. "No," he then said decisively. "That's too deep for me. Which humorous side? Who could expect me to laugh at my own misfortune? Do you laugh when you break a leg? Is your own sense of humor that big?"

"Maybe," she replied, and his excitement made a greater impression on her than his words.

"I don't believe that entirely," he contradicted. "In any case, I can't imagine that you'd think being spit on is a good practical joke."

"No, I would not!" She sounded indignant. "What kind of preposterous idea is that?"

"It's not my idea, but let's leave it be."

They looked at each other in silence. "I see that there is a certain resemblance," she then said quietly. "He also has this dry earnestness."

"Who? Ah . . . your lawyer?"

She didn't answer. Then she took out a cigarette, which he lit for her. That brought them closer together, and their eyes met once more. He sat back in his seat.

"If I weren't Jewish," he said almost casually, "and naturally if I weren't married, I would tell you how appealing I find you."

"Really?" she asked, and smiled. "And why do you say it when you really don't intend to?"

"I don't know," he replied. "The words just spoke themselves."

"Why don't you simply get a different passport?" She changed the subject. "If your passport was in the name of Gottlieb Müller, everything would be very easy for you. I saw that once in a film, a man changed his identity, I think that's what they called it. So isn't it really just a—technical issue? No one would think you're Jewish if you weren't named Silbermann. It's actually quite simple."

"I don't have any experience with that kind of fraud," he explained, annoyed at her playful way of treating his most serious worries, matters of life and death. He scrutinized her with a look that was both insulted and insulting.

"But why? It would be self-defense. With a name like that you could live and work. You'd be rid of your worries."

"It's a good thing your friend the lawyer can't hear you. His hair would be standing on end!"

"Yes, my husband is also so horribly upstanding and upright. Always everything by the book. Only capable of doing what other people have done before. But at the moment isn't it a bit difficult for you to live your life according to some grand guiding principle?"

"In any case they've stolen whatever chance I had to live according to mine. But the fact that crimes are committed against me doesn't entitle me to take such steps."

She looked at him mockingly. "Yes I know, I know," she

said. "'Noble be man, helpful and good.' Of course when a man is just plain scared of everybody else, then being a virtuous citizen is all he can do, right?"

"It's not a question of being scared, or even of morality, it's a question of intelligence and a sense of responsibility. Addicts usually end up in the sanatorium, swindlers in jail, while respectable or reasonable people . . ."

"On the run." She helped him and looked at him.

He had to laugh. "I've only been running for three days," he said, "don't forget that. A criminal is on the run his entire life, even if he's just rushing to his next crime. The normal person strives for stability in life. He tries to overcome exceptional circumstances, but not by making his life one enormous exceptional circumstance. No one is up to that for the long haul."

"But an outsider can also manage to . . ."

"Perhaps," he interrupted. "But that's not who I am at all. I cannot and will not change who I am. I was born a middle-class citizen and will die a middle-class citizen. Perhaps as one on the run, but a proper citizen nonetheless, that is certain."

"Following your high morals, I'm sure you managed to save a large part of your fortune," she suggested.

He didn't know immediately how to answer that. "That doesn't have anything to do with it," he said at last.

"It has everything to do with it," she maintained. "After all, sooner or later you'll have to risk it and take a chance. You won't have any choice."

"Yes I will," he replied decisively. Then he added, "I like you very, very much, madam. I don't think you can imagine how much. But when it comes to life, I think you understand about as much as I do about novels. Don't be cross with me."

She shook her head. "None of you have any inner zing," she said, without indicating that she had been somehow offended by his attitude or his words.

"Zing? I was brought up to live in normal circumstances. I need order! Clarity! A system, if you will. You have to have grown up with mess and muddle to know how to deal with it."

"Be glad for once that you're forced to shed your old skin," she said with thoughtful cheerfulness. "Of course it's a terrible misfortune, but in my mind it's also a boost for your vitality."

Silbermann laughed so hard he started to cough. "You're very touching," he then said. "A person can be on the brink of death and you manage to congratulate him on his sensations."

He bent over and placed his hand on hers, which was resting lightly on her knee. She let it happen, although her smile disappeared, and she now looked at him through eyes that were almost languid, unmoving, waiting. He stroked her hand several times, then kissed it.

"How interesting you have made yourself," he said, suddenly switching to the familiar *Du*—and his voice was a mixture of genuine admiration, gentle irony, and authentic warmth.

EIGHT

I shouldn't have done that, Silbermann thought. I have no
right. After all, I love my wife! It's just the fault of the circumstances, no question about it. But precisely the circumstances
should make me more disciplined. By now I could already be
in Küstrin, I should have been there a long time ago!

He looked at his watch. It was 3:40.

A rendezvous, he thought, how long has it been since I
had a rendezvous? And now of all times . . . He had pro-
posed to meet her in the Café am Zoo at 3:30.

He slowed his pace.

I'll simply show up too late, he decided. Then everything
will be over before anything ever began, and there won't
even be the bad feeling of having missed out on something.
Besides, it's perfectly possible that she won't have come.
This way I won't know if she did or didn't.

Anyway, what can this Ursula Angelhof mean for me?

An affair? As if I needed that. I have plenty of problems already.

He slowed his pace even more, and stopped when he caught sight of the Gedächtniskirche.

I have to gather my wits, he resolved, and focus on the circumstances. Surely that will convince me to stop and turn around.

He kept going.

This woman really doesn't mean anything to me at all, he thought. I already know her better than I ought to.

He picked up his pace. It was already 3:50.

She's bound to have left by now, he thought, and didn't know whether he was bothered or reassured by the idea. I'm actually counting on her not being there!

He stopped once again.

Even I realize how ridiculous I'm being, he decided. She's nothing but a little sensation seeker. And is that what I really want? A chance to be her sensation? Does a man risk the fate of his family for a pair of will-o'-the-wisp eyes?

He stepped into the café.

"Hopefully," he mumbled to himself, not knowing exactly what he meant. He strolled through the large room, scanning the tables, but there was no sign of her. She won't even have come, he told himself. An insignificant incident on the express train, that's all it was. But that notion didn't suit him, either, nor did he want to have come in vain. I could have spared myself the trip, he thought, annoyed, then sat down at a table and ordered a coffee.

He found the orchestra very irritating.

When all is said and done I feel like such a clown, he mused. On the one hand, I'm hoping she'll come and at the same time I'm persuading myself I no longer expect her, and the truth is I believe both things at once.

He placed a coin on the table and stood up.

Adieu, Ursula Angelhof, he thought, taking his leave in silence. It's fine with me that it all turned out this way. That you didn't come. Besides, he consoled himself as he left the café, if I absolutely want to see her again I can always look up her address in the telephone book. But it's really not that important to me.

He headed to the train station. On the way he faulted himself for having thought too little about his wife during the past few days.

On the other hand, he rationalized, I'm sure Elfriede's all right, I've written to her, and I've sent her telegrams. I've also thought about her, quite often as a matter of fact! But really I should have thought about her more. We've been separated for three days. Outwardly our family may be torn apart, but inwardly we should be united. Well . . . we've lived together in the past and we'll live together in the future, but it's genuinely hard to imagine everything will be the way it once was, the way it was just four days ago.

And even if things do calm down outside, will I ever be able to recover the calm I had on the inside? Everything has changed, after all. That inner security is now gone, and my life is nothing but a series of accidents—I'm completely at the mercy of chance. It's almost as though the subject has become the object.

He had reached the train station and purchased a ticket to Küstrin.

As he climbed up the stone stairs to the platform, his thoughts again turned to Ursula Angelhof: How beautiful it could have been. Why did I show up too late? I missed her on purpose, and she could have made such a difference. She could have helped by providing some connection to the times we're in. After all, she belongs to the times, she accepts them as they are, and she seems more than a match for them. Yes indeed, he thought, now getting angry: brutality plus romanticism. Ignorance plus insolence. She may have a motion-picture soul—that's the character of the times—but she is charming! Which is something that can't be said about the times.

He took his seat in the train and was leaning back into the plush cushion when he remembered that he'd forgotten to telephone his sister. I'll call her from Küstrin, he decided. Then he started reading the paper.

After stepping off the train in Küstrin he stayed on the platform, unable to make up his mind about what to do next.

First I'll call Ernst, he thought. Then again, if he isn't home I'll end up having to explain myself to a housekeeper.

The stationmaster, who had an empty but self-important expression, was pacing up and down the platform with his hands behind his back. It was clear he didn't want to interrupt this activity, so Silbermann was forced to walk alongside him to inquire about a telephone, and had to repeat his question before the man emerged from the fog of his officialdom and finally led Silbermann to a small booth.

Silbermann picked up the receiver, put ten pfennigs in the slot, and dialed the number. Then he turned around and looked through the glass pane only to see the stationmaster still standing there, watching him with watery blue eyes.

When he noticed Silbermann looking at him, he saluted

by touching his red cap, then did an about-face and resumed his pacing.

Strange, thought Silbermann, with a bad feeling in his stomach. Maybe I shouldn't have asked, who knows?

His brother-in-law answered.

"Hello, Ernst," said Silbermann, agitated. "It's Otto. You're probably surprised, am I right? I just arrived in Küstrin. How are you all? How is Elfriede?"

Ernst Hollberg didn't answer right away. Finally he said, "I see. Thanks, we're all doing well. Elfriede and Hilde just went into town half an hour ago to do some shopping. That's a pity, because otherwise you could talk with her yourself."

"Has she calmed down? Did anything happen to her?"

"No, there's nothing for you to be worried about. And how are you doing?"

Hollberg had never been especially animated, nevertheless Silbermann felt more than a little irritated by how unconcerned he sounded.

"Perhaps you can imagine," he replied reproachfully.

"Yes, well . . . so what do you intend to do? Not that it's any of my business. Nor do I particularly want to know the details! But what are you thinking, looking ahead?"

"If it's fine with you I'd like to spend a few days at your place, to gather my wits. It's been three days since I slept in a bed."

"I see. Well, that won't really work, you know. You don't have to worry about Elfriede at all. She can stay with us for as long as she wants, but in your case I'm afraid that won't be possible. I hope you understand. If the party caught wind of it I'd be finished. However, if you need money—I can't offer very much at the moment, but of course I'd be happy to give you a few hundred marks."

"I want to speak with Elfriede!" Silbermann was practically shouting. "As far as I'm concerned she's not staying one more hour at your place. This is utterly absurd! Now when I need you and ask for a ridiculously small favor you turn me away! Have you completely forgotten what I did for you?"

"Please don't get so worked up, Otto," said Hollberg, whose voice now sounded annoyed. "I can't wreck my whole life to let you stay here two or three days! No one could expect me to let you bring about my ruin just because you helped me out once upon a time. If the party finds out that I'm related by marriage to a Jew, and that I even let him live in my house, then I might as well straightaway get packing."

"Do you have any idea what I've been through?"

"Listen, Otto, there's no point in being so dramatic! Be glad that Elfriede's taken care of. Where is she supposed to go? Do you want to drag her along all up and down across Germany? Be reasonable, will you? I find it very egotistical of you that you're willing to put your wife in danger just because you're in danger yourself. That you won't allow her to stay with us simply because you can't. No, Otto, I would have expected you to be more—manly."

"Are you trying to teach me about character? Elfriede has been married to me for over twenty years. Why don't you ask her if I've ever knowingly exposed her to any danger?"

"I realize that, Otto. Don't get angry. Understand that it just won't work! You're putting us in jeopardy! Elfriede can stay. She's my sister after all, but you . . . That's something entirely different."

"Good-bye," said Silbermann and hung up.

"I'm putting them in jeopardy," he mumbled, helpless. "Jeopardy." He repeated the word so often that it began to lose sense. Then he rushed out of the booth and walked up to the stationmaster.

"When's the next train to Berlin?" He was shouting.

"In ten minutes," said the official, who stopped and looked at him as though he expected some explanation for Silbermann's unusual behavior.

Silbermann didn't pay him any attention. He dashed through the gate and hurried to the ticket counter.

"One ticket to Berlin," he shouted. "One to Hamburg, one to Cologne. One to . . . what else is there? Well come on, make a suggestion!"

The clerk stared at him, frightened.

Silbermann tossed down a thousand-mark bill and shouted, "Tickets, tickets! Did you not understand? I want tickets!"

"Second class to Berlin?" the clerk asked, trying to facilitate the matter.

"I couldn't care less, just give me some tickets."

The clerk looked around for help.

He thinks I'm crazy, thought Silbermann. Maybe he's right, maybe I've already gone mad. He regained his composure and tried to laugh.

"Just give me the ticket to Berlin," he managed to blurt out, since the clerk was staring at him as though he might call for help at any minute. The man shook his head and attended to the ticket Silbermann had requested.

"Why are you screaming like that?" the clerk then asked in a surly voice, after he'd concluded that the customer might well be mad but wasn't actually dangerous.

"I drank a bit too much," Silbermann explained haltingly, now that he realized what a dangerous situation he'd put himself in.

"That's no reason to scream at someone. Don't you have anything smaller?"

Yes he did.

As he walked away from the counter and headed to the platform, Silbermann took pains to sway a little as long as he was in sight of the clerk. This is all so stupid, he thought, so incredibly stupid. Disappointment and rage began to well up inside him once again.

They're all backstabbers and sellouts, he thought, every single one of them. No one resists. They all cringe and say: we have no choice, but the truth is they're happy to go along because there's something in it for them. The "opportunities" everyone keeps talking about—what would they be without people willing to take advantage of them? Why is Elfriede staying at her brother's? Doesn't she realize I'm putting him in jeopardy? Did she not think to bring up the idea that he should also take me in for the time being? Or does she agree with his position? No, that's impossible!— What's impossible?

I'm on the run, and there's her brother, with all his reasonable arguments. Perhaps she regrets having married a Jew. The times have definitely changed! We've become a business opportunity for our enemies, and a danger for our friends. And in the end we're blamed for our own bad luck. What else do I have to offer except my misfortune?

A ticket for the express train, that's all.

There may have been times when I didn't behave as people might have wished. Incidents I thought were completely forgotten are now coming back. Did I not hesitate before agreeing to be his guarantor? But in the end I agreed. Now he's forgotten about that, but not about the fact that I hesitated and he had to wait! And I can be reproached for a lot of other things as well, mostly trifles, but taken together they inevitably add up to a Jewish character trait. Because the truth is I don't have the right to be an ordinary human being. More is demanded of me.

He angrily tossed away the cigarette he'd just lit. Whatever I've done in the past, he thought, looks different today than it did back then, because now my humanity is called into question, because I am a Jew.

He climbed aboard the train that had just pulled in.

Is it going to go on like this forever? The traveling, the waiting, the running away? Why does nothing happen? Why don't they detain me, arrest me, beat me? They drive a person to the brink of despair and leave him standing there.

Through the window he saw a clean, charming little farm village go flying by.

That's all just a backdrop, he thought. The only thing that's real is the hunting and the fleeing.

He leaned back in his seat.

Why did I get there too late? he asked himself, turning sad. I could have been a human being again. He pictured her face, her eyes. I have to see her again, he thought, and resolved to locate her address as soon as he was in Berlin and then look her up.

Back in Berlin, as he was leaving the station, he heard

someone calling his name. "Silbermann," said a familiar voice. "You're still alive?"

He turned around. "Ah, it's you, Lustiger," he said, not exactly pleased.

They shook hands.

Herr Lustiger was around sixty years old. He was hard of hearing and always held his head cocked a little to the side, which gave a compassionate if also overeager impression. He had very Jewish features and had already been attacked on the street: a member of the Hitler youth had punched him for not raising his arm when some marchers carrying the party banner had paraded by. Lustiger had fought back and wound up losing both of his two remaining front teeth. Since that time he was easily spooked, and his crooked face now bore a very obliging expression. He clutched Silbermann's arm.

"If I live to be a hundred, God forbid," he said, "this is a joy I won't forget."

"What joy?" asked Silbermann.

"Running into you. You look like a goy, you know. Being with you is safe. Come, Silbermann, let's have a cup of coffee together. Incidentally, they arrested Heinz."

"Which Heinz?"

"My son!"

"Oh! Well, they'll have to let him go soon."

"That's what you think! I'm not so sure."

They left the station hall and Silbermann spotted an SA man staring at Lustiger. "Keep your voice down," he requested.

But Herr Lustiger was hard of hearing. "What did you

say?" he asked, in the same loud tone. "So, how are you getting along? You seem to have been lucky! Most of the others have . . . well, I'm sure you know! Tell me, where do you plan on going?"

They entered a café, where many eyes turned to Lustiger. After they sat down he scooted his chair very close to Silbermann's and said, as quietly as he was able: "That bit of fun cost me two thousand marks."

"What bit of fun?"

"When they stopped me on the street, of course. What I haven't been through! Yesterday I was in Duisburg, then in Essen, the day before I was in Munich. They also arrested my brother-in-law. My heavens. And for that I get to live to sixty! For that."

"How's your business doing?"

"Business? Business? There's no such thing anymore. I don't dare set foot in the bank to get money. What will happen if the people call the police?" He turned to the waiter: "Coffee with milk for me. Do you have any newspapers here? Perhaps the *Frankfurter Zeitung*?"

"No," said the waiter. Silbermann had the impression the man was eyeing Lustiger in amazement.

"What may I bring you?" the waiter asked Silbermann, his tone noticeably friendlier.

"I'll have a cold platter."

"I'll have one, too," Lustiger interjected. "So tell me, Silbermann, what are you doing now?" he asked. "Are they leaving you alone?"

"I took off and haven't stopped traveling since . . ."

"You know something? Let's stick with each other. We

can travel together. I feel safe with you. Besides, I'm not as limber as I used to be. This was the last thing I needed. Imagine turning sixty just to have some rascal knock your teeth out? My heavens. I should have had myself buried a long time ago. I missed the right moment. Rosa, now there was a smart woman, she died in good time. You were there at the funeral, autumn of thirty-four. Do you remember? Since then I've had nothing but troubles. In any case, she hasn't missed anything. Still, I always say"—Lustiger was again speaking too loudly—"that I'm happy I'm already an old man. The young people these days, I feel sorry for them, whereas at least I've had . . ."

"I know what you mean," Silbermann cut him off, somewhat testily. "Excuse me a moment, I have to make a quick call."

He stood up.

"The fact that I ran into you!" Lustiger said again. "Finally I have a chance to speak my mind. But go on."

Silbermann hurried to get to the phone booth. He found the encounter with Lustiger increasingly irksome. He's attracting everybody's attention and that means they're also looking at me, he thought, and on top of that there's all this tired, bland prattle. My mood's already gloomy enough without having to listen to that.

He opened the phone book and looked under the letter A. "Dr. Hermann Angelhof, Attorney and Notary," he read. That's her husband, he thought. I can hardly call him to ask for her address. Silbermann asked for a postal directory at the buffet counter, but they didn't have one. He was annoyed that old Lustiger was keeping him from getting on with his research.

When Lustiger saw him coming back, he called out

across several tables: "Silbermann, see if you can't dig up a newspaper somewhere."

Silbermann didn't react to that. With a pinched expression he returned to the table and took his seat.

Lustiger put down the bread he was holding. "What's the matter?" he asked, his head more crooked than usual. "Is there a problem?"

Then he slapped his forehead. "I shouldn't have called out your name," he said out loud. "I keep thinking things are like they were, meaning that I'm always forgetting how things are now. I'm an old man. The goose leg is excellent, by the way. They really know how to do that here. I'll give them that much."

Silbermann ate with subdued appetite.

I wanted to be with her, he thought, and here I am with him! He looked on as Lustiger chewed with his sunken cheeks, making light smacking sounds that Silbermann found almost repulsive.

"I'm telling you," Lustiger said, misty-eyed, "this goose leg helps you forget a lot!"

A few minutes later he clapped Silbermann on the shoulder. "We'll stick together," he said cheerfully.

"You're putting me in jeopardy," Silbermann exclaimed, both agitated and annoyed.

Lustiger stared at him. His face lost the look of contentment it had taken on while they were eating, his eyes widened, and his mouth opened as if he wanted to say something, but he was silent. He lowered his head until it was practically lying on his right shoulder. Then he stood up without saying a word, took his hat and coat off the chair next to him, and started putting them on.

"Lustiger," said Silbermann. "I didn't mean it that way. It just came out like that. I'd be very happy to stay with you. Of course I would. I wasn't serious. I didn't want to upset you, I really didn't. But Lustiger, don't be silly, stay. I really do believe you'll be a little safer with me. Don't take it so . . ."

Lustiger grimaced. "You're right," he said. "Of course I'm putting you in jeopardy. But one always only thinks of oneself. Good-bye."

He reached out his hand. Silbermann held it tightly.

"Stay," he requested. "I'm all wrought up. Just so you know, someone said the same thing to me today. Only a few hours ago. Now I see there's no difference between me and the others. Sit down, please. Stay."

Lustiger shook his head. "No, no," he said, very calmly. Then he tapped his hat once more and said, "Another time, then . . ."

Silbermann watched him leave.

I can no longer complain, he thought. Becker, Findler, Hollberg didn't behave any worse than I just did. I can't even claim any moral outrage: I've forfeited the right. I really ought to run after the old man, hold on to him, stay with him. Perhaps my wicked words will do him in. For being a sensitive man, I'm plenty brutal. I stay in my chair, I watch him go, and despite everything I'm glad to be rid of him.

Distraught, he looked around the café. What actually separates me from you, he thought. We're so alike it's downright frightening.

He finished eating, paid, and left the café.

Will-o'-the-wisp eyes . . . he tried thinking about the

woman. Her eyes really were so . . . But suddenly he was no longer interested in her. He pictured old Lustiger, his tired gait, his enthusiastic eating, and thought he could hear him say, "And for that I get to live to sixty?"

Once again Silbermann found himself in front of the train station.

I wanted to look up the address, he remembered. But he was already in line at the ticket counter, with people in front and behind him. Where to? he asked himself.

"One ticket to Munich second class, please."

He left the counter, ticket in hand, and smiled.

At least I'll get to know Germany, he thought.

NINE

Silbermann made his way through the cars, stopping for a moment to listen to two soldiers playing accordion in a third-class compartment.

This train should be in Dresden a little before noon, he thought. If I hurry I can make the connection to Leipzig. But why hurry? What's there for me to do in Leipzig? Ride back to Berlin, then on to Hamburg, and from Hamburg . . . So why rack my brain about that now? Maybe I'll change trains en route. The more often I switch, the safer I'll be. I should have bought a pass for the whole network. As it is I've practically become a permanent fixture of the German Reichsbahn.

There was a man on board whose bearing and general demeanor reminded Silbermann of the fat police spy in the train from Dortmund to Aachen. Silbermann had already run into him three times, and when he saw the man once more heading his way, he opened the door to the compartment with the soldiers and took a seat.

"Keeping spirits up I see, eh?" he said in a lively voice.

The two soldiers smiled awkwardly and paused their playing. The man Silbermann wanted to avoid stopped in the corridor, so that Silbermann could see his back through the compartment window.

"That's right," Silbermann exclaimed excitedly. "Life in the army. There's still something wonderful about it."

He glanced at the man's back.

"When I was a soldier—you were probably just born—I saw all sorts of things. I was there at Verdun. You have no idea what that was like. Drumfire, that's something else I tell you!" He laughed.

The two soldiers looked at him, embarrassed. They didn't know what to make of him or how they should respond.

Silbermann kept his eye on the man's back.

"Of course in those days you were still infants," he said fiercely. "Infants, and now it's your generation that's in control. Let me tell you something"—he continued his rather disjointed speech—"you may very well have a chance to experience a war someday . . . and you have every right to. Just make sure you enjoy yourselves now because afterward it's too late. Ha ha . . . In our company there were four of us friends, two are still alive . . . Becker and myself . . . But it was an experience all right . . . the war was an experience . . . it's definitely an experience . . . as long as you don't drop dead. You'll see . . . You'll see. It will either make real men out of you . . . or else corpses. An experience, no doubt about it . . . I was at Cambrai, too, fighting the tanks. A tank like that's a lot more sturdy . . . than a hallway mirror for instance . . . You'll see for yourselves! I'd like to join you . . . I'd like to go along once more, just to see how you take things . . . ha ha . . . Because it's not as simple as you think, ramming a bayonet into another man's stomach . . . especially when the other guy has one, too. There are two types of bullets, you see . . . the ones you shoot and the ones that come back . . . like I was saying . . . maybe you'll experience that . . . the returns . . . but I won't. But why did you stop playing? Go on and play . . . we always had music in my company, always! Becker had a harmonica . . . He could play that thing to where you completely forgot there was a war on . . . so keep playing, men, go on and play!"

The train slowed down, and the man's back was no longer to be seen.

"I have to get off," Silbermann said. "A pity . . . there was so much I could have told you . . . I was there . . . also in Russia. The 1914 advance. Trenches. Foxholes . . . Twice wounded, badly . . . well, but I have to change here . . . I have to change quite often . . . Ha."

He dashed out of the compartment, ran down the corridor, and jumped off the train before it came to a stop. Clinging tightly to his briefcase, he hurried across the platform.

"The train to Leipzig?" he asked a porter as he ran. The porter pointed the way.

Nice fellows, Silbermann thought back to the soldiers. What was I saying, anyway? It doesn't matter. I'm sure they didn't understand a word. I'm thinking of going to Leipzig, but I could just as well go back to Berlin. Why Leipzig of all places! Especially considering I never found the Saxons all that agreeable.

He stopped another porter. "The train to Berlin?" he asked.

"It leaves in twenty minutes."

Silbermann thanked him almost exuberantly, ran down the stairs, hurried to the ticket counter, and purchased a ticket to Berlin. Then he stepped out of the station for a bit of fresh air. Dresden, he thought. I've been here so many times. Isn't this where Solm & Co. have their headquarters? Good clients. I could drop in and say hello. Better not, though. And they're not very good when it comes to paying on time, either. Always insisting on bills of exchange. Just thinking about what happened to Fanter & Son makes me dizzy. Sixteen thousand marks they lost in one blow. What could they have been thinking? Such a solid old firm and then all of a sudden . . .

He went back inside the station. Out of habit he approached the ticket counter. Then he remembered that he'd already bought a ticket. He pulled it out of his pocket along with a jumble of banknotes. The Reichsbahn really ought to give me a discount, he thought. All of a sudden he felt ill, and the station hall began spinning around him. He saw trains arriving and departing, heard horns honking, bells ringing, wheels rattling, words close by and far away, loud and quiet . . .

He fell to the floor.

A woman screamed. Officials came running and people pressed close to see what had happened. One man bent over him, opened Silbermann's coat, jacket, vest, and shirt and placed his ear to Silbermann's chest.

"His heart's fine," he said calmly. "It's just a passing weak spell."

Then some medics arrived and picked him up and took him to an ambulance.

When Silbermann came to, he was puzzled to find himself

in a hospital room. He sat up, looked around, stroked his forehead, felt a dull pain, and wondered where he might be.

I was traveling, he remembered. I had been in Munich . . . no, I went back to Berlin . . . then I was in Dresden . . . then . . . no, I must still be in Dresden.

As if reassured by that supposition, he let himself slide back into the pillows. Apart from the fact that my head hurts, I'm fine, he was somewhat pleased to note. Then he gave a start.

"Where's my briefcase?" he asked loudly.

He noticed a call bell hanging by his bed. He pressed the button two, three times. An older nurse came in.

"Nurse, where is my briefcase?" Silbermann asked immediately, as he sat up in the bed.

"Calm down," she answered, holding her palms out.

"I want to know where my briefcase is!" Silbermann demanded.

"I'm sure they have it in safekeeping."

"Nurse, I want to point out that there are approximately thirty-five thousand marks in that briefcase!"

"You don't mean it!" she said, surprised.

"Yes I do," he bellowed, excitedly. "Thirty-five thousand marks. And don't think for a minute I'm going to let that—"

"Don't make such a racket!"

"I demand to speak with the director immediately!"

"What director? Do you mean the doctor?"

"I don't care who it is. I want my briefcase back! Besides, I'm healthy and what's more . . ." He stuck his legs out of the bed. "I'm not staying here," he declared.

The nurse clapped her hands together. "Now, now," she said reproachfully.

"I demand my briefcase!" Silbermann repeated sharply.

"If you have a briefcase here, I'm sure you'll get it back."

"And my suit," he added. "I want to leave. But before I do perhaps you could have them make something for me to eat. I simply forgot to eat, that's all. I can pay, too!"

"Please lie back down in your bed," the nurse requested in a commanding tone of voice.

He obeyed.

"Nevertheless I would like to speak to the doctor right away," he said. "I'm completely healthy. And I don't have any more time. I have meetings, important meetings! Please have him see me at once!"

"You're in a hospital, not a hotel! And please stop shouting. Show some consideration for the other patients."

"No one shows me any consideration," Silbermann countered, already noticeably quieter.

"If you had a briefcase when you were admitted," the nurse continued, "then you'll get it back. You're acting as though you've fallen into a robbers' den. No one's holding you here against your will."

"Please have them make something for me to eat," Silbermann repeated, "and I'd like a bottle of red wine, too. I always cure myself with red wine." His voice was now completely calm.

"You'll probably have to stay here another few days, though," the nurse said.

"Have to?" he asked, once again more agitated. "Have to? They can't force me. After all, I'm not that helpless! In any case I want my briefcase back at once!"

The nurse put her hands on her hips. "Now you listen to me," she retorted angrily. "Some people saved your life, or at least they came to your aid. They didn't bring you here to rob you but to help you, and you're acting as though . . ."

Silbermann jumped out of the bed. "I don't want any help!" he called out and glared at her. "I don't want anything at all! All I want is to leave! I refuse your—help!" He hurled the word at her as though it were an insult.

She left the room and he lay back down in bed.

Calm down! he commanded to himself. I absolutely have to act more calmly. He felt his pulse and touched his forehead. I don't have a fever, he established. I simply should have eaten something. I've been eating too little and far too irregularly. And on top of that there's all the commotion of the past few days.

He pulled the covers up to his chin.

Actually it's nice just lying here, he thought. I really should stay a couple of days. Once again he examined the room. Nice and clean, he determined. I really ought to stay. No! No! It's a prison. Or the prelude to prison! They nurse you here so they can thrash you there!

The nurse came back. She was carrying a large sheet of paper and a pencil. Silbermann looked at her mistrustfully.

"Your briefcase is here, of course, along with your money," she said. "Here's the list of all your personal belongings. Please look it over and let me know right away if there's anything missing."

Silbermann took the list and studied it without much interest, since he knew his essential possessions had been found.

"Incidentally, the doctor is also of the opinion that you can be discharged," the nurse added.

"That's good," said Silbermann, relieved. "Many thanks."

The nurse started for the door, then turned around and asked, "Are you Jewish?"

Silbermann started. "And what about it?" he asked back.

"Oh nothing. Calm down. Nobody's going to do anything to you here. If you like you can easily stay another few days. But perhaps it's better . . ."

"I want to leave," Silbermann said quickly. "I'm sure you mean very well, but I want to go. Besides, I'm completely recovered. It was just a minor passing weakness."

She had already left the room.

What's going to happen now? Silbermann wondered. Will they really let me go? Will they give me back my money? Or perhaps . . . ? There are so many possibilities. After all, they're not going to let a Jew with money slip away. He got out of his bed, walked to the door in his bare feet, opened it, and peered out into the corridor. Now I've fallen into the trap, he thought. Now they have me! And above all they have my money! Everything's part of the same system, even this hospital. The state in all of its totality is turned against me—against me!

He saw an orderly round the corner and quickly scurried back to his bed.

Maybe if I stayed here I'd have some peace, he thought. But how can I be at peace when I don't know what's in store for me? And the longer I stay, the greater the danger! That money is a temptation . . .

He poured a glass of water from the carafe on the nightstand and gulped it down. I'm hungry, he thought. Why aren't they bringing me anything to eat? What do they intend to do with me, anyway?

Another orderly came and draped Silbermann's clothes on a chair.

Why didn't he bring my briefcase? Silbermann brooded. He felt his pockets but they were empty.

"Where's my passport? Where is my money?" he said to the nurse when she came in, bringing his meal on a tray.

"They'll give it to you later," she reassured him. "You're among honest people here. What on earth are you thinking?"

"Is this a state hospital?" he asked, mistrustful.

"No, we're a municipal one."

"Nevertheless!" he said and began to eat. In the middle of his meal he suddenly paused. I'm practically begging them to rob me, he thought fearfully. Besides, I'm making myself look suspicious. Who knows what they think of me. He quickly wolfed down the rest of his food. I can't let that happen again. Passing out in enemy territory . . .

Half an hour later he left the hospital. They'd returned all his belongings and he was so astonished—practically moved—that he gave the nurse a hundred marks. She was reluctant to accept it until he indicated that he'd be seriously offended if she did not.

No sooner had he taken a few steps than he regretted having left, because he still felt weak and woozy. He first went to a post office where he sent his wife and his sister each an insured letter containing two thousand marks. Afterward he felt relieved, not only because in his mind he'd taken care of an obligation, but also because he'd lowered the risk associated with his briefcase and thereby lessened his responsibility for any potential future loss.

He wondered whether he should head back to Berlin or stay in Dresden awhile longer, and ultimately decided on the latter. After wandering aimlessly through the city he boarded the funicular train and rode up to the Weisser Hirsch resort. On the way he recalled Ursula Angelhof's advice: . . . enjoy myself enormously . . . start living as though each day were my last. Even if he had serious doubts about his ability to follow through on an idea so foreign to him, perhaps his constant movement would seem a little less grindingly senseless if he tried to get to know the places at least a little bit—the places through which he was being blown by an evil wind.

I've been in Dresden a dozen times, he recalled, but I've never been up to the Weisser Hirsch. And they say it has such a wonderful view.

As the funicular climbed the hill his thoughts alternated between his wife and his acquaintance from the express train. I absolutely have to see her again, he thought, and felt an intense yearning for her. For her sympathy, her carefree attitude, her silly advice, her playful manner. She certainly isn't someone who just sighs and lets things happen. Thank God. And suddenly he had a new plan, namely to find her under all circumstances.

When he got to the Weisser Hirsch he tried to behave like an ordinary tourist. He looked down at Dresden, which was spread out in the half-dark with only a few lights discernible, and tried very hard to admire what he could see.

What a pity that Elfriede isn't here, he thought. She loves beautiful vistas, and I'm sure she would have enjoyed the short ride on the funicular. Silbermann sighed. She really is the only person who means something to me.

He entered the restaurant, sat down at a table, and asked for some postcards. "I'll have a bottle of Mosel," he then reassured the waiter, who had probably feared Silbermann would content himself with the postcards.

I'm still alive, Silbermann thought, and tried to smile.

He took his pen out of his pocket and wondered what to write his wife. Shall I tell her that I'm sitting in the Weisser Hirsch with a bottle of Mosel wine and am struggling very hard to talk myself into a decent mood? If her brother sees the card he'll say, "You see! Evidently he's doing pretty well!" And perhaps she'll feel reassured by that.

But I don't want to reassure anyone!

In a fit, he tore up the postcards. "It won't work," he muttered. "I can't pretend to be someone out for a day trip!" He summoned the waiter, paid, and left.

He took the funicular back down to Dresden. Once in town he rushed onto a streetcar and headed for the station where he hoped to catch the express to Berlin.

When all's said and done I still feel most comfortable in a train compartment, he thought, when he boarded the train a minute before it departed. He chose a seat in a second-class compartment, where there were two gentlemen and an older lady. Silbermann immediately began reading the novel he had purchased at the kiosk. After half an hour he felt tired and leaned back and closed his eyes. Soon he was asleep and didn't wake up until they had arrived in Berlin.

The two gentlemen were already gone, and the elderly lady was tugging his arm. "Thank you," Silbermann said, still very sleepy. It took effort to stand up. The lady left the compartment, and Silbermann clumsily put on his coat and hat and started to follow her out when he suddenly sensed he was missing something. He thought for a moment and then remembered his briefcase. He hurried back to his compartment, but it wasn't there. He quickly stood on a seat to examine the luggage rack, but all he could find were newspapers. Then he rushed out of the compartment.

Is it possible I left it in Dresden? he tried to remember. No, when he bought the novel in the train station he had stowed it in his briefcase. So someone must have stolen it while I was on the train! he concluded, as he ran toward the station exit.

The elderly lady?

But in that case she hardly would have wakened him, and anyway all she was carrying were her purse and a small suitcase.

The two gentlemen!

But what did they look like? He thought he remembered one having a mustache, a blond mustache. People with blond mustaches are somewhat rare.

He stopped a crewman. "I've been robbed," he called out. "I've been robbed by a blond man! My briefcase, my money!"

"You have to report it to the Bahnpolizei," the man said, then went on his way.

If only I'd memorized their exact features! Silbermann thought, in desperation. I don't even know what they looked like, all these damned ordinary-looking faces.

He hurried through the gate and stopped just past it.

Maybe they have yet to pass through, he hoped. I'll wait here. Then he realized they were bound to be faster than he. So he hurried down to the station hall and decided to wait outside the exit. But the station had several exits, and he couldn't make up his mind which one to watch. And by that point there were only stragglers, since most of the passengers had already left. Despondent, he collapsed onto a bench.

It's pointless, he decided. After all, a thief doesn't wait for the person he's robbed to wake up and chase after him. He's sure to be gone by now.

A policeman strolled slowly past him. Silbermann jumped up and ran over to the man.

"I've been robbed," he explained, his voice faltering. "In the train from Dresden. They took approximately thirty-one thousand marks. A briefcase, a leather briefcase."

The policeman stopped, stared at him for a moment in disbelief, but then seemed convinced.

"Have you inquired if the briefcase—your money was in the briefcase, correct?—wasn't handed in to the conductor by chance? In any case it's outside my jurisdiction. You have to go to the railway police. See the sign there? Go right away and report your loss. You also need to check with lost and found."

"The railway police?" Silbermann asked quietly.

"Of course! That's what they're for. Just don't wait too long, hurry."

They had been walking together and were now standing across from the police station. "Don't waste any time explaining things. Go make your report."

"I don't know," Silbermann said, his voice sounding anguished and undecided.

"What don't you know?" asked the constable, growing suspicious. "Did you have a briefcase or not?"

"Of course I had one. With over thirty thousand marks! But maybe I'd better go back to the platform and check if someone hasn't turned it in there."

"You can check to your heart's content, but anyone who

goes to the trouble of stealing thirty thousand marks isn't going to be so quick to return it."

"But maybe someone found it."

The constable scowled at him. "You just said it was stolen from you! How can anyone be expected to find it?"

Silbermann's situation was getting somewhat critical. At the moment he was just as scared of the railway police as he was of losing his briefcase.

If I file a report, he thought, then not only will I have lost my money, I'll lose my freedom in the bargain. On the other hand, if I don't file a report I have no prospect of seeing my briefcase or my money ever again. Either way I'm done for. That briefcase was my last remaining asset. But then he again felt a glimmer of hope, thinking that someone might have found the briefcase and handed it in—as unlikely as that might seem.

"I'll ask one more time," he said, and went back to the platform. Bewildered, the constable shook his head and watched him leave.

He was already at the gate when he realized he hadn't bought a platform ticket, but to his great relief he saw that the train was still in the station. He hurried to a vending machine, paid for the ticket, then ran to the platform and asked for the conductor.

"Did anyone find a briefcase?" he said, nearly out of breath from running. "I lost my briefcase. With over thirty thousand marks!"

The conductor puffed out his cheeks in surprise. "Thirty thousand marks," he said, impressed. "Good lord!"

"Has someone turned it in?"

"Not to me. But you need to file a report with the

lost-and-found bureau. Incidentally if you want to know my opinion there's not much point. Thirty thousand marks are enough to turn an honest man into a scoundrel. Where were you sitting?"

"In second class," said Silbermann, now hoping he had somehow overlooked the briefcase when he had searched his compartment. They boarded the train, but Silbermann could no longer tell which compartment he had been sitting in. So they made their way through all the second-class smoking compartments, with no result.

The conductor asked about the other passengers, and Silbermann described them as best he could. "The man with the blond mustache," Silbermann answered. "He did strike me as a little suspect, but perhaps I'm only imagining that after the fact. There were two men, one with a blond mustache, like I told you."

"And the lady? You didn't ask the lady?"

"Ach!" said Silbermann, unhappy. "I didn't even think of that. And she might have been able to give me an exact description."

"I'm sure she would have," the conductor agreed. "You should have asked her."

"But I can describe her. She was wearing a gray skirt suit . . ."

The conductor looked at the clock.

"Go to the railway police and the lost-and-found bureau," he suggested. "As you see, I've done what I could. There's nothing more I can do. If you'd like, I can have someone show you the way to the police."

He leaned out the window and looked around.

"No, thank you," Silbermann was quick to respond.

"There's no need. It's very kind of you, but I know the way. Good-bye."

He left the compartment and clambered out of the train car, gripping the handrail with weak hands, then headed slowly back to the gate.

The truth is that all I've lost is time, he tried to persuade himself, a little time off my life. Nothing else. Not even the money could be of any real help. I've already seen that.

But this reasoning brought no consolation, because Silbermann realized beyond all doubt that he'd been dealt a decisive blow, that along with his money he'd been robbed of his ability to resist, his one point of support. Compared with this disaster, which he believed would determine the rest of his life, all the other dangers he was facing seemed completely insignificant.

For the first time something has happened that can't be rectified, he thought, and even when he tried to escape into a listless indifference as a kind of self-defense, he was unable to do so completely. He walked down the stone steps. Along with the money I've lost all hope of buying time, he thought: there's no more time in my account.

He stood outside the door with the sign: BAHNPOLIZEI.

Silbermann turned the door handle, opened the door, and looked into the room.

A surly voice greeted him with "Heil Hitler!"

"I'll be right back," he said, then turned around and went to the bench where he'd been sitting earlier.

Should I file the report? he wondered. Report the thief? To whom? He let out a helpless, angry laugh. They'll just arrest the person who was robbed and put him on trial instead of the thief!

He sank back into the bench so it made a slight cracking noise. He rested his hands flat on the seat, splaying his fingers. I'm done for now, he thought. Completely finished! Then he jumped up and took a few steps in the direction of the station. "I'm going to report the thief," he muttered. "I'm going to report the thief to the robber!"

The door to the station opened and an official stepped out. He looked at Silbermann questioningly: "Is there something you want?"

Silbermann turned around without saying a word.

I have to think it through, he thought. No hasty decisions. He went back to his bench and sat down. The official observed him for another moment, then went on his way. Silbermann watched him leave.

"My briefcase," he whispered to himself. "I want my briefcase back! This can't be! I had it just an hour ago!"

His head sank onto his chest.

This can't be, he thought again. I'm only imagining it. A week ago I was still the owner of Becker Scrap and Salvage Co. . . . and a few hours ago I was still a man with over thirty thousand marks . . . a man who still had many prospects, in spite of everything. A man with thirty thousand marks is still fully capable of living. I had endless possibilities . . . I just ought to have taken advantage of them! All the travel, the struggle, the worries, the self-torment, the brooding . . . it was all in vain. My entire life has been meaningless, everything I've ever achieved . . . There I was running around Berlin as the merchant Otto Silbermann . . . I had a family . . . I had friends . . . I had a wonderful life . . . I was rooted . . . No, I wasn't rooted, I only imagined I was . . . this is the only life that's real, that's genuine . . . this bench here . . . the empty pockets . . . the police station where I don't dare enter . . . that is the authentic Silbermann existence . . . I'm perched on a bench in the void, and when they close the station they'll kick me out and I won't even have that anymore.

His hand stroked the wooden seat.

This is what I have accomplished, he thought. For this I sneaked across the border and begged two gendarmes for a little air. Ach, if I'd only given it one more try! He sighed, lost.

Then he suddenly leapt up.

"I want my money back," he growled. "My thirty thousand marks!"

Once more he went over to the station. I'll show you who I am, he thought, in desperate fury, only to stop again outside the door.

He looked at his wallet to see how much money he had left. "Two hundred twenty, two hundred thirty, two hundred forty," he counted quickly, in a low voice. He still had bills worth two hundred eighty marks.

Tomorrow, he decided, and turned away from the station and headed toward the exit. Tomorrow . . .

A low-level employee, he then reasoned, can live off two hundred eighty marks for several months. What will the thief do with my money? He has no idea it belonged to a Jew, so it's possible he's afraid they're trying to track him down, and maybe my briefcase is roaming with him all across the country.

He headed out of the station but stopped at the exit.

In 1919, when we opened the firm Seelig and Silbermann, my investment amounted to thirty thousand marks, he recalled nostalgically. Twenty thousand from Father, and ten thousand that I borrowed from Bruno. Those thirty thousand marks were my beginning! And now they are my end. Up to this point I'd only lost what I'd earned, but now I've lost the source of those earnings, and what might have let me earn more in the future.

I shouldn't take it so tragically, he then thought, because really all I've lost is the last piece of my past, which no longer properly belongs to me anyway. After all, did the money guarantee my safety? He tried to console himself for his loss. No! It only provided the illusion of security.

Ach, nonsense, it was more, much more! It was my entire future. I've lost twenty years of my existence, twenty years! How ungrateful I've been. My wealth has shielded me from poverty for an entire lifetime. And for a few days it's no longer been able to help—at least not to the extent it had. But now I've lost my very existence! Now I've let my entire life get stolen! I am a dead man—utterly and absolutely dead.

He left the station, went to a waiting taxi, and gave the driver the address to his apartment, since he had decided to sleep in his bed one last time before going through with his suicide, which is what he considered filing the report on the theft to be.

When the car passed a telephone booth, Silbermann had a new idea and tapped his finger on the pane separating him from the driver. "Stop," he said. The driver stopped the car some hundred meters past the telephone, and Silbermann climbed out. He paid and walked back to the booth. He stepped inside, opened the phone book, and searched through names beginning with *A*. When he came to Angelhof, attorney, he underlined the number with blue pencil, as was his habit, and dialed.

He had to wait some time before a sleepy voice finally answered: "Hello, who's calling?"

"Herr Angelhof?" Silbermann asked as calmly as he could.

"Yes, that's me, but . . ."

"May I speak with your wife?"

"My wife? At this hour? Who are you? What do you mean calling like this?"

"It's imperative that I speak with your wife," Silbermann explained emphatically. "It's very, very important!"

"Fine, but will you first tell me who this is and why you're bothering me in the middle of the night—that's never happened to me before in all my life."

"Your wife left her purse in the train," Silbermann lied, passing over the first question, since he would have been hard-pressed to invent a name. Where did I come up with a lost purse? he asked himself. Ah, my briefcase, of course. "I found her purse," he continued slowly. "And I would like to return it to her."

"Then come and give it to me tomorrow," the attorney suggested, his tone slightly more gentle.

"Unfortunately I'm just passing through, it's a very short layover."

"But tonight? It's already very late. Couldn't you have called earlier?"

"Unfortunately not, besides I have my own business to attend to," Silbermann said brazenly.

"Of course . . . I understand . . . It's very kind that

you . . . but perhaps you could come by early in the morning?"

"Early in the morning? Yes, that would work. I have a train to Hamburg at nine twenty." By now I have all the departure times in my head, Silbermann was surprised to note. Which can be very useful in certain cases, such as this one.

"So if you'll be so kind as to come by at eight," the lawyer suggested very politely.

"Where do you live?"

"Kurfürstendamm 65."

"Right, I have that address from the telephone book. But the purse has a letter to your wife at a different address. I think . . ."

He stopped, hoping the lawyer would mention the address, but he didn't.

The man just growled reluctantly. "So?"

"Well," said Silbermann. "Now I'm in an awkward situation. I have no idea what to do. I believe your wife implied in conversation that you're living in separation."

"So why are you calling me?"

"Well I don't know exactly, either. I'm not so precisely informed about your family affairs, which are none of my business. I only wondered where I ought to take the purse, since I really should return it to your wife."

"Bring it to my office tomorrow morning."

"I don't know if I have the right, if you are . . ."

"So then leave me in peace! Do what you want. Take it straight to her for all I care. Perhaps that's best."

"I'll simply deposit it in the lost-and-found bureau." Silbermann made one final try. "I don't know if the address is still valid. Then the bureau can look up your wife."

"It's all the same to me, but maybe you should take it to Pension Weler, that's where she's staying, if you don't want to entrust it to me. What address is on the letter?"

Silbermann quickly opened the phone book.

"Let me see," he said. "Maybe I can manage that, if I have enough time."

"What address is on the letter?" The lawyer repeated his question.

"I'll have to check," Silbermann said. "Please excuse my having bothered you. Good-bye."

He hung up. Full of hope, he leafed through the phone book. Perhaps I should have asked for the street, he thought. If that pension isn't listed—I can't call him again. But he found the address and wrote it down. Then he went back onto the street. An escapade, he thought, almost angrily. A romantic escapade!

He took a taxi. When he reached the boardinghouse he had to ring several times before someone finally opened the door.

"I'd like to speak with a Frau Angelhof," he said.

The maidservant looked at him, astonished. "At this hour?" she asked, incredulously.

"Yes," he said decisively. "I'm only passing through and have something to give her," he added by way of explanation.

"Can't you give it to me?"

"No," said Silbermann, then reached into his pocket and handed her a three-mark coin. "Will you be so kind as to tell her she has a visitor?"

The girl let him in and showed him to the reading room. By the time Ursula Angelhof entered some ten minutes later, Silbermann had nearly fallen asleep in the comfortable armchair. She examined him calmly. It seemed she was neither pleased nor particularly surprised, just perhaps a little taken aback. Silbermann jumped up.

"Good evening," he greeted, no longer knowing exactly why he had come.

She seemed not to know, either.

"I wanted to see you again," he explained, using the familiar *Du*. "I didn't meet you in the café because I came too late."

"But how did you find out my address?" she asked, using the formal *Sie*.

"From your husband." Silbermann stuck to the familiar form.

"Ah," she said, and it seemed to Silbermann as if she smiled for a moment approvingly. But then she became serious. "You shouldn't have done that"—here she switched to *Du*—"you know how things are between us."

"But I wanted to see you again," he said quietly.

"Why?" she asked. "It doesn't make any sense. Which is why I didn't keep our appointment."

Silbermann couldn't help smiling. Of course, she hadn't kept their rendezvous.

"Maybe you're right," he then said.

She shook her head. "And?" she asked.

"It's . . . I don't know how to go on. I have no idea what to do. No idea! I'm done for. They stole my money in the train from Dresden to Berlin."

Her eyes widened, appalled. "Your money?" she asked.

"Now I don't know why I came . . . I wanted to see you . . . But . . . it doesn't make any sense . . . it's just that . . . I don't know."

He stood up, took her hand, looked at her closely, and finally kissed her hand.

"Good-bye," he said.

"But I don't understand," she said. "There was something you wanted. What was it? Can I help you . . . I mean."

"No, no, no," he cut her off, almost testily, and shook his head. "Besides, there's nothing you can do to help." He sighed.

Slowly he walked to the door. Then all of a sudden he felt her hand on his shoulder. He turned to her and looked at her questioningly.

"Do you want to stay here?" she whispered.

He gazed at her with empty eyes.

"I don't know," he said. "I think . . . perhaps it's better . . . if I go."

"As you wish," she answered calmly. "But what are you going to do?"

"I'm not going to do anything anymore!" he answered. And then he left.

TEN

———✦———

Silbermann was taking a walk with his family through the Tiergarten. He would have preferred to go to Potsdam and visit the park and palace at Sanssouci again, but Eduard had wanted to go rowing on the Neuer See and had persuaded his father to change plans.

Because of that, and because now he'd even gotten his father to agree to go to the circus, Eduard was in a fantastic mood, and Silbermann was also happy to have stayed in Berlin, since he had set up some important meetings for Monday and wanted to get to bed early.

The weather was very good, and they were discussing the trip they planned to take in the summer.

"Eduard needs another new suit," said Elfriede, looking in his direction.

"When I was a boy," Silbermann said, "I took better care of my things." Then he turned to his son. "By the way, have you done your homework, Eduard?"

"Right," said Eduard, looking away.

"Right isn't an answer," said Silbermann. "Don't forget to show it to me tonight."

After a moment's silence Eduard spoke up. "I didn't completely understand the math assignment."

"That really is the limit." Silbermann was indignant. "And you dare go out walking in the park? And tonight you want to go to the circus? Honestly? Until you've solved all your math problems, don't even think about going with us to the circus."

"But he spends so much time on his schoolwork." Elfriede tried to mediate.

The doorbell rang. Silbermann gave a start.

"Eduard really ought to . . ." he said, in a daze. Then he looked around. He was lying in his bedroom, but he was all alone.

"So," he said, and closed his eyes again.

The doorbell rang again. Slowly he climbed out of bed, slid into his slippers, and went to the door, rubbing the sleep from his eyes.

They certainly don't waste any time, he thought, assuming the police had come to take him away. He opened the door.

"I'm here to collect for the milk," said a female voice.

Silbermann studied the woman.

"So," he said slowly. "You're here to collect for the milk."

"That's right," the woman answered. "I've already been by four or five times. But no one answered. Today I made a special point of coming to the front door, since I thought the doorbell in back might not be working." She was eyeing him as though he'd committed some evil deed directed against her.

"It comes to nine marks seventy-five," she said firmly, and handed him the bill.

"Please wait," he said.

He went to his bedroom to fetch the money.

"Shall I keep delivering?" asked the milk lady, when he was back. "Because I see the bottles are still just sitting out by the back door. It's been three days since I . . ."

"We'll no longer be needing any delivery," he interrupted. "But you can give me that bottle there."

"Shall I go ahead and put the thirty-four pfennig for it on your next bill?" she asked. "Then again, if you're not going to be having me . . ."

"Thirty-four pfennig," he said—"that's a lot of money."

"Milk costs the same everywhere," she responded. She sounded bitter, presumably aggrieved at the perceived challenge to her integrity.

Silbermann was alarmed and said, "I don't doubt that in the least."

Then he paid, closed the door, and took the milk bottle to his bedroom. The milk lady is deeply offended because she assumes that I think her milk is overpriced by one penny—and that's something she won't put up with. Whereas I . . . I . . .

He opened the bottle and took a big swallow.

Now I'd like to have a coffee, he thought as he wiped his mouth and headed to the bathroom. He turned on the hot water and mindlessly watched it fill the tub. Then he undressed and took a bath.

I didn't realize how much I've missed this, he thought, stretching out contentedly in the water. He stayed in the bath for half an hour, then shaved and slowly got dressed.

No sooner had he tied his tie than he heard the doorbell ring again, this time in back.

I suppose that's the bread delivery bill, he thought, almost amused at the idea.

It was the bread delivery bill. He paid and a few minutes later he left his apartment and went to the pastry shop across the street. He drank his coffee and took his time eating breakfast.

When he was finished he decided to do what he couldn't bring himself to undertake the previous evening. Outwardly he was completely calm when he stepped into the police station.

"I want to file a report," he explained, without returning the official's "Heil Hitler." He stood right at the barrier rail and propped himself up with both hands.

"What's it about?" asked a disapproving official voice.

"I was robbed."

"That's not my jurisdiction. I only handle residence registrations."

Silbermann waited a moment, then said, "Nevertheless, you might take it upon yourself to advise me who is in charge of that jurisdiction?"

The official bristled. He was familiar with that tone. He studied Silbermann, presumably wondering whether the latter was in a position to get away with such high-handedness. But he evidently accepted it, and then said in a significantly more polite manner, "Room 3 if you please."

"And where may I find Room 3?" asked Silbermann.

The official stood up, stepped to the barrier, pointed to a door, and said, "The first door there in the hall."

Silbermann thanked him and a moment later was standing in front of Room 3.

He knocked.

"Come in," said a gruff voice.

Silbermann stepped inside. Sitting behind a desk was a thickset man in civilian clothes, who put down the newspaper he was reading and picked up a dossier.

"I've come to file a report," said Silbermann, coming closer.

"Heil Hitler," said the inspector, and looked at him expectantly.

"Good morning," replied Silbermann. "As I said, I've come to file a report."

"Are you a German?" asked the inspector, looking at a document.

"Of course," Silbermann replied.

"Then kindly use the official German greeting. That's obligatory here!"

"I'm a Jew."

"So then you're not a German!" The inspector closed the dossier and looked at him.

"Let's deal with that another time," answered Silbermann, making an effort to stay composed. "I've come to file a report!"

The man stroked his chin. "Are you aware that filing a false report is a punishable offense?"

"I have no intention of filing a false report."

"In any case I advise you to carefully consider what you say."

"Won't you first hear my report?" asked Silbermann.

"So, you're a Jew!" the inspector stated, nodding his head at his own remark.

"I came here to file a report!" Silbermann repeated for the fourth time.

"It is my duty to inform you that you'll be liable for punishment if you . . ."

"Someone stole my briefcase on the train," Silbermann interrupted, and his face started changing from pale to red. "It contained thirty thousand marks. Will you take my statement?"

The inspector placed a large paper form in front of him. "How did you come to have the thirty thousand marks?" he asked. He dipped his pen in the ink, carefully tapped it against the inkwell to knock off a small blob, and relaxed back into his chair. He observed Silbermann awhile, then leaned forward again and began writing.

"Name?"

"Otto Silbermann."

"Do you have an ID?"

Silbermann handed him his passport.

"Good," said the inspector and wrote down the number of the passport and various dates.

"The address that's listed is still valid," Silbermann explained.

The inspector registered that without comment. Then he looked up and said in a sharp voice: "I asked you how you came to have the money. Are you refusing to answer?"

"That money is what's left of my estate," Silbermann answered. "I was once a rich man."

"And you go lugging it around inside a briefcase? That's

a little odd, I'd say! In which train is this supposed to have occurred?"

"In the train from Dresden to Berlin. In a smoking compartment in the second class."

"Did you file a report with the railway police?"

"No, but I informed the conductor."

"Why didn't you file a report with the railway police?"

"Because I wanted to do it here."

"Strange. So, you allege that on the train from Dresden to Berlin, in a second-class smoking compartment, you were robbed of a briefcase along with its contents of thirty thousand marks."

"I'm not alleging, that's exactly what happened."

"I can't know that for sure. Do you have a particular suspect in mind?"

"I was traveling with an elderly lady and two gentlemen. One of them had a blond mustache."

The inspector laughed or coughed, it was impossible to tell. "Is that all you can tell me?" he asked. "Would you recognize them?"

"I believe so."

"What did the briefcase look like?"

"It was brown leather with a steel lock. Here, this is the key."

"Did you note the number of the train?"

"No, unfortunately I didn't think to do that."

"At what time did this supposedly occur?"

"It was the last train to Berlin, I think."

"You think! What time did the train arrive in Berlin?"

"Toward one AM."

"Is that all the information you can provide? You claim

that on the last train from Dresden to Berlin you lost a briefcase . . ."

"It was stolen!" Silbermann cut him off.

"Don't be so rude! I'm not deaf."

"What do you intend to do?" asked Silbermann.

"We'll have to see."

"I'd like to add a finder's fee of ten percent of whatever amount I receive when the perpetrators are apprehended."

"First you have to get your money back, second you have to have lost it, and third . . ."

"You don't seem to be taking my report seriously. Do you think I'm joking? Is that it?" Silbermann interrupted the inspector. As he did so, he sat down in the chair opposite the desk, having waited in vain to be offered a seat.

The inspector viewed this uninvited gesture as disrespectful, but didn't exactly know how to respond. "Kindly let me finish," he snapped. "My opinion on the matter is not at all up for discussion. You have filed a report, and my job is to examine it and pass it on. Will you now please explain why you were traveling around with thirty thousand marks in your briefcase?"

"Who said I was traveling around?"

"In any event you were in Dresden."

"Don't I have the right to travel to Dresden?"

"I'm the one asking questions here! And what I want to know from you is"—he paused and glanced at the paper he had just filled out, then suddenly looked up and asked—"were you planning to take the money out of the country?"

"Do you want to look for the thief or cast suspicion on the victim?" Silbermann retorted, having anticipated that particular line of attack.

"As I've already told you, what I want or don't want isn't the issue. Here in this office I am not who I really am, but a public official. Otherwise you might be surprised at who you're dealing with!"

"I am not who I really am," Silbermann repeated sarcastically, no longer able to suppress his rage. "Who are you then, if you're not who you really are? Since when do German officials suffer from split personalities?"

Furious, the inspector pounded his fist on the table. "How dare you!" he roared. "Do you think you can get away with your Jewish jokes here?"

Silbermann jumped up.

"Perhaps it's also a Jewish joke," he shouted, "that I'm reporting a theft to the very people who are stealing all my rights. Because the German reality is that instead of looking for the thief you presume to treat the victim with such insolence. You . . . Herr Inspektor . . . I want to get my money back . . . my thirty thousand marks . . . and I want it immediately . . . So see to it . . . I've filed one report . . . Now I wish to file a second . . . A gang of bandits broke into my apartment, destroyed my furniture, hurt my friend Findler . . . here . . ." He reached into his pocket and held out the swastika pin. "The criminals forgot to take this . . . Kindly take my statement. What are you waiting for? . . . This second report is even more important than my first, it's much, much more important. Go ahead, start writing . . . don't just stare at me like that. Or perhaps you think I wrecked my own apartment? Write this down: Findler, Theo Findler . . . he's my witness, he was there . . . They injured him . . . He was there to squeeze what he could out of me . . . What are you waiting for? Why aren't you writing? After all you're the official here, that's what you told me. It's your job to protect the rights of all citizens, Herr Inspektor ... Crimes were committed: burglary, home invasion ... bodily harm to Findler ... on November ninth of this year a vast gang of criminals perpetrated crimes not only in my house ... but everywhere ... why aren't you writing? I'm telling you: murderers, Herr Inspektor, intruders, highwaymen ..."

He was talking himself more and more into a rage.

"Does the fact that I have traveled make me suspicious? Does it? I was fleeing from criminals, Herr Inspektor, kindly don't forget that. Doesn't a citizen have the right to flee from criminals? And doesn't he also have the right to take his money with him? Or is that not the case? And yet evidently he's allowed to file a report? Ask Findler, just ask Findler ... He was there ... he'll corroborate everything ... he's a witness ... Set up a meeting in my apartment ... establish the facts ... conduct an investigation ... at other people's homes, too ... not just mine ... unlawful detention ... bodily injury ... And what about the police? Isn't their job to intervene? So why don't they? I'll tell you why, it's because ..."

He glared at the inspector as if he were going to pounce on him at any moment. His mouth was foaming, and spittle was dribbling down his chin. Two policemen took hold of him and dragged him off to a holding cell.

"Thieves," he shouted. "I want my money back! ... Accessories after the fact! Receivers of stolen goods, all of you! ... Bribed ... Corruptible ... Criminals ... Accomplices ... Thirty thousand marks ... You're divvying up my money ... my money! ... I demand the police ... This is ... there are laws ..."

The policemen locked the door of the cell behind him. Silbermann drummed against it with his fists.

"Open up," he roared, completely beside himself. "I demand to speak to the inspector. I have a report to file . . . I have witnesses . . . I have witnesses!" he kicked the door. "Give me my money back!" he cried. "I'll leave the country! I promise you . . . I'll leave the country . . . but I want my briefcase back!"

The door was torn open.

"Shut your mouth for once," said a guard, who, losing his temper, grabbed Silbermann and shook him. Silbermann went silent. The guard let go of him and left the cell. Silbermann staggered against the wall, threw himself onto the bunk, and cried. He lay there for about ten minutes. Then he jumped back up, ran to the door, and roared, "There are laws! There are laws!"

He kept repeating these three words. Finally the door was yanked open once again.

"Have you gone completely out of your mind?"

"There are laws!" Silbermann repeated, intimidated to speak in a much quieter voice.

"They'll haul you off to the asylum, if you don't shut up!"

The next day Silbermann was taken to the same inspector who had received his report and who had witnessed his fit of rage. As a precaution the officer had retained two policemen in the room.

"You realize," the inspector began with a dry voice, without looking up from his files, "that yesterday you were guilty of directing the grossest slander not only against me but against the entire service. Moreover, you made defamatory statements that are offensive to the German people as a whole." At this point he looked up. "What do you have to say to that?" he asked.

Silbermann said nothing.

"Do you want to be sent to a concentration camp?"

Silbermann said nothing.

"You'll be put on trial!"

Silbermann said nothing.

The inspector jumped up. "What on earth are you thinking?" he roared. "I advise you to open your mouth!"

"I filed a report," Silbermann said, in a husky voice. "I was robbed of thirty thousand marks! They broke into my apartment!"

The inspector sat back down. "Why won't you listen to reason?" he asked more quietly. "Surely you realize this stubbornness will get you nowhere."

Silbermann looked past him out the window.

"If I want, I could have you sent immediately to a concentration camp. You're practically forcing me to. There they'll teach you some manners!"

"Did you follow up on my report?" asked Silbermann. "Have they recovered the money?"

"Are you starting again? Don't speak unless you're asked a question!"

He picked up Silbermann's service record, which had been taken from him along with his other papers when he was put in the cell.

"So you were a soldier," said the inspector, more mildly. "I'm guessing of course you were rear echelon, am I right?"

"Is that what it says in the papers?" asked Silbermann.

"Papers can be falsified."

Without answering, Silbermann shrugged his shoulders.

"I didn't say that they are falsified. I just said they can be falsified," the inspector explained. "So, what should I do with you? What do you suggest?"

"I demand an investigation into the whereabouts of my briefcase."

"Of all the nerve," said the inspector, not without a note of respect. "So, I will have you sent to the concentration camp! There you'll recover your senses and learn how a Jew is expected to behave these days! Don't think for a minute they won't have their own ways of dealing with you."

"On the contrary," Silbermann answered. "I'm quite convinced of that."

"So why are you acting like this?"

"I lost a briefcase with thirty thousand marks. I came here to file a report."

"You behaved outrageously and you . . . Now I really am going to place you under arrest!"

"That's what I thought," Silbermann said calmly. "I knew that before I came here."

"So why did you come here?" the inspector asked, curious.

"Because I no longer care what happens to me. Because I have dutifully paid my taxes year after year and now I'm requesting that the police also fulfill their duty to me as a citizen."

"The police aren't here to serve you!" The inspector studied him thoughtfully. "Western front?" he then asked. "How long?"

"What does that have to do with anything?"

The inspector laughed. "Go to the devil," he said, in a

strong voice. "But don't ever show your face here again. Now move, get out of here!"

"They stole thirty thousand marks from me along with my briefcase."

"So it's no, then, is it!" said the inspector. "You simply can't keep your trap shut. Meier, take him away. And here I wanted to put mercy before justice . . ."

"Let's go, Jew, come here," said the guard, grabbing Silbermann by the arm.

Silbermann brushed his hand away. "Do you mean me?" he asked. "My name is Silbermann. I will not tolerate . . ."

"Ha ha ha," the inspector laughed. "He got you there, Meier! So just throw the man out. Let him go. He fought on the front line and . . . well something of that always stays, even with a Jew."

The guard ushered Silbermann to the door.

"Just keep your dirty trap shut," he recommended. "You won't be so lucky a second time."

Silbermann looked at him fiercely.

"Tell your master he should kindly attend to my report. I'll be back."

And with that he gave one more sullen glance at the guard and left.

"What bad luck," he muttered to himself. "Now I'll have to kill myself with my own hands, while they could have easily done it for me."

He wandered aimlessly about the city for an hour. Suddenly he found himself in front of the building where his lawyer lived. He went inside, took the elevator up to the third floor, and rang the doorbell.

Löwenstein himself opened. "It's you," he observed. "I assumed it was the police . . ."

"I thought you'd been arrested," Silbermann replied grumpily.

"So why did you come here?" Löwenstein asked, inviting him in. "As it happens they just let me go today."

"And what are you doing now?" asked Silbermann, and started to take off his coat.

"I'm leaving the country. My train goes in one hour."

"Do you have a visa?"

"No, but I have the address of a man who can take me across the Dutch border. You should come with me, Silbermann."

"I've already done that! Besides, all I have left are two hundred marks. They robbed me in the train and stole thirty thousand marks. When I passed by here, I thought: maybe Löwenstein knows how I could come by some money."

"But if you were robbed . . . God forbid. How can anybody let thirty thousand marks get stolen! A person has to be careful. On the other hand, everyone's going to lose his money sooner or later. At least you don't have to die on that account. Be glad you're in one piece. So, are you coming?"

"I'm sick of travel," Silbermann said slowly.

"Do you think I enjoy it? You have to decide right now though, please. I don't have any time. I have a hundred things to take care of, and my train leaves in an hour. Well?"

"I don't have enough money."

"I'll loan you some. After all, you're still good for two hundred marks."

"Very nice of you. Good-bye."

Löwenstein took hold of him. "So?" he asked. "What is it?"

"I wish you the best of luck," Silbermann replied. "But I've had it up to here with traveling. It bores me."

The lawyer looked at him uncomprehendingly.

"What's wrong with you?" he asked. "It bores you! Did I hear that right? It's a matter of life and death, my man. Don't you realize that?"

Silbermann stared back at him.

"I want my money back!" he said. "Thirty thousand marks! I demand . . . I . . . have to think it all through again . . . Don't let me detain you."

"Something's no longer right with you," said Löwenstein.

"Yes," Silbermann said calmly. "I often have that feeling these days . . . the world has gone mad . . . that is to say I no longer know what to make of it . . . Which really means that I myself . . ."

"Oh come on." Löwenstein interrupted him. "A sensible man like you. So are you coming? I'm afraid you have to decide right away."

Silbermann shook his head, then held out his hand and said good-bye.

As he slowly went down the stairs, he wondered what he should do. I have no choice but to keep moving, he thought. But on my own . . . Löwenstein talks too much for my taste. I'll simply go to Hamburg. That was always a nice ride. I always felt best in the compartments on the train to Hamburg. Although I could go back to Dortmund. At least then I could get some sleep.

He stopped outside the entrance to the building.

Löwenstein will make it, he thought. He's a capable soul . . . not easily intimidated. I really ought to join him . . . but what about my money? What will happen to that? What if they find it . . . and then I'll be out of the country and won't have a penny!

He boarded a streetcar.

I'll go to the office, he thought. I have to check to see what mail has come in the meantime. I haven't been paying any attention to my business . . . that's practically criminal negligence.

He hopped off the streetcar.

What business? It no longer exists, he remembered.

He hailed a taxi and gave the driver Becker's address.

Maybe he'll give me some money, a few thousand marks, who knows?

After just one block he had the driver stop and he got out.

It's pointless, he felt. Everything is pointless.

He jumped onto a passing streetcar.

"Where are you headed?" he asked the conductor.

"Adolf-Hitler-Platz."

He paid for a ticket.

What am I supposed to do there? he asked himself.

He got off two stations later.

Where to? he thought anxiously. Where to? I'm insane, I should have gone with Löwenstein. But I'm so sick of traveling.

He went into a pub, sat down, and ordered a glass of beer.

I am insane, he concluded once more. Maybe that's actually the best thing for me, the most reasonable. The times are enough to drive a person mad all on their own. However, these and similar musings led him to conclude that he was still of sound mind, and was therefore obliged to think rationally.

How am I supposed to cope with all of this, he despaired. Reason dictates I should kill myself. But I want to live. Despite everything, I want to live! And that requires all the wits I have, but they aren't enough, because the same reasoning is pitting me against myself. It negates my existence. So where does that leave me? It's because I understand, he thought unhappily, that I despair. If only I could misunderstand. But that's something I'm no longer able to do. And the only thing I have left in life is the list of all my losses. Apart from that I have nothing, absolutely nothing.

"Nothing left!" he said so loudly that the few people in the pub turned toward him. "Nothing left, absolutely nothing," Silbermann said again, out loud.

A waiter brought his beer. He got up and paid.

I'll go get arrested, he thought. I'll go back to the police station. Have them detain me. The state has murdered me so it ought to bury me as well.

He went back out to the street and waved a cab over. "The nearest police station," he said. But no sooner had he climbed in than he regretted his decision.

Maybe, he thought, just maybe . . . You never know . . . Shouldn't I give it a go with Löwenstein after all? He rapped on the pane and gave the driver the lawyer's address. He's probably already gone, Silbermann then thought.

When the car stopped, the driver had to wake him because Silbermann had succumbed to his fatigue and had fallen asleep. He took the elevator back upstairs.

I'm sure he's left by now, he thought, as he pressed the doorbell.

Löwenstein answered just moments later. He was dressed for travel and carrying a small suitcase.

"Did you reconsider?" he asked Silbermann, as he stepped out of the apartment and locked the door behind him. "I was delayed. You're lucky. Come on!"

They went into the elevator and rode downstairs.

"I took far too much time," the lawyer explained on the way, annoyed.

"What will become of your things? Your money?"

"Gone is gone," Löwenstein answered very calmly.

Silbermann couldn't help but admire such an attitude. When they reached the ground floor, they noticed two men waiting by the elevator. Silbermann was the first to step out into the hall. He passed the men and walked on five or six steps, assuming that Löwenstein would follow. Then all of a sudden he heard the word "arrest." He quickly turned around.

Just at that moment one of the two men was putting handcuffs on the lawyer, whose face had gone completely pale. With his eyes he signaled to Silbermann to go on.

Silbermann stayed where he was. "What's this about?" he asked quietly.

One of the men grabbed him by the arm. "You know this man?"

"Of course. He was my lawyer."

"Then you're coming to the station immediately. Are you also a Jew?"

"Yes," said Silbermann.

They were led away.

ELEVEN

"My name is Schwarz," said the inmate, as he went up to Silbermann to shake hands. "I'm completely normal," he added right away. "And what did you do wrong?"

"Nothing," said Silbermann, and sat down on the bunk.

Schwarz followed him. "I see what you're doing," he replied. "I get it."

Silbermann wrinkled his forehead. He didn't find his cellmate particularly sympathetic. His face alone triggered a certain repulsion: it was spongy and lacked structure, with heavily bloodshot eyes.

"What I'm doing?" Silbermann asked and lay down.

"Your ploy. The reason you wound up here and not . . . Everybody wants to get off the hook by pretending to be mad. I did as well! But I'm completely normal."

"I believe it," Silbermann replied, closing his eyes.

Schwarz shook his shoulder. "They're planning to sterilize me!" he said, frightened.

"What are they planning?" Silbermann sat up.

"They want to sterilize me. I stole a handbag and then I pretended to be crazy. And now they want to sterilize me! But I'm not going to let them. I'm not schizophrenic. I'm normal. I have a fiancée. I . . ." Schwarz paced back and forth inside the cell.

Silbermann pressed his hands against his temples. "I have a headache," he said.

Schwarz interrupted his pacing. "I see what you're up to!" he stated. "But they're going to sterilize you as well!"

"Nonsense," said Silbermann calmly.

"It's not nonsense! What did you do? Tell me what you did wrong!"

"Nothing at all," Silbermann repeated, irritated. "I'm Jewish, if you really want to know."

"So that's your ploy," Schwarz declared. He leaned over Silbermann's bunk. "Racial defilement, eh, is that it?" he asked, and smiled idiotically.

Silbermann turned to the wall. The trusty opened the door and shoved some food into the cell.

"You," said Schwarz. "This man's a Jew. I refuse to put up with that. I'm a National Socialist. I don't want to be in the same cell as a Jew . . ."

"You better pipe down," said the trusty. "Pretty soon now they'll be taking you to get sterilized."

"No!" Schwarz roared. "No!"

The trusty grinned and shut the door. Schwarz paced up and down the cell. Then he went to the door and started drumming.

"Jews out!" he shouted. "Jews out!"

His shouting was picked up by other insane inmates, and

soon there were dozens of jumbled voices shouting: "Jews out! Jews out!"

Silbermann leapt from his bunk. "Shut up," he screamed.

Schwarz looked at him, frightened, and went silent. But the others kept shouting: "Jews out, Jews out!"

"They're going to sterilize you, too," Schwarz whispered, and huddled in the corner, scared. "They're going to sterilize you for sure!"

The guard's key jangled in the lock.

"What's going on here?" he asked.

"I don't want to be with a Jew . . ."

"What you want or don't want doesn't matter here . . ."

The prisoner was silent. After the guard left, Schwarz started shouting again: "Jews out! Jews out!"

Silbermann lay back down and stopped his ears with his thumbs. "I'm going to leave soon!" he said loudly.

"What are you going to do?" asked Schwarz, stepping closer. "What are you going to do?"

"Why are they making such a racket?" Silbermann asked quietly.

"Idiots, all of them are idiots," Schwarz explained. "But I'm the one they want to sterilize!"

Silbermann stood up. "I don't want to stay here," he said. "I want to leave! . . . There's a train to Aachen at seven . . . and at eight ten there's a train to Nürnberg . . . and at nine twenty there's one to Hamburg . . . and one to Dresden at ten . . . There are so many trains . . . so many trains and trains . . . I want to get away from here!"

"I see what you're up to," said Schwarz, convinced. "Come on and let's shout together: Jews out . . ."

AFTERWORD TO THE
GERMAN EDITION

———

Peter Graf

On October 29, 1942, Ulrich Alexander Boschwitz was approximately seven hundred nautical miles northwest of the Azores aboard the MV *Abosso*, when the German submarine U-575 torpedoed the passenger ship that was being used as a troopship by the British government. The unescorted vessel sank at 11 PM Central European Time. Ulrich Boschwitz was just twenty-seven years old when his life—along with the lives of 361 other passengers—was extinguished. He was carrying his latest manuscript.

Several weeks earlier, he had sent what would be his last letter to his mother, Martha Wolgast Boschwitz, in which he spelled out what should be done with his published and unpublished manuscripts in the event of his death, including his novel *The Passenger*, which had come out in England in 1939 and in America the following year—only to quickly disappear. In this letter dated August 10, 1942, Ulrich

Boschwitz informed his mother that he had thoroughly revised the book, and that she should expect to receive the first 109 pages of the corrected manuscript from a fellow former prisoner who was on his way to England. The remaining revisions were still pending.

The author advised his mother to engage someone with literary experience to incorporate the revisions, as he was convinced that the changes would greatly improve the book, and thereby increase its chances of being published in a Germany that would hopefully soon be liberated. Writing in English, he closed his notes with the words: "I really believe there is something in the book, which may make it a success." Evidently Martha Wolgast Boschwitz never received her son's revisions: in any case they are not included in the fragmentary "Ulrich Boschwitz Collection" currently housed in the Leo Baeck Institute in New York. Nor does his niece and closest relative, Reuella Shachaf, know anything about their whereabouts.

My first contact with Reuella Shachaf came as the result of an interview I gave in December 2015. Avner Shapira, literary critic of the Israeli daily *Haaretz*, had asked me to discuss Ernst Haffner's 1932 novel *Blood Brothers*, which I had rediscovered and which had just come out in a Hebrew translation. After the interview appeared Reuella sent me an email, in which she mentioned her uncle from Berlin Ulrich Boschwitz, whose books had been published in several languages but never in his own native tongue. One book in particular, she wrote, might be of special interest—namely the 1938 novel *Der Reisende*, whose original German typescript was not with the remaining papers in New York, but since the late 1960s had been housed in Frankfurt, in the

German Exile Archive of the Deutsche Nationalbibliothek. It all sounded so interesting that I traveled to Frankfurt a few days before Christmas 2015 and spent an entire day absorbed in the first and only original copy of the novel.

I quickly found myself riveted by the text, but it was also obvious that the typescript had never been edited, and that a proper editing would only enhance the book's quality. Furthermore, because Ulrich Boschwitz himself had seen the necessity, and since as mentioned above he had continued to revise the text following its release in England and America, I decided to seek his family's consent and edit the manuscript just as I would any other text I publish or edit— the only difference being that no exchange with the author would be possible.

But it was inside that little bare room in the otherwise impressively large Nationalbibliothek when I first followed the fate of Otto Silbermann, as he wandered aimlessly across Germany, frightened in the wake of the November pogroms, always in danger of being arrested or denounced. By the time I left the library late in the afternoon it was already dark, it was drizzling outside, and everything I took in as I walked back to my hotel near the train station seemed incredibly dreary and reinforced the enormous sadness I felt after reading the novel. Back in my room I began to refresh my knowledge of the events that occurred in Germany and Austria between November 7 and 13, 1938, and I set out to learn more about Ulrich Boschwitz, whose novel was likely the first literary account of these atrocities.

Today it has been amply documented that the excesses of violence were not the expression of spontaneous popular outrage that Joseph Goebbels claimed had spilled over because a Polish Jew had shot Eduard vom Rath, the third secretary of the German embassy in Paris, who died from his wounds two days later. The assassination carried out by the seventeen-year-old Herschel Grynszpan simply served as the pretext for members of the SA and SS—many disguised in civilian clothes—to set fire to synagogues and plunder Jewish businesses. It was a signal to begin the all-out systematic persecution of Jews, following years of a more piecemeal deprivation of rights.

A survey of the international press coverage of the pogroms reveals how little credence was given to the official pronouncements of the Nazi regime. In 1938 there were still a lot of foreigners in Germany, and journalists, embassy personnel, businessmen, as well as other eyewitnesses reported directly to their home countries. The outrage sparked by these accounts was universal, but it did not lead, as one might expect, to a greater willingness to help, by granting more Jews the possibility of immigrating abroad, for example. Quite the opposite.

Overnight it became clear to the Jews remaining in Germany that flight was the only way left to save themselves, but the doors were gradually closing. Legal immigration to European countries such as France, England, or Switzerland was practically out of the question for Jews. And obtaining visas for the United States or South American nations was virtually impossible—even apart from the horrendous costs that such a venture entailed. This is precisely the hopeless situation in which Otto Silbermann finds himself. But Ulrich Boschwitz was not only describing the trap into which hundreds of thousands of Jews in Germany had fallen, he was also writing in despair about his own fate, and incorporating some of his own family history.

His protagonist Otto Silbermann is a prosperous Berlin merchant of Jewish ancestry who considers himself very much a German. He had fought on the front lines in the First World War and had been awarded the Iron Cross, and prior to the Nazi takeover was considered a respectable member of Berlin's middle class. Ulrich Boschwitz's father, who died a few weeks before the birth of his son in 1915, was also a well-to-do merchant. His Jewish background, which would ultimately determine his family's fate, had been of no importance before 1933. He had in fact converted to Christianity, and so Ulrich and his sister Clarissa grew up in a household shaped by Protestantism. Their mother, the painter Martha Wolgast Boschwitz, was descended from the Plitt family of Lübeck, whose members included various senators and influential theologians. Consequently the exclusion from society, the stigmatization and increasing persecution of the Jews—to which Ulrich and Clarissa Boschwitz were also subjected—came as a great shock.

After the Nazi takeover Clarissa Boschwitz deliberately embraced her Jewish roots and in 1933 fled Berlin on a night train to Switzerland. She joined the Zionist movement, and settled on a kibbutz in Palestine. Meanwhile Ulrich and his mother stayed in Germany until 1935, but immediately after the proclamation of the Nuremberg Race Laws they left the country and immigrated first to Sweden, and then in the following year to Oslo. There Ulrich Boschwitz wrote his first novel *Menschen neben dem Leben* (*People Parallel to Life*), which was quickly published by Bonnier in the summer of 1937 in a Swedish translation, under the pseudonym John Grane, and which received an enthusiastic reception in the Swedish press.

The success of that book enabled him to move to Paris, where he spent a few semesters studying at the Sorbonne. In *The Passenger*, Paris is also where Otto Silbermann's son lives and where he tries unsuccessfully to obtain residency permits for his parents. Because this effort fails, Otto Silbermann attempts to cross out of Germany illegally and is captured by Belgian border guards. Evidently this scene, too, is drawn from the author's life: Reuella Shachaf recalls family stories about how her uncle Ulrich Boschwitz was once detained by customs officials on the border of Luxemburg.

Many of the events in the novel can be linked to autobiographical or familial experience. As can the despair and hopelessness that overcame Otto Silbermann in the wake of the November pogroms. Boschwitz began writing *The Passenger* immediately after Kristallnacht, and finished the book in a feverish four weeks. An English version appeared in the spring of 1939 with the London publisher Hamish Hamilton under the title *The Man Who Took Trains* and in the following year Harper published the book in the USA as *The Fugitive*. Evidently Ulrich Boschwitz felt compelled to fight his own looming sense of powerlessness by writing, by bearing literary witness to the crimes being perpetrated in Germany and Austria—crimes that the world was treating with terrifying indifference or, at any rate, appalling inaction.

Boschwitz's protagonist Otto Silbermann puts a face on the nameless victims. But he also mirrors the author's own inner turmoil. Silbermann is not a completely sympathetic person—among other things he even scorns his fellow sufferers—nor are all the "Aryan" Germans he encounters as he vainly tries to outrun his fate bad people. He meets the most diverse archetypes of German society: those who bear active responsibility for the crimes being committed, fellow travelers, frightened people who duck and dodge, as well as courageous, empathetic individuals who offer assistance. This panorama informs his view of the country and the people to whom he still feels a sense of belonging.

Ulrich Boschwitz's literary estate reveals a similarly tormented ambivalence to his native land, as can be seen in several poems penned in 1936. Lines such as: *As long as there are German Germans, the country will again be free* display a hopefulness that he had not yet abandoned. But there are also more bitter entries, such as "The Club of the Upright Citizens," which begins:

True-blue eyes and trusty hands
double chins and strong broad chests
ready to receive commands
and march in good Germanic step

Another, entitled "The Legend of Joseph," is devoted to Joseph Goebbels, and ends like this:

Joseph was a jobless hack
who scribbled here and there
and yet today—imagine that!
he is a millionaire.
Spreading his crippled soul's infection
onto the German nation's grand elite

he fashions history from fiction—
his work paid off—that's no small feat!

These are all angry, if clumsy, attempts to express his contradictory feelings. There are also lines where he is clearly trying to buck himself up:

He who hopes will go on living
while he who sees no road ahead
has just given up his spirit
long before he's met his death.

At that point Ulrich Boschwitz was twenty-one years old. A young man sitting alone in Paris, frantically writing as a way to counter the looming catastrophe. Death or Life—both options were equally likely, as he was very well aware. But before the curtain fell, fate had a few more twists in store for him, both terrible and absurd.

In 1939, shortly before the outbreak of the Second World War, Ulrich Boschwitz followed his mother into exile in England. Like practically all of the Germans who fled the Nazi regime, he and his mother were placed in internment—25,000 people on the Isle of Man alone. In July 1940, Ulrich Boschwitz was sent to an internment camp in Australia aboard the former troop transport *Dunera*. The ship was grossly overfilled; Jewish and political refugees were mixed in with German and Italian prisoners of war, and the conditions were catastrophic. In addition to the overcrowding, passengers were mistreated and robbed by the crew. The fifty-seven-day ordeal became an inglorious page in British history. Among the "Dunera Boys" were many Jewish intellectuals: one of Ulrich Boschwitz's former fellow prisoners wrote a letter to Reuella Shachaf in which he described the important role that culture played in the prison camp.

After 1942, some internees were able to regain their freedom—first and foremost those who were willing to serve in the British army and fight against Nazi Germany. Ulrich Boschwitz hesitated for a long time, for fear of the war and of the long passage, perhaps also for other reasons we can no longer know. He wrote incessantly, confessing to a fellow prisoner that he was more afraid of losing his last manuscript than his life. Sadly, this final work of his perished aboard the *Abosso* in 1942. This makes the publication of *The Passenger* all the more noteworthy, as it gives readers around the world a chance to discover the author Ulrich Alexander Boschwitz—since its republication the book has been translated into nineteen languages.

I should note that this is not the first attempt to have the book published in Germany: we know for instance that it was turned down by Fischer Verlag. None less than Heinrich Böll—one of the most passionate advocates for a humane society and against forgetting—campaigned on its behalf, as can be seen in a letter preserved alongside the typescript and other documents in the German Exile Archive. Böll recommended the text to his own publisher. But even his endorsement wasn't enough. Decades had to pass before this novel could appear in its original language. I thank Reuella Shachaf for alerting me to the text and for her trust in allowing it to appear in the present form. Now, decades after Ulrich Boschwitz died at sea, his novel is at last available to the descendants for whose grandparents and great-grandparents it was actually intended—the "German Germans" who remained committed to humanitarian ideals.

I am convinced that in revising the typescript I have proceeded with the utmost respect and in accordance with the underlying original version. And I want to believe I'm not mistaken in this judgment, and that I am able to present a version that allows all the qualities of this important work to come to light. Astoundingly serene and well-observed, Ulrich Boschwitz's *The Passenger* is both an important literary testament from a dark chapter in human history as well as a timeless—and timely—plea for greater humanity.

THE PASSENGER
ULRICH ALEXANDER BOSCHWITZ

LEARNING TO TALK TO PLANTS
MARTA ORRIOLS

AT NIGHT ALL BLOOD IS BLACK
DAVID DIOP

SPARK
NAOKI MATAYOSHI

THE ENCHANTED NIGHT
MIKLOS BÁNFFY

ISLAND
SIRI RANVA HJELM JACOBSEN

ARTURO'S ISLAND
ELSA MORANTE

ONE PART WOMAN
PERUMAL MURUGAN

WILL
JEROEN OLYSLAEGERS

TEMPTATION
JÁNOS SZÉKELY

BIRD COTTAGE
EVA MEIJER

WHEN WE CEASE TO UNDERSTAND THE WORLD
BENJAMIN LABUTUT

THE COLLECTED STORIES OF STEFAN ZWEIG
STEFAN ZWEIG

THE EVENINGS
GERARD REVE

AN UNTOUCHED HOUSE

WILLEM FREDERIK HERMANS

ODESSA STORIES

ISAAC BABEL

RABBIT BACK LITERATURE SOCIETY

PASI ILMARI JÄÄSKELÄINEN

ISOLDE

IRINA ODOEVTSEVA

BEAUTY IS A WOUND

EKA KURNIAWAN

BONITA AVENUE

PETER BUWALDA

IN THE BEGINNING WAS THE SEA

TOMÁS GONZÁLEZ

COIN LOCKER BABIES

RYU MURAKAMI

BINOCULAR VISION

EDITH PEARLMAN

THE SPECTRE OF ALEXANDER WOLF

GAITO GAZDANOV

JOURNEY BY MOONLIGHT

ANTAL SZERB

TRAVELLER OF THE CENTURY

ANDRÉS NEUMAN

BEWARE OF PITY

STEFAN ZWEIG